REMEMBERING ME

Ruby Eyre

KDP Publishing

For Mam.

To Niamh,

thank you for
supporting my first
book!

Happy reading,

Ruby Eyre

EDITIOR'S NOTE

You are about to embark upon an adventure inside the heart and mind of a soul that survived World War II. But the story begins long before and ends long after that devastating war of wars. The story must begin and end this way for all those who live through wars are humans like you and me. And war, being a characteristic of humans, touches and changes the way we remember ourselves forevermore.

My name is Janet Still. I am an author and an editor by trade. Editing Ruby Eyre's novel *Remembering Me* is one of the more appreciated gifts of my occupation. This is Ruby's first book to pen. Yet as you read, you will quickly recognise that this is surely not her first effort at weaving a story. Ordinarily an editor finds little trouble remaining detached as they work through a book. This is the editor's role. *Remembering Me* tested my detachment from start to finish of each chapter. And I thoroughly enjoyed the experience.

Ruby chose me specifically to work with her through the edit, because close family of mine also lived through World War II, here in England, the setting of Ruby's tale. I am also an advanced practice nurse. This came in decidedly handy as *Remembering Me* takes place through the eyes of nurses on the frontline during wartime.

Ruby wrote this story straight from her creative imagination, partly inspired by people she met when traveling. She shared with me the alluring feeling all writers look to experience...that the story would not leave her. She had to write it down and get it all on the page. The main character is unveiled within her subjective dialogue, written in a unique voice that is solely Ruby's creation. So, although I proofread and edited this book, I turned over the decision of which edits to keep and use to its author. More than that, I will not share because this tale deserves to be read without expectations.

I have not read Ruby's changes yet. I await my own copy to read from cover to cover, not as an editor, but as a lover of good storytelling.

-Janet Still-

JULY 1998

Delicate rays of the summer sun shine through the trees and find my face. I feel young again. If only momentarily. My wooden garden chair holds me as I listen to the chirping birds around me, harmonising with the gentle summer breeze flowing over my skin. I am reminded every so often that this life is not a nice nostalgic dream. This is my life and I am at peace with it.

Sounds of summer gently bring me back to reality. I open my eyes and take in the blooming garden in front of me. It is filled with flowers of every colour with luscious bushes and trees, whose leaves rustle in the wind, creating its own symphony. The addictive smell of my garden sweet peas climbing up the chicken wire fills my nostrils.
I created this haven.

For many years, I spent my time down on my hands and knees, pruning, weeding, planting, and talking sweetly to these plants hoping they will grow. And they did grow. I can see that now. Time always knows what it is doing, even if we do not.

My children, Mae, and Teddy sit on the patio drinking tea. They too have grown and have children of their own. The melodic laughter of my six grandchildren fills my ears and brings such happiness to my recently lonely and sad heart. As of late, the days feel like years to me.

My husband, and best friend, Will died two months ago. Today would have marked his 80th birthday. My children and grandchildren decided to mark Will's birthday with a small party. No matter how hard I try, I cannot join them in the celebrations. I feel as though I have lost a limb. The phantom limb is still attached to me, tugging me every now and then, but I can never see it. With each day falling from the calendar, my phantom limb pulls me more and more. It is trying to tell me something, bring me somewhere, maybe even take me with it.

Life feels incomplete without Will by my side. For over fifty years of my life, I have lived it with Will by my side. Then one day I woke and he was gone. It is not surprising to many, maybe not even surprising to me, that he is gone. He was almost eighty, did I expect him to live forever?

No, but I hoped he would. Or at least let me go before him, so I would not have to deal with this pain.

How selfish of me to think that. This is not the first time I have experienced such emptiness. Heartbreak is something I am all too familiar with. But the last time I felt such emptiness and heartbreak, it was my darling Will who helped me from the depths of my despair and refilled the gaping holes inside.

But I was younger then. I healed more quickly. Now that I am old, pain seems to take me down quicker and hold me there for days until I am barely capable of standing up again.

I have always needed time on my own to recharge, to think or to figure things out. But I never thought that I would need Will when I wept. I never knew I needed Will to help me mourn him. That is when we need our loved ones the most, when they are gone. Every little thing that I seem to do reminds me of Will.

I want to go to him. I know he is waiting for me.

At 78 years of age, I never imagined that I would be looking back at my life and mourning a lost time and a lost person – my lost self. When did I lose myself?

Over the last two months, I have had a homesickness for a vanished time and place. I have lived a long life, I would say. A good life. I was lucky enough to have experienced everything that I wanted to do and to achieve. It is these things that make me feel even more ready for death, as I know I have lived a life I have loved.

Mae's harmonious laugh brings my attention back to the garden. I admire her throwing her head back laughing with Teddy. Just like Will, Teddy and Mae never let a day go by where laughter was not had. I admire their strength and courage to find a reason to smile and laugh on difficult days.

That is a rare quality to possess.

Their laughter grows louder and it brings a smile to my face. My job is done. There is not much more that I can do in this life. I am not needed anymore.

They have their own lives, their own children, and will be fine without me. They will be okay without me. They do not need me anymore. They do not understand or see this, but one day they will. I suppose when one reaches this age, one develops a new perspective on life and the people in it.

I know that my family want me around, but they do not necessarily need me. And it is often the things that we want the most that we do not actually need.

It is such a peaceful sight to sit back and watch the family I made sitting and laughing with each other...to look at the house and gardens I worked hard to make into a home, now flourish in the summer sun...to sit and look at the life I made and see the impact and outcome of it. It is in this moment that I feel most at peace with myself.

I have received a chance that not many of my generation was granted - I survived World War II. I lived to make a family of my own and watch them grow. I lived to see the world be rebuilt. I lived to see the world change. Too many young men, women and children died. Some of these deaths I witnessed. When the war ended, I promised myself that I would cherish my life. I would live my life to the fullest in honour of those that did not the chance. I think I have fulfilled this promise. I hope that I have honoured those that have gone before me.

It makes me smile to think of all the people that have passed on, that I will meet again soon like a bittersweet reunion.

My eldest granddaughter, Emmy, moves across the lawn with her youngest sibling Nell. My eyes follow them and I smile as I watch them laugh and joke. Despite an eleven-year age gap between the two, Emmy dutifully cares for Nell and Nell always looks adoringly at Emmy. Their sisterly bond is quite striking. From the moment Nell came into the world, an innate part of Emmy awakened where she proudly took on the title of being the 'big sister.'

Emmy has grown into a beautiful young girl who is slowly coming into her own essence of being a woman. Her long, curly, golden blonde hair bounces down her back with every movement that she makes. Her downturned green eyes - wise eyes - are shaded under her thick eyelashes. Emmy's view of the world is my favourite sight. With a sharp mind, courage of a lioness, and the warmest heart, Emmy is beautiful inside and out.

At 19, Emmy has a mind of her own and a determination to go and get what she wants. She reminds me of me when I was nineteen. It is strange to look at Emmy and to think that at her age, I went to train to be a nurse. More specifically a nurse for war. I see Emmy's innocence and I cannot begin to imagine letting her go out into the world, but she must do it. I know she will live a wonderful life.

Emmys youth, innocence, and gentleness will never be taken away from her by a world driven mad with war. Why did I ever want to lose my carefree and youthful days to help a war that should never have started? That is a question I have battled with all my life. But still, I would not change a thing. For I never would have arrived here if I did not live this life.

As Emmy and Nell enter the house through the patio doors, I begin to wonder how life looks through their eyes.

EMMY

Granny's house folds itself around me, like a comforting hug with a warm cup of tea rolled into one. The house is Granny and Granny is this house. I have always adored hearing the story of how she found it. I must have asked her a thousand times growing up to tell it to me over and over again and to never leave anything out. Of course, she knew if she did forget something, I would instantly remind her.

One thing for sure is that my grandparents always made the house colourful, inside, and out.

Over the years, they painted the outside of the house in many colours of the rainbow. I have seen pictures of the house in the sixties painted a mysterious dark purple with a white rim on the windows, fascia trim and front door; a lovely forget-me-not blue in the seventies with black rims; and a blushing pink with cream rims in the eighties. Now the house is classic white paired with blue rims around the windows and fascia trim, completed with a glossy red door.

My grandparents became known to their neighbours as the 'eccentric couple in house 4.' I am always proud to admit I am their grandchild.

There is something about this house and the history of it that is important to me. It is a part of my family history, my lineage, my being here in this world. This house, and my grandparents, hold a history and stories of how my life has come to be. I cannot explain what I feel, but I have this desire to know more about the history of this family and specifically Granny's story.

Granny paved the way for our family to be how it is today. But I want to know the full story behind this journey, not just snippets, so that I can possibly appreciate it and understand it better.

I wander into the kitchen. This was the only room in the house that was habitable when my grandparents bought the house. They lived in the kitchen for some time until they renovated the other rooms. To this day, the kitchen is still the heart of the house. It opens onto a conservatory which is the dining room. The kitchen and conservatory catch the sun from dawn till dusk, shining a spotlight onto different parts of the rooms. I like to think about all the cups of teas and meals that were had in here. All the laughter, conversations, and the precious moments that the house witnessed.

From here, I see Granny sitting away from the family in her garden chair, under the oak tree sheltered from the sun. Her eyes fall onto each member of the family, as she slowly takes them in. Is she beginning to forget our faces? Why does she stare at them like so?

I move from the window and wander through the old Victorian house with Nell by my side. I feel as though my body is being taken back through time and old memories. This house is residence to old memories and stories. It has always made me feel safe and secure, luring me in and wrapping its warm arms around me as I try to follow the trailing breadcrumbs of each story to find out more.

Each corner, hallway, and room are decorated with trinkets and photos. My favourite photo is a black-and-white framed photo of my grandparents after Victory-in-Europe-day. It is placed proudly on the wooden table in the main hall, beside a vase filled with beautiful daisies of every size.

I believe daisies are Granny's favourite flower.

Nell smells the daisies while I try to memorise the picture even more. Grandad Will was a handsome young soldier with the biggest smile on his face. He stood tall with broad rowing shoulders, sandy blond hair, and sun-kissed skin. His charming smile in the photo was utterly contagious. The type of smile that you fall in love with.

Granny was a young nurse with an equally big smile. Her hair was tied in a low bun at the nape of her neck, with loose strands of hair framing her round face. His arm securely wrapped around her waist, caught Granny in the middle of a laugh. Their exhaustion from the war hid behind their beaming smiles. They looked so happy, so in love.

The way that Grandad looks at her and the way Granny looks at him, is what every relationship strives for. They are completely and utterly besotted by each other. I hope someday I can find a love like that.

I have often been told that I resemble Granny in both looks and personality, which is the highest compliment that could ever be given to anyone in this family. My mother, Mae, called me after Granny's mother, Esme, which makes me feel that bit closer to Granny.

I have also been told that I get my determination and stubbornness from Granny and Esme, which can act both in my favour and against me.

I have my mother's green downturned eyes and golden-brown hair. But I take after Grandad with my sense of humour and curiosity, which lately seems to be of a great comfort to Granny. She seems to want me around the house with her more and more since Grandad's funeral.

We all miss him, but Granny seems utterly lost. I have never seen her like this before. The day that we placed Grandad in the cemetery and said our final goodbyes was the day Granny could no longer find her way back to us. She is slowly regressing more and more into her mind with her eyes searching for Grandad, always searching. The family hoped today would help her, but it seems she is slowly slipping away from us. Maybe when we bring out the cake and say a small toast to Grandad, she might manage a smile.

Since the funeral, Granny watches each of our faces as if it is the first and last time. As though she will never see our faces again. When she hugs us, it is as if she is holding on that extra second. Over the last two months, we have all tried to help her, to cheer her up and bring back the woman we all know and love. Maybe if I make her think she is helping me with something, some project, it might bring her out of herself?

But what project? College is over for the summer, there are no holidays or celebrations coming up that I can convince her to work towards. Maybe I could tell her I want to make a scrap book or a memory book? Maybe a book of Granny's memories?

Even though our family is extremely close, we only know fragments of Granny's past.

I begin to climb the carved wooden staircase in the front hall as Nell takes two steps at a time, bobbing along beside me singing a song. As I wander past the bedrooms upstairs, I see that Granny's bedroom door is wide open.

Nobody is in here, but something on the floor by her side of the bed catches my attention. It seems to be a piece of paper, but as I come closer to it, I realise that it is an old black-and-white photo. The photo is frail, slightly torn at the corners and damaged by the years, but it is still clear. It has crease marks, as if it has been folded up time and time again, hidden away. It is a picture of a handsome young soldier. He has dark curly hair and dark eyes. I have never seen this photo or this man before. There is no name on the back only 'A' 1941.

"Who's that Emmy?" Nell asks, whilst trying to balance her weight on one leg.

I place the photo carefully back on the bedside locker. "I'm not sure Nell." I mentally make a note to ask Granny about the picture later tonight. "Come on, let's leave Granny's room."

Nell skips out of the room singing to herself. I turn to close the door but take another look at the unfamiliar man in the picture. There is something about him that draws me in and wants to know him.

We continue to walk around the house, admiring the beauty of it. Maybe I might stumble upon something that I can use to help Granny come out of her shell and talk to us.

The glass doors to the back garden are open wide. Nell drops my hand as soon as she sees dessert has arrived and runs to the rest of the family at the round picnic table.

Even though I love the house, the gardens are my favourite part. They have a unique ability to make me feel as though I am walking into the world of *Alice in Wonderland* or entering *The Secret Garden*. So many twists and turns lie within this garden.

Little metal archways, dripping with colourful clematis and ivy, stand here and there breaking up the garden. A concealed glasshouse lives at the bottom of the garden near the small stream. Beautiful old trees of every kind are sprinkled about the garden, adding to the mysteries that you might find in this Eden. A small pond, with goldfish swimming happily, lives among the wild meadow dedicated to the worms, ants, and bees. Each pathway, flower and tree fill my nostrils with sweet and fresh aromas. It is simply breath-taking no matter what the season.

I look at Granny sitting comfortably in her garden chair watching everyone with a melancholic smile on her face. I walk towards her and feel the grass tickle the skin on the tops of my feet. I take the seat next to her.

"Granny? I found a large pile of your old photo-albums in the living room."

Granny smiles with a smile. "Gosh Emmy! I have not looked at them in a long time."

"Well, I wondered," I mumble, "if you could tell me who some of the people were in the photos. I am trying to make a family tree and learn some things about the people in past generations of this family. Maybe we could make a memory book?"

"That's nice dear! I will try my best to remember all the faces in the pictures, but I think Mae would be better suited to that. You should ask you mother, her memory is much better than mine. Oh, looky here, tea and cake have arrived!"

I help Granny out of her chair, and she hugs me. I notice how frail she has become. Her arms are thinner and she shakes with every slight movement. For the first time when I look at her, I see an old woman. Granny was always young, free, healthy, and strong with an equally strong mind and character. But since Grandad died, we are seeing less and less of this.

Granny links arms with me and we slowly walk to the picnic table. Tea and cake are shared around the table with smiles and laughter. Once we are finished, Granny asks me to take her inside.

I walk her through the French patio doors into the living room overlooking the garden and help her into her floral armchair as I take the couch opposite her. She slumps into the armchair and stares at the photographs on the walls. After a long silence has passed, she asks me to fetch the photo-albums. I quickly bring them to her and place one in her lap.

I watch her intently as she opens the first album. She begins to laugh and smile admiring the pictures of her parents. But the smile quickly fades and she hands me back the album.

"Here," Granny sighs, "you take it since you want to know who the people are in these pictures. It sometimes pains me to look back at faces who have gone."

Maybe bringing these albums to her was a mistake. But maybe, just maybe, these photo's might be the thing to bring back the Granny we know and love. I carefully take the photo-album from her frail grasp and open the first page. The photos are so old and worn. Some of these photos date back to the early 1900's. I wish I could jump into the photos, take me to that lost time to see how life was then. I look up and see Granny is smiling at me.

"You always were such a curious girl, like a sponge soaking up everything," she laughs. Granny sits forward and places her hand gently under her chin. A gentle smile forms on her face as she carefully stares into my eyes for a few moments, almost as if she is trying to memorise my face and features.

"So, you were born 1920? It must be amazing to have lived through and witnessed with your own eyes so many moments in history. Even fashion alone, you have seen, and probably worn, so many different styles. It's incredible!", I exclaim as I eagerly fingered through the old photo-albums.

"I have always felt that I was born in the wrong generation. I find the 1920's right up to the '50's so fascinating. From the music to the fashion, to the way of living. Everything! I don't understand today's music, fashion, or way of living."

Even though Granny is smiling at me, her eyes tell another story. They looked tired and sad. "Where do you want to begin?"

"The beginning is always good. Let us start with this one," I point to a photo of a couple standing before a large country estate. "They are your parents, yes?"

"Yes."

"Tell me your story, Granny."

LUCY

Since my dear Will's death, my family have taken their turns to stay with me and keep me company. I think they fear that I will not be able to cope with the empty house, but I love my peace and quiet as it gives me the chance to relive some of my memories. But as of late, I am finding that grief is playing tricks on my memory. Out of all my family members staying, I enjoy it the most when Emmy is here as I feel like I am in the company of my younger self but with Will's humour.

I realise that the room has fallen silent. I look up to see Emmy staring at me, awaiting my response. What was her question again? Oh yes, my parents.

"Yes dear, I was born in 1920 to Esme and Charles Webley in Buckinghamshire. A lot has changed since then and you are right, in my 78 years that I have lived through and witnessed many historic moments. Some I was right in the middle of. That picture that you are looking at is my parents standing outside my family home," I reply.

Emmy sits back into the couch, adjusting the goose-feathered cushions to make herself comfortable.

Nostalgia can be an amazing thing wrapped up so lovely and appealingly, inviting you in, waiting for you to unwrap it. However, nostalgia can be quite painful to unravel. I have not thought about my parents in such a long time and they too have now become yet another thing that I am mourning for.

"I can still hear my mother's voice screeching at my father - 'Charles!' - as if she were constantly outraged at something. Of course, she did come from a time where one used to gasp, 'where are my smelling salts?' as a reply to anything remotely upsetting. I remember as a girl, my father's reply to my mother's cries of outrage was - 'yes my darling' - ever so softly and he would gently rub her hand. But over the years he became amusingly used to her cries and he would roll his eyes at me, hide behind his newspaper, and sarcastically say, 'good heavens, what now?' My parents had quite a humorous relationship," I joke, as the memories pile in, one on top of the other.

My mother always loved telling me the story of her delight on the day of my birth. My two brothers, Arthur and George were lovely of course, but a daughter was something she had to herself.

My mother used to say, "Charles has the boys for hunting, fishing, and other things, and I felt excluded. But now I have my very own daughter whom I can do womanly things with, and he may accept that!"

I became somewhat her own doll or a project in which she invested all her time and effort.

My surroundings fade out as I allow my memories to lure me in ever so gently, folding its warm and welcoming arms around me, ensuring that I am comfortable.

THE WEBLEY'S

My parents were at the top of society. Moulded into being a well-respected lady since birth, my mother seemed to carry a regal air about her that people were instantly drawn to. She expertly beheld the 'perfect' image of a lady. She stood tall and slim, beautifully dressed, and moved so delicately.

Mother's golden-blonde hair, always pinned up prettily with one of her many different types of hair-combs, made her beauty angelical. My favourite one of her hair-combs was of a delicate blue and green gemstone butterfly. She would carefully slide the hair comb into place at the top of her low bun and smooth any fly away hairs. Turning her head to each side, she would take in her beauty with an air of assurance. I adored sitting on the end of her bed and watching her get ready, admiring her long golden hair as she brushed it and expertly pinned it in place. I happily observed her every move as she applied her makeup. My mother was mesmerizingly beautiful and she knew how to use this beauty. I prayed that I would grow up to be half as beautiful as her.

Mother had the most enchanting green eyes. My father used to exclaim how he felt he could have a whole conversation with her just by looking into her eyes. My mother was a great painter, charming singer, satisfactory pianist, and an eloquent speaker. She loved to write. She had the ability to write letters in such a way that you felt like she was there beside you, having a conversation. She was the epitome of Edwardian society and from birth, I knew I had to try and live up to this.

My father came from a long lineage of wealth, that was accumulated through the breeding and racing of horses.

Webley Stud and Farm were well known around the world, and to say that one's horse came from Webley Stud was definitely something to boast about. Webley Stud ensured the estate rarely ran into financial difficulties. But financial difficulties were often the least of the family's worries when scandal befell onto the family name.

Fortunately, the Webley family moto was simply, 'Perseverance,' and every member certainly did just this. It was in the Webley nature to thrive in difficult situations.

When my father took over the estate and began his family, he wanted another source of income for the estate, and a form of distraction, so he established 'Webley's Whiskey' in 1923.

He received a helping hand with his whiskey business from a questionable man named, Freddie Blackwood, otherwise known as Black Freddie. He attained his name from dealings with the Black Market and how most of his work that he did took place in the dead of night. Mother naturally did not approve of or appreciate Black Freddie and the talk that came from his presence on the estate. However, Black Freddie and my father held an unbreakable bond – they fought alongside each other in the Great War – and that was something that could never be forgotten.

Like my mother, father appeared as a regal man who proudly sat by the fire in his grand emerald-green armchair every evening after dinner and happily drank his fine whiskey while puffing his cigar. Father's magnificent imperial moustache and great head of brown wavy hair made him stand out. Even when he grew older, he still had a youthful air to him. He came from a long lineage of men with magnificent moustaches, and they all began to grow their moustaches as soon as they came of what Webley men called - 'moustache age.' The Webley moustache was an unspoken tradition and must be abided.

My father dressed in immaculate suits. I do not think he ever wore anything other than a suit in his entire life. A pipe hanging from his mouth, a book or newspaper in his left hand and a pondering look on his face and that was Charles Webley. His great companion, Chester –

a stunningly loyal golden Labrador – always accompanied my father. You would often see Chester plodding along and know that Papa was not far behind. He loved Chester so dearly and certainly treated him as if he was royalty.

Like the men that came before him, my father attended Eton College and afterwards he became an Oxford scholar, all of which engrained 'gentlemanliness' into him from such a young age. Yet another Webley tradition to uphold.

At the age of 23, my father fought in World War 1, along with the Cavalry division. Of course, Webley horses were used. He became a Captain and grew respect among his men. Unfortunately, during the Battle of Somme in 1916, he fell from his horse injuring his left leg. Luckily for him, he went back to England to recover in the Westcott stately home, which opened its doors to recovering soldiers. He had an attentive woman to nurse him back to health – Esme Westcott - who quickly became Mrs. Charles Webley.

In November that year, Arthur arrived. George followed in October 1918, I arrived in May 1920 and my sister Nell was born in January 1922. Sadly, Nell died on the night of her fourth birthday from tuberculosis. After her death, my parents clung to me even more so and they could never bring themselves to say her name let alone talk about her. Over the years it was as though Nell never existed as no one dared mention her name. Only one photograph of Nell remained and it was locked away in my parents' room, never to be seen again. I often fantasised what life would have looked like if Nell had lived.

Being the eldest of the Allister and Adelaide Webley's four children, father inherited everything. Webley Hazelton Manor became his kingdom. He was the eighth generation of Webley's to own the house. The family home was an establishment and business first before anything else. Decorated in a red-brick baroque style stately home, Webley Hazelton Manor was built in 1671 with extensions being added on over the years. Lined with lime, sycamore and chestnut trees, the long avenue up to the house looked beautiful in every season of the year. The gardens were a tasteful mix of the Italian romantic, French landscape, and

English renaissance. Together they made a very pleasing view.

Yet another thing my family proudly showcased.

My family were a prestigious family and they needed an equally prestigious house to show this. Each generation dutifully needed to bring something more to both the family name and house. Webley Hazelton Manor was more than just a place of dwelling. At the height of the Webleys power, wealth, and glory, it represented the family's history and status. It was an integral part of the family's being.

Not only did the house have a history, but the name itself held many stories. Everything in the house oozed history. Everything in it, including the people, always felt like artefacts to me.

By being a Webley, I had to carry the weight of the name on my shoulders from birth. It was not something that I did lightly. If I wanted to do something, I would have to think about the consequences it would have on the family name. Even something so trivial as what shop I should enter could spark gossip about the family. I often felt trapped growing up as from a young age I had to think about the family name before I thought of myself or what I wanted to do.

After all, family always came first.

LILIAN

Emmys delicate voice brings my attention back to the room.

"Oh, look how beautiful your mother was on her wedding day! She looks like she belongs in an old movie or a history book." Emmy gently moves her hand across the photos as she turns to the page with photos of my mother. Emmy holds up the picture of my parents wedding day to me and smiles.

My parents married in the spring of 1917. Mother wore a floor-length, white, lace gown, with a nine-foot-long cathedral lace veil. Her mother, Lady Agatha Westcott, gave her a string of pearls which was a family heirloom worth a small mansion as a wedding gift. Mother of course had a handsome dowry as well.

Kitted out in his fine military service uniform, my father stood handsomely by my mother. Their wedding became the talk of the season. Many women strived to have the 'Lady Esme Webley' look on their wedding day. Even as a young girl, I heard the village continue speak about my mother on her wedding day.

"Did you know you were named after my mother? Mae loved the name Esme, but the first day I saw you I nicknamed you Emmy," I smile.

"Yes, Mam told me that I was named after her, but I never knew it was you that nicknamed me Emmy. Why did you?"

"I nicknamed you Emmy because it is a softer name for a child," I laugh. "But the main reason was that I felt Esme was a big name to live up to and big shoes to fill. You would have had to carry the weight of 'Esme Webley' all your life, which is something myself and my two brothers were forced to do growing up...carrying the weight of the Webley name on our shoulders...It may sound simple, Emmy dear, but it is not. I did not want you to have to do that from the second you were born, so I thought you deserve to make the name your own. To be Emmy."

It can be hard trying to explain to your grandchild a concept so inherent to you and the era you grew up in and to try make a girl who is desperately yearning to be from that time understand the old ways.

"How come you call Nell as it is, and not give her a nickname?"

"I had a younger sister, called Nell, who never got the chance to live her life like she should have rightfully done. I often wondered what she would have accomplished in her life," I lament.

"So, when Mae said she wanted to name her last child if it was a girl 'Nell', it brought tears to my eyes. I felt as though my little sister was finally going to be able to live her life. And so, I call your sister Nell because she is bringing life to a name that rarely surfaced after my sister's death."

"Does Nell look anything like your sister? Or remind you of her in any way?"

I turn to look out the patio doors and watch Nell gently swinging on the tire seat hanging from the chestnut tree.

"Yes! Her big warm blue eyes remind me of my sister's and the slight auburn tint in her hair is similar."

Growing up, losing a sibling was not uncommon. That did not make it any easier to accept. I am glad to say that I found my sister in my friend, Lilian, whom I met during my nursing years.

Lilian Comerford, born and raised in County Kilkenny in Ireland, became my sister. Before the war broke, she moved to England and began nursing. Even after all these years, Lilian still has the same gentle melodic midlands accent that makes me smile every time I hear it. I never thought I would find a sister in another, that I would love another more than I loved my own kin, but Lilian changed that.

Emmy and I sit in silence looking through the next photo-album. I smile to myself as I see the old familiar faces stare up at me from the worn pages. The sun is slowing dimming and it will be a magnificent sunset soon.

I love the way the sun shines through the stain-glass window on these patio doors, casting dazzling colours all around the room. One of my favourite things to do with Will was to sit on the plump couch that Emmy is sitting on, chat and watch the shadows casted from the sun move about the room like clockwork, becoming enthralled by the colours. No matter what the weather, in here was always charming.

"Mam, you have a visitor," Mae shouts from down the hallway, "it's Lilian."

"We're in the living room," I call out.

Lilian walks through the door from the hallway with a warm, kind smile on her face. "Hello! How are you doing? It feels as if it has been ages since I've last seen you."

"Everything seems yonks when you are old!" we both laugh. "Emmy has been jogging my memory about some old photographs. Do you remember this one? It's around the time that we first met."

I hand the black-and-white photo to Lilian of two young and very innocent looking girls, who were proud to be wearing their new nurses' uniform.

"Gosh, we were so young, weren't we? Bright eyed and bushy-tailed," Lilian laughs. "I don't remember looking *that* young in my uniform. Isn't it crazy to think we were the same age that little Emmy is now? Well, not so little anymore." Lilian continues to admire the old photo in her hands. "I've always thought it...but doesn't your grandmother have a marvellous chin."

Emmy chuckles as Lilian points at the picture to reaffirm her compliment.

I tap my chin and laugh. "You've always had a way at giving the strangest compliments Lil!"

Mae arrives back in the room carrying a tray full of tea and biscuits, and places it onto the small chestnut table in front of us.

"I see Emmy has been quizzing you on your photo-albums," Mae teases while gently patting my shoulder. "She has been asking both Teddy and I who is who in the photos around the house and wanting to know the history of everyone in those photos, and the history of *every little thing* in this house."

I reach out to hold Emmys hand. "You know Emmy, your curiosity reminds me so much of your Grandad Will. That too is a lovey thing to see live on in someone else."

Lilian raises her cup of tea to a picture of Will on the wall. "Happy eightieth birthday to you, Will."

Mae and Emmy follow Lilians example and raise their cup of tea to Will's picture. We all take a moment to quietly think of Will before I revive the conversation.

"Why don't we go back out to the garden, it'll be sunset soon. The tea will keep us warm while we can admire nature's simplistic beauty!"

"Oh, how very grand we are!" Lilian imitates my accent while smirking at me.

I playfully pinch her as we link arms and begin to walk out to the garden.

We are instantly hit with the smell of French lavender. The rest of the family still sit around the yellow picnic table, filling the garden with joyful sounds of melodious conversations and laughter. Lilian, Mae, and Emmy join them, but I take my time walking towards them as I wish to admire them all for a few moments – take a photograph of them in my mind. Add it to my own private collection.

My six grandchildren are at the age where they are not quite young enough to be playing games with each other, yet not old enough to be involved in adult conversations. However, they all become children when they are in each-others company, laughing about their inside jokes and playing pranks on one another.

I admiringly watch my son Teddy, with his charming wife Gwen, and their two children; Art who is my oldest grandchild and is twenty years young, and Milly who is fifteen. I look to Mae who is laughing with her husband Harry and their four children. Such a beautiful sight, I wish I could bottle this moment.

I believe that when you are a parent you are constantly

looking ahead, focused on the next thing you must do or making sure your child is okay; that they are behaving themselves or giving them a helping hand in some way. I have done that. However, when you are a grandparent, you live in the moment not the future with your grandchildren. It is more relaxed, and you can appreciate the little things that you may have missed with your own children.

I love observing my grandchildren and watching their different personalities blossom and to see them discover themselves. But what I really love is when they do something or say something in such a way, even the slight way they move their face, however small, and I can see a resemblance of their parents. I see this now as I watch Art and the way his face almost explodes when he laughs, just like Teddy. Or how Nell crinkles her nose when she is trying to observe something from afar, just like Mae.

It is in these simple moments that makes me feel at peace with myself and my life. It is exactly these moments that I treasure, just being surrounded by the family that I created. Growing old is only for the lucky. I know that now.

SIBLINGS

After sunset, the family said their goodbyes except for Emmy, Mae, and Lilian. We walk back into the living room and sit on the couches to continue where Emmy and I had left off.

"I want to know more about your family when you were growing up. What were you brothers like? Where did you go to school? What was it like growing up in a house like Webley Hazelton Manor? Do you miss that lifestyle?" Emmy asks.

"I'd better make more tea as I see we will be settled in here for the night," Mae laughs as we make ourselves comfortable.

"I'll give you a hand, Mae," Lilian calls out.

"No, you're okay, Lil, you stay there. You are our guest after all!" I smile at Mae and gently squeeze her hand as she passes me.

"Well, my brother Arthur was the eldest, which meant that he naturally inherited the family estate and money."

Emmy sighs, "It's unfair if you think about it that just because he was the first male, it meant that he got everything."

"It is unfair, especially when the male heir is a distant cousin and he gets the estate and all of the money," Lilian adds matter-of-factly. "That's what happened in *Pride and Prejudice.*"

I nod along in agreement. "For Arthur, he was the first born and the male heir which bore a lot of responsibility since birth. From his first breath, Arthur was practically trained to fill the role of my father."

I take a moment to look at the picture of Arthur as a boy, dressed in his Sunday clothes as he proudly stood beside his horse, Noble. Emmy hands me a picture of George and I immediately chuckle.

"George on the other hand was quite the character. He always cracked jokes and instantly brightened up any room that he walked in. As children, George and Arthur were inseparable, so much so that George became known as 'Arthur's Shadow.'" I look at the fading photo of my brothers, with their arms around each other, both caught in a laugh.

"They both loved to call me 'Lucy Loo' repeatedly in a sing-song style, which drove me insane! But...I'd love nothing more than to hear them say it now."

Emmy outstretches her hand to me with a picture of Arthur, aged thirteen, dressed in his school uniform as he leaned on his big wooden trunk.

"This picture was when Arthur went off to boarding school. Of course, he attended Eton College like my father, and after that he went onto Oxford University. Both of which were a family requirement or societal expectation. Our family name alone was enough for him to get in -"

"Did you send Uncle Teddy to boarding school?" Emmy interrupts.

"I let Teddy make that decision for himself – we didn't force it upon him. Your Grandad and I told him that he could go to the local school here or to a boarding school. Boarding school was not going to be a family requirement in this household. And Teddy decided to go to the local school, it was where all of his friends were."

Mae returns with a tray full of tea and biscuits.

"So has the tradition ended where our family attends boarding school, like some rite of passage?" Emmy asks Mae.

"The option was always there if you wanted to go, but it's not forced upon you or your siblings like Granny's generation," Mae replies. "I was always glad I never went to boarding school, I would have missed home too much!"

Lilian, Emmy, and Mae continue to look at the photos of Arthur and drink their tea. I hold the warm mug in my hand and take a small soothing sip, gently re-entering my old memories and letting them tell their story. I longingly try to grasp a time that I have naturally lost due to growing up. I fix the cushions behind me on my armchair and allow the sweet, peaceful sensation of my nostalgia to encompass me.

ARTHUR

Being the topic of conversation among many of upper society circles, my brother Arthur was greatly sought after. Arthur was a gentleman with impeccably good etiquette, who charmed everyone around him. He fluently spoke French, German as well as Latin. He could speak about almost any topic which made him immensely popular and sought after.

Arthur could talk to my father's circle about business, politics, and horses, then move onto my mother's circle and charm them with poetry and good manners, and finally move onto people his own age and comfortably fit in there too. Arthur went on the seasonal hunts with my father's Gentlemen's Club and played Polo. Both, of course, showcased Webley horses. He played poker, occasionally smoked cigars, and drank Webley Whiskey with father. However, as a sister I always managed to bring out the worst in him.

As a sister, seeing Arthur being anything but perfect - even it was only for one minute - was humbling. Arthur held a high standard and a high pedestal in my family and George and I felt obliged to desperately meet this impossible standard.

Arthur was perfect. He was a natural all-rounder. He was effortlessly charming in every way. He stood tall, as though he owned the world. He had my mother's golden hair and father's piercing blue eyes which naturally all the debutants swooned for his attention.

For a girl, to be seen talking to or sitting beside *the* Arthur Webley would immediately spark rumours of a courtship. For men and women to have their name associated with Arthur instantly made them exceedingly popular, as not only was he a sought-after eligible bachelor, but he was a Webley.

Being associated with the Webley family opened doors for many people. For me, being a Webley closed many doors.

Arthur took after mother in that people were naturally drawn to him. He was that rare type of person that made you feel special when near him. When you left his company, you were always smiling – it would be bad news for him if you were anything but happy when leaving him. Arthur had a reputation, status, and name to uphold after all.

Despite all this, I always believed that Arthur was a boy in a man's suit. He tried so hard to fit in with every crowd, especially my father's, that he became a perfectionist, extremely arrogant and condescending at times especially to both George and me. Most importantly Arthur became a pompous idiot!

Arthur tried so hard to be what everyone else wanted him to be that sadly he forgot who he was. Obsession with high society and the constant strive to be at the top of everywhere he went, was the cause of Arthur's unhappiness.

As Arthur grew older, his unhappiness grew into arrogance. He began to look down on people, especially those less well off than him. He obnoxiously called them 'poor people,' almost spitting out the words. It infuriated me when he would say this. At times, I felt embarrassed to be his sister. I feared what he would be like when he would inherit the estate.

But I accidently stumbled upon the reason for Arthur's arrogance and obnoxious behaviour one summer's evening, as I walked through the garden. Sworn to absolute secrecy, I reluctantly agreed to keep Arthur's secret.

I came upon Arthur kissing a maid who worked on our estate. Her name was Molly Coyle. We grew up with Molly. Her mother worked as our maid and her family lived in the village. It seemed Arthur loved Molly since childhood, and she loved him too. As children, they played together in the garden or in the village. As they grew up, their social statuses grew further apart but privately friendship blossomed into something more. Unfortunately, society would never allow them to be together. It just simply was not possible.

A Webley could not marry a maid - it would ruin the family's reputation.

Arthur became frustrated with the life he had chosen and fell into a depression as he watched the woman he loved walk around his house, work for his family and pass him every day in the hallways. Never could he be with her as he longed to. So, to make himself fit into to his social box and leave Molly behind, Arthur turned against 'poor people', almost making up an image or story in his head to make Molly less desirable to him.

When Arthur was in the company of his people, he would belittle those like Molly. Often, he would belittle Molly especially as to make sure it was seen that he was equally being rude to all those lesser than him. But what Arthur needed the most was Molly's kind of people, as they accepted him. He did not need to prove or do anything to be accepted by them. Unfortunately, his gratitude for their kindness was insults.

Despite this, Molly foolishly stayed around and believed things would change. Arthur thought that he could love Molly, keep her as a maid in the estate where he could have her for herself, but marry a woman of status for show.

When I discovered his "ingenious plan" as he called it, I expressed my disgust. Arthur replied, "Lucy darling, don't be so terribly dull. This set up has been done for centuries."

I firmly took him by the arm and sat him down a wooden bench in the garden and began my lecture. But Arthur did not see the errors of his plan or why it upset me. He could not see the problem in stringing along Molly for the rest of her life. That Arthur would marry another woman and parade this in front of Molly yet expect Molly to still wait for him. This was normal in Arthur's eyes. This was what all his friends would do or were doing. Arthur did not see how it would break Molly. I knew Molly would waste her life waiting for Arthur, hoping they would someday be together. But someday never comes.

Once I finished my lecture, I wondered what battles Arthur fought inside, for he bowed his head and stared only at the ground.

After a long silence of neither of us acknowledging the others presence, he said, "You have never been in love, Lucy, experienced love or know what it is to have another hold the key to your happiness…you just don't realise how unfair this all is. I love Molly and have loved her since I was a boy. I will continue to love her till the day I die, and I must accept the fact that I will never be with her because I am a bloody Webley…worse I am the heir to the bloody Webley estate."

Arthur's anguish and turmoil brewed inside him like a storm. His emotions never betrayed him. Emotions could never be shown. His eyes welled and reddened, but like a true Webley, he pushed the sorrow back into his neat box. Our father's voice stubbornly rang through our ears – "Webley's don't cry."

I understood Arthur, but I did not necessarily agree with his plan. Instead of arguing further with him, I sat with him and I decided to help Arthur and Molly meet up in secret.

When the war broke out, advertisements appeared everywhere calling men to fight, to join the army, to save the country and king. Arthur turned 22 that November and he decided to join the Royal Air Force (RAF). He was positioned in the High Wycombe base. He was close to home and came home often to visit. He made everyone so proud. Our father was especially proud. Like a true Webley gentleman, Arthur followed tradition, honoured the family as he fought for his country. Arthur became even more perfect in everyone's eyes.

But when I looked into Arthurs eyes, all I saw was a scared little boy trying so hard to please everyone and to do the right thing. His biggest fear was failure.

GEORGE

Emmy gently turns the page of the photo-album, revealing pictures of George and Mae's face brightens.

I joyfully look at the old pictures. "Now George on the other hand was light-hearted, relaxed, and easy going. A bit too easy going at times! He was the second born, second being the important word. George unfortunately was second to Arthur in everything. People nicknamed George 'the Other Arthur', but mainly people called him 'Arthur's Shadow.'"

Emmy frowns. "That's not fair. Imagine being known as someone's shadow and not having an identity yourself."

"Despite this Emmy, George and Arthur were the best of friends. They had such an admirable brotherly bond," I continue.

Being the second born had its perks. It meant George did not have the same weight on his shoulders like Arthur. George had more freedom to do what he pleased. He had the luxury of going wild if he pleased. And he did.

During his fifth year at Eton, George snuck some Webley Whiskey into his dormitory and had a midnight soiree with the other boys in his dorm. George of course got caught when many of the boys spent the following morning horrifically vomiting in the bathroom. George did many things like this at school. But at the same time, he still had many pressures to present himself at a certain level of grace and to uphold the Webley name.

After more incidents like this, Father encouraged George to join the rugby team at Eton. Father believed it would discipline George, that both the sport and exercise would tire George out and he would not have the energy to misbehave.

However, George found his type of people in his teammates. They each exchanged their mischievous ideas and helped each other carry out their many pranks.

George had a natural sense of humour and charisma which helped him get out of many an unfavourable situation that he had somehow put himself into. He adored making people laugh. George was at his happiest making those around him laugh and smile. Even if his pranks and jokes were not well received, people always found themselves laughing. He had the most infectious bellyful laugh that I have ever heard.

One of his favourite pranks to pull on me involved tea.

I remember one afternoon when both Arthur and George were home from Eton. The family sat in the Orangery drinking tea with our Grandmother Agatha and Great Aunt Anne. I could see George looking around the room with that mischievous smile of his, as he slowly stirred his tea. Our Grandmother Agatha sat beside me and questioned me on my education and ballet. I felt a burning hot sensation on my hand and I let out a yelp. I quickly turned to see that George had placed his hot teaspoon on my hand.

My mother exasperatedly shook her head at me as she hissed at me to behave. She profusely apologised to our visiting family while sneakily shooting me another warning look. All the while, George and Arthur sniggered at my embarrassment. I tried to stretch my legs under the table and kick them both to stop them from laughing but instead I kicked Great Aunt Anne. George and Arthur's laughing grew worse. That was their favourite part of the prank - to see me flustered.

I got my revenge though when dessert came around. Apple pie with cream dolloped on top arrived on our plates. I told George that I thought the cream on my slice of pie smelt strange. As he leaned in to smell it, I pushed his head and he landed face first into the cream and apple-pie.

George heartly laughed as he spat cream and crumbled pie at me. "You little minx! Well played. I have taught you well!"

That was the highest compliment I could ever hope to receive from George. I felt immensely proud until my Grandmother Agatha cried for her smelling salts. My mother sunk further into her chair as Great Aunt Anne disgustingly declared that I needed a stricter governess and to be separated from Arthur and George.

I sheepishly looked at my parents and my mother held a scalding look in her eye. But my father bit his lip, holding in his laugh. He picked up his teacup and winked at me before raising it to his lips. My mother elbowed him, removing the smile from his face, as she hissed – "Do not encourage her Charles."

I always believed George used his humour to make up for his insecurities of being second to Arthur. It saddened me when I watched George strive to prove himself or work so hard to achieve something, and he would be met with "didn't Arthur do that" or "I'm sure Arthur helped you greatly."

Like Arthur, George attended Eton and Oxford and received a great education, but again it did not match Arthur's.

George was tall, solidly built, and muscular from playing rugby throughout his years of education. He took after father with his brown wavy hair, but he had Mama's green eyes. He had the most fabulous smile, the rare type that made you feel so special and warm inside when it was directed at you. He was handsome and he soon became an eligible bachelor though most young ladies sought after Arthur because they knew he would inherit the estate and not George.

When war broke out, George did not immediately join the fight as he wanted to complete his studies at Oxford first. Well, it was more to do with - "I am having too good of a time, that I don't want to give it up and fight some war."

This was noted, and George was unfortunately met with a highly disapproved father.

Our parents reminded George that Arthur joined the RAF and honoured both his family and country. At that time, it seemed the only words our father ever said was - "You're a Webley, George, and Webley's fight for their country."

But George stood his ground, completed his studies at Oxford, and then joined the Royal Navy in 1940. He was based in Southampton and we rarely saw him. George received an opportunity in the Navy to get away from being Arthur's little brother, to finally be seen as George Webley.

George wrote lovely, innocent, gentlemanlike letters to my parents while he trained with the Navy. He told them all about how hard he was working, how much he loved serving his country and how dearly he missed them. My parents were beyond proud of this version of George. However, they never received letters as I did from George telling me about all the mischievous behaviour that he and his shipmates used to get up to. He would begin his letters with – *Lucy Loo* – and I would instantly know he had done something.

A favourite joke of his was to shave off one eyebrow when people were sleeping, as they would be faced with the dilemma of either drawing on the missing eyebrow or shaving the other. I do not think George ever grew out of being a trickster and getting into trouble, it just was not in his nature. His letters always made me laugh though, which would soon be followed by sorrow as I longed to hear his laugh and stories in person.

I missed both of my brothers when they were away. But I particularly missed George. I was used to their long absences when they went to boarding school, but this was different. An uncertainty hung in the air. No plans could be made or committed to. Everything could change at a moment's notice.

Mae chuckles as she admires a photo of George in his Navy uniform.

"It's funny to think of Uncle George and his trickster ways, fighting in the Navy. I just cannot imagine him being serious for one second!"

"That was exactly everyone's thought when George first joined the Navy. We all believed the Navy would discipline him and straighten him up, but it didn't," I acknowledge. "But I am rather glad that it didn't. His humour helped a lot of people during those tough years. My parents were proud of their boys off at war, honouring the family name and their country until George sent an interesting letter home in late autumn of 1942."

"Did your parents find out about a prank? Or did he accidentally send his letter for you to your parents?" Emmy smiles.

"Not quite."

George had been away for some time with the Navy, fighting in the Mediterranean Sea and North Africa. But

33

he did not spend all his time on the ship fighting for his country. He had secretly married a German woman called, Margot Von Adler, whom he had met during his time in the Mediterranean Sea.

Margot resided in one of her family homes in Monaco. Margot's father was a member of the Nazi Party and her brothers fought in the German army. She did not want to be affiliated with her family and Nazi Germany, so she fled to Monaco. George assured our family that Margot's father only became a member of the Nazi party to keep his family safe but did not necessarily agree with the Nazi way of life.

George adamantly made sure we knew this and assured us that Margot's family had morals like ours. Margot's family were just trying to survive like everyone else. George wanted my parents to understand that Margot was not her father and to not hold her responsible for what her father had done or was doing during the war.

When my parents discovered that George's new bride was a Nazi's daughter, it was safe to say he was safer in the Navy than on our family estate. To make matters worse, Margot gave birth to a baby girl, Adelaide, very soon after the marriage. My mother was bed ridden for a week after George's letter, crying about the talk and gossip that would follow from the news.

My mother belonged to a prestigious ladies' group and desperately desired to be valued and highly thought of by her fellow ladies. It became her life mission. Lady Margery, in particular, held the key to the dominant opinions of the ladies group. Her opinion was the only opinion. If one was rejected or disapproved by Lady Margery, one was rejected by everyone in society.

Great Aunt Anne also belonged to my mother's ladies' group. She introduced my mother to these women. Great Aunt Anne held more than social superiority to my mother, as she often gifted the family with money. Therefore, it was of upmost importance that Great Aunt Anne thought of us in a high regard or else the money would cease to come. If any scandal fell onto the family name, Great Aunt Anne would be sure to remove us from her will.

My father particularly felt insulted and angry with George's impromptu marriage. To hurt George, my father wrote him a long letter, telling him of his anger and disappointment. How George let the Webley name down. Father told him that he felt the most disappointment in George's first born who belonged to the weaker sex. Father did not mean this at all, but when anger overcame him, he became very childish and directed his anger at people's weaknesses. Father also informed George that he was not to be affiliated with the Webley estate as long as he was married to a Nazi.

"That's awful!" Emmy sympathises. "Poor George fell in love and only wanted to marry Margot. I am glad he did not listen to your parents and stayed with his wife."

"Those were different times, Emmy dear," I reply. "Society, ladies' groups, and people like Great Aunt Anne called the shots, and you had to obey. Or else, ostracism would befall you."

Emmy passionately holds her hand to her heart. "I would gladly be ostracised if it meant I married the man I loved!" Mae, Lilian, and I share a smile and chuckle at Emmy's dramatic way of seeing life.

Emmy blushes and continues to look at the pictures to hide her embarrassment. "What did Arthur have to say about George's choice of wife?"

Mae shakes her head at Emmy to stop her from asking more question, but I am too lost in thought to answer her just yet.

FEBRUARY 1941

February 1941 arrived with an early spring. The sun shone through the oak trees and the birds happily chirped. I adored this time of year. The smell of fresh, crisp Spring air lingered in the air. The freshly polished staircase guided my way through the house to the Great Hallway. The front doors opened wide onto the garden, allowing the sun to light up the dark hall. The two maids, Mary and Daisy, spring cleaned the front porch as more staff ran through the house opening the windows. Spring had once again brought a new sense of life to the estate.

Gravel crunched and rustled in the driveway which turned my attention to a black car driving through the gates of the estate. I made my way out the doors to greet the unexpected visitors.

"Miss?" Mary sheepishly called while looking to Daisy. They both stood beside me and tried to cox me back inside. "Master Webley should deal with this visitor."

"Why ever so Mary? I can greet them. But, Daisy, do inform Papa in case he is expecting visitors."

Daisy quickly turned on her heal and disappeared down the hallway. Mary lingered behind me. Something in her presence gave me a sense of strength and comfort. Two men in military uniform stepped out of the car and walked towards me.

"Hello gentlemen, how may I help you?"

"We are looking for Lord Webley."

"He is on his way, but he might be a while. I believe he was out in the stables. Can I be of any help to you? I can take that envelope. Would you like to step inside while we wait for my father?"

They lowered their hats to me and handed me the

envelope and looked away. I glanced down at the thin paper in my hands and saw a black telegram. I hesitantly opened it and gently pulled out the piece of paper, looking up to see if my father was nearby.

The men began to speak but their voices faded to nothing as the muscles in my legs no longer knew how to work. I collapsed onto the hard gravel, cutting my knees. An agonising scream arose around me. It originated from my mouth. I did not know I was capable of making such a sound. I raised a hand to my mouth to stop further screams from escaping.

Mary rushed to help me, but I could not hear her.

The only thing I could see was the name 'Arthur Webley.'

My parents rushed out from the front door and saw me crouched on the yard crying. They desperately tried to calm me. But when they saw what was in my hand, they looked to the two men for confirmation. My mother joined me on the ground and sobbed, while my father stood tall and proud, not a tear in sight.

My father proudly spoke to the military men, as though addressing an auditorium. "Arthur died valiantly for his country," was all that he said. "Arthur died valiantly." So valiantly. My mother continued to sob into my arms as she stared emptily at the telegram.

❊ ❊ ❊

"Oh, I am sorry," Emmy lowers her head. "I just wanted to know what Arthur thought of Margot…I didn't mean to upset you, Granny."

I had not realised tears were falling from my eyes. Lilian hands me a tissue and I gently wipe the corners of my eyes.

"Oh, look how silly of me. Crying after all this time. It is okay, Emmy. If you do not ask, you will never know. Arthur's plane was shot down during the Blitz in February of 1941, so he never knew of George's wife."

"I never knew what happened to Arthur, only that he didn't live to see the end of the war," Emmy softly says. "I had no idea that Arthur fought during the Blitz."

"There are quite a lot of things people don't know about Arthur," I think aloud.

SECRETS

In the village, news spread quickly that Arthur had died after his plane was shot down during one of the many Luftwaffe bombing attacks. Everyone spoke of how valiantly he had fought and how brave he was. I wished their words could have comforted me, but they angered me.

I walked with my parents to the small local church for Arthur's memorial service. People gave me sympathetic looks and shook my hand as I passed them, each one offering their condolences. So many families had been hit with the unfortunate news that their son, brother, father, husband, uncle had died. Life was beginning to look grim.

I noticed one person trying ever so awfully hard not to break down in tears. It was Molly.

Molly's devastation drowned her. Her brown eyes no longer looked bright, warm, or full of hope, they were completely sunken into her face with bulging dark circles under them. Life exhausted her now.

When Molly heard the news of Arthur's death, she could not react any differently from anyone else. She had to commit to the secret or she could potentially lose everything.

Molly pulled me aside while everyone passed by to go into the church. We walked over to the old graveyard gateway so that we were out of earshot. Molly would not look at me at first as she was afraid that at any moment she would break down in tears. So, we waited until everyone had gone inside before we started talking.

Molly confided in me that she was nearly three months pregnant with Arthur's child.

"Did Arthur know about the baby?" I questioned.

"Yes, I told him four weeks ago when I met with him," she replied while trying to hold back her tears. "That was the last time we saw each other."

"Four weeks ago? Where did you meet him? How did he take it? Did you two discuss a plan? How did you two meet? Where did you meet?"

Molly picked at a piece of skin on the side of her nail. "I met him at your family town house on Cornwall Terrace. We often used to meet there whenever he got a day or weekend pass. He was shocked at first when I told him, but he then said that he had never felt happier." She held her hand up to her mouth as she began to sob.

I handed her my handkerchief and gently rubbed her arm to stop her from wailing.

"He asked me to marry him...and I said yes. We were planning on eloping the next time he got a day off." The tears streamed down her face. "But now he's... and I...and I am left...our baby...What am I to do?"

I held her tightly in my arms and tried to remain strong for her.

"It'll be okay. We will figure something out Molly. Don't you stress yourself," I tried to reassure her. But she continued to cry heavily into my chest. I continued to repeat these three sentences until she stopped crying.

"No man will want me...I will be the talk of the village, and I will bring shame upon my family and yours. Both will want nothing to do with me. My parents will definitely throw me out," she began to panic. "My father will kill me with his own hands if he finds out. I will be ostracised...I have seen it happen before," Molly paused to look up at me. Her eyes were bloodshot. "Lucy, what am I to do?"

I did not know how to answer her. I held her in my arms and tried my best to comfort her as she cried.

"You could move to London? I could help you find a place to live and get some work. I can try and get some money together to help you. We will figure this out together. You have to remain strong now Molly, if not for you, do it for your child."

The Vicar's voice echoed out from the church as the sermon begun. I began to quietly walk into the Church followed by Molly, who pulled her hat down, covering her face. After the service, Molly and I went our separate ways. I desperately tried to think of a way to help her. But I could not think of anything other than her moving to London to start her new life there with her baby. She could tell people that her husband died during the Blitz and nobody would be any wiser.

However, a letter arrived for me one day a few weeks after I spoke to Molly. It was a wedding invitation.

Molly quickly married a man called, Ned Finche, from the village. The day of the wedding, Molly did her best to conceal her growing bump. She distracted everyone with her dazzling smile which everyone believed was pure happiness and bliss for marrying a man that she loved.

But I knew it was relief that she and her baby had been saved. Molly cared for Ned, but unfortunately, she did not love him.

Ned adored Molly and worshipped the ground she walked on. He loved her with all his heart. When Molly gave birth to a healthy baby boy, she him named Arty. Ned suspected that Arty was not his, but he never uttered a word as he feared he would lose the family he had always wished for.

1998

Mae looks at me with wide eyes. "Arthur had a son?"

"Did Ned or anyone else ever find out that Arty was Arthur's son?" Emmy inquires, with a sympathetic look on her face as she holds Arthur's RAF picture in her hand.

"No, nobody but Molly and I knew...But, I have a feeling that Ned had his suspicions about who the real father was. He never said anything. He was a gentle and kind man Ned, who hated the idea of hurting someone, even if they hurt him," I sadly reply.

"I first met Arty when he was a toddler and he looked strikingly like Arthur. He had Arthur's golden-blond hair paired with Molly's soft, brown eyes," I pause and smile to myself while I picture the little boy in my head. "And I watched him grow into a very handsome young lad."

"Did Molly and Ned have any more children?" Mae asks.

"For a while there was only Arty until they had a little girl. Molly was very fond of Ned, but they were more friends than husband and wife. Ned adored Molly and he settled for what he had. He was a gentle soul. On her death bed, she called for her dear Arthur," I solemnly reply.

"What about your parents?", Emmy asks. "Did they ever know about this? Or suspect anything?"

"No, never. My parents never knew, and I can't imagine how they would have reacted to the news. It would have tarnished their lovely memory of Arthur, and it was those memories of him that gave them comfort after his death."

For me, knowing Arthur had son made me smile to think that part of him lives on.

"A person's memory and spirit never really die when people are named after them or when people continue to talk about them. They almost carry the deceased with them."

Lilian kindly smiles at me and gently pats my hand.

"It never gets easier talking about those we have lost. But I think it's lovely Emmy that you are so interested in learning about your lineage and wanting to know about your grandmother's life."

"I just feel that Granny is the last connection we have to these people and even her life-story. I want to pass on her memories and stories of these people, so that they are never forgotten."

Mae and Lilian smile at Emmy as she continues to flick through the album. I know that Emmy is doing this to help with my grief. Since Will's death I have become weighed down with grief that I am slowly beginning to forget things. It frightens me.

Every morning I wake, I still think Will is beside me in the bed. Every time that I turn to say "good morning" I remember that he is not there. It is taking longer and longer for me to realise this. I am slowly forgetting how to live.

It truly brightens my heart to know that Emmy, Mae, Lilian, and the rest of my family want to help me remember.

"Well, I am enjoying it too as I have never really heard you talk about your family before in such detail," Mae adds. "Most of what you have told, I have never heard before. How come you didn't talk about your family or your brothers?"

"I've never been asked," I simply reply.

Emmy continues to look at the photos and arrives onto the next page.

"Granny, who is this woman standing beside you? Do you remember her name?"

I look at the Victorian dressed woman, holding a stern and hateful glare that still makes me shudder even in my old age.

"Unfortunately, that is a woman I remember all too well."

MADAM SPEIRS

Growing up, my parents hired a governess for me. My mother felt the house was too empty with Arthur and George away at school, that I was kept at home. My mother spent her days obsessively thinking of the past, with Nell taking centre stage of her mind. Most days, my mother became inebriated with migraines and required silence. But it was the silence of the house slowly that burnt her nerves to insanity.

My governess, Madam Speirs, became my prison guard and I felt utterly alone and isolated at home.

Madam Speirs was the most insufferable, fearful, dreadfully ugly looking thing that I have ever come across in my entire life. I once heard that governesses must be unattractive and frightfully ugly as to scare the children into learning their lessons, but also so that the governess would not tempt the husbands! There were many stories of husbands running off with governesses – but mother could always rest assured that her husband would not be tempted by Madam Speirs.

I often found myself unknowingly staring at her, trying to figure out what could be changed about her to make her somewhat appealing, but unfortunately there was nothing that could be done.

Madam Speirs stood tall like an oppressive building, always peering down. She was rather plump around the middle, with thick muscular arms and large feet. Her long, pointed nose veered to the left of her face and her blue, close-set eyes pierced into your soul whenever she set her gaze upon you. She had thin, chapped lips that stretched into a tight smile which surfaced when she was about to make you suffer. Inflicting pain and keeping a person in a state of suffering was her pastime. She had a protruding chin and a thick neck which tightly squeezed into her starched, white collar of her

Victorian blouse. She strangled her brittle, black hair into a bun at the crown of her head, drawing more attention to her grumpy face. Her hands were chapped and rough, with stumpy fingers and severely cut nails, perfect for slamming onto desks to emphasise her point.

Madam Speirs was not known for being nice and gentle. Her harsh, cold, crude, and volatile reputation exceeded her. She hated children with a passion and would only qualify a child as a person once they turned 18 years of age. Madam Speirs was a firm believer in punishing a child for something that they 'could do' - meaning you "probably have the thought to do something naughty, therefore I am punishing you for your future-self's actions."

This constantly frustrated me as I would have to painfully endure hours of writing lines, suffer a few belts from her splinted wooden ruler, or she would make me stand in one spot for hours, reciting poetry and Shakespearean quotes with my arms outstretched barely able to breathe. Many of my toys became victims of her anger as she would break them in front of me, for the simple reason that she could.

If ever I defied her or annoyed her, mainly by being in her presence, I would shortly hear – "left palm up" - followed by a sharp dull pain and the cursing woosh of her cain passing my ear.

Madam Speirs had a strange ability of blending into her surroundings and then popping out when she had caught me doing something I should not have been doing. It was one of her more special talents.

One afternoon forever sticks in my memory. I escaped a lesson with her on needlework. I tip-toed along the corridors and into the kitchen and stole a freshly baked shortbread biscuit. It was so quiet as all the kitchen staff were on a break. As the intoxicating smell of the warm biscuit hit my nose, I opened my mouth wide and shoved the entire biscuit in my mouth.

Madam Speirs, ever so smoothly, stepped out from the olive-green wall and bitterly announced through gritted teeth, "Lucy. Annabelle. Webley."

I never understood how Madam Speirs blended into the

wall or how she could terrify a person without raising her voice.

She grabbed me by the chin and forced me to spit out the biscuit and watched as I struggled to breathe. Once I got my breath back, Madam Speirs made me clean up the crumbling biscuit mess around me. She skilfully remained calm until we were back in the library. There she unleashed her cain.

Her job, as my parents instructed, was to teach me "to be a fashionable and socially savvy young lady who can have elegant, coherent conversations with potential suitors." Because that was apparently all my parents aspired for me in life was to be a wife, while they sent Arthur and George off to boarding school and then onto college to be whatever they pleased.

My days and weeks were mapped out for me. I attended piano and violin lessons in the morning, followed by reading poetry aloud with the focus on my diction. French and German lessons were interchangeable after lunch, followed by lessons on literature and art. Shakespearean plays were included in these lessons, and ballet lessons were before dinner with needlework reserved for the evening.

I also had to have impeccable morals, learn about social graces, decorum at social gatherings, what is considered fashionable and good etiquette along with daily elocution lessons. All of this kept me busy, but not entertained.

The only part of my day that I found my joy and solitude in was when I was playing the piano in the evening times, as I could finally be alone. My favourite piece to play was *Chopin's Nocturne op. 9 No. 2*. However, mother always insisted that it was a melancholic piece and too advanced for a young girl to comprehend. I thought it was rather reflective and relaxed my busy mind.

The music was so gentle and flowing, taking me away into its world. The waltz-like rhythm soothed my ears, gently rocking me along to its melody. With gentle tremolos, decorative tones and trills which enchanted me further into its melody, the free-flowing right hand fully captured me in its story.

From the moment that I opened the piano lid, I

immediately entered my own world. A world that was always peaceful, like a calm summer's evening as the sun melted into magnificent colours across the skyline. My thoughts instantly fell away, quietening and allowing my hectic mind to stop for a while. Doors of my unconscious mind opened and effortlessly flowed through me. All my aches and pains faded away with each note that I played.

When the piece would end, I would be reminded of my reality. Madam Speirs would find me once again and I would leave my little corner of happiness.

Every day became the same, with the same timetable and layout. Similar conversations, just different dates. My childhood slowly slipped away from me without my knowing. Adulthood was almost upon me. I could feel my life slipping away from my grasp. I knew exactly where my life was heading. The road paved neatly before me, all I had to do was follow. I hated the drowning feeling of knowing what my life was going to be before I even lived it. I hated knowing that I had this life planned without my say, without my input. My life was not mine.

I desperately desired to do something worthwhile with my life that would matter or help others. I wanted something that was completely my own, that I had decided to pursue.

Throughout the second half of the 1930's, there was constant talk of war breaking out in Europe. Nobody believed that it was possible, as the great war that was fought in 1914 to 1918 was supposed to be the "war to end all wars."

If anyone was caught talking about a possible second war, they were met with angry glares and disapproving noises. Nobody wanted to admit what the world would become if we had to face another war.

In 1937, I turned seventeen. Serious talks of an approaching war were discussed in almost every conversation. I was told to focus on things that would matter more, like finding a suitable husband and "not to worry my delicate mind with such worldly matters."

I decided that if a war came it would be my chance to do something. So, I decided I wanted to be a nurse and then I would be of practical use to society.

One Spring evening after dinner, I brought up the subject of nursing to my parents. My mother's favourite word – "no" - surfaced and there it stayed all night. I could not understand what was *so* wrong with wanting to be a nurse.

Why was it so shameful?

"But you were a nurse during the great war, why can't I train to be one?" I retorted.

My mother pinched the bridge of her nose. Another headache surfacing. "Those times were different, Lucy. My family opened our estate house to recovering soldiers and it was, therefore, my duty to help and nurse the men as they were our *guests* at the estate. I was not necessarily a nurse but a hostess. You on the other hand want to *actively* pursue a career in nursing, which is not for people like us. Not many potential suitors will want a lady who has touched blood and God knows what else. You will be exposed to diseases. Who knows what other ghastly things you would have to do? Nursing is not for people like us, Lucy, end of."

I tried my best to remain calm but with each sigh and shake of her head, an anger began to rise within me.

"Charles! Do you hear this?" my mother wailed as father absent-mindedly sat on his armchair reading the newspaper.

Father sighed, taking another puff of his pipe. "Yes, my darling I hear. Lucy do listen to your mother."

"It's very charming of you wanting to give something back to society, but you should know that a girl like you is not made for a job like nursing. You wouldn't last two seconds even in training," my mother laughed while patting my arm.

I took in a deep breath to calm my frustration, but my face betrayed me.

"Don't look at me like that, Lucy! Think of what people will say about a Webley girl wanting to be a nurse. You will have no chance of marrying, because no family will want a girl who does a degrading job for a living. It would be like letting their son marry a maid!" she laughed yet again.

I felt so small and patronised by my parents. I abruptly stood up which shook the table and at the tip of my tongue I considered yelling them that their son was in fact in love with a maid and wanted to marry her, but I knew that would not help anyone. So, I left the room and tried to plan how to bring up the subject again.

For weeks, I consistently brought up nursing to my parents. They tried to make me consider studying a small course at Oxford, but I wanted to do something more practical and useful. I found advertisements in my father's papers for training to be a nurse, and I highlighted them in red ink each morning before he got the paper. I also went into his study, opened books on pages that had nursing on them or were about something medical, drew a red cross by them and placed them on his desk.

His patience slowly wore thin. I knew that if I continued to annoy him in little ways he would break and then I would move onto my mother. But in the meantime, I also worked on her by bringing up her past nursing experience and how she met my father through her nursing.

My mother's reaction stayed the same each time. Nursing was a degrading job in her eyes. I tried to explain to her that by allowing me to nurse, she would gain an advantage with her competitive ladies group. It would make her appear as a modern, forward-thinking woman with modern values, who allowed her daughter to pursue a career...rather than oppressing her daughter and forcing her into marriage.

My mother's ladies group spent their days trying to out-do each other and to be the leader. Allowing me to nurse might be her chance to be seen as ahead of the curve. I tried to show my mother that if a war did break out, that it would provide comfort to her ladies group, that their sons would be cared for by someone like me. Someone from their own background. She contemplated this.

After our conversation, my mother went to luncheon with her ladies' group and subtly turned the topic of conversation to nursing. Lady Margery spoke highly of how every woman should embody their compassionate and caring nature, but she did not fully believe in a woman nursing people that were not her kin. Nevertheless, she had great admiration for them.

Like sheep, the group of ladies agreed with Lady Margery. When Mother arrived home, she had a new perspective on nursing.

By Autumn 1937, my parents allowed me to complete a course in first aid so that I would get a flavour for what nursing would be like. But I believed it was only because their patience was growing short with me. Well, they did raise me to be stubborn and to persevere!

I attended a first aid day-training course in the town near us for a month. A new First Aid Textbook arrived from America and we studied it. I learned the basics of first aid, such as, how to dress a wound, what to do when someone faints, vomits, chokes on something and how to treat a minor burn wound.

Even though it was the basics that I was learning, I was hooked! I loved caring for someone and knowing that what I was doing was of some help, that I helped to make someone at ease in their pain or illness. After this training, I began to help at the local doctors and at the small convalescent hospital on the outskirts of town. I mainly had cleaning duties or giving the patients a cup of tea, but I knew that nursing was the job for me.

1938

In May 1938, I turned eighteen and I was allowed apply to be a nurse.

I filled out the forms, bought the stamp, walked to the post-box, and posted it. I made sure my forms were safely delivered and not 'mishandled' by any of the staff at the house. I did not trust anyone else to do this.

Even though my mother saw how happy nursing made me, I knew she would fail to post my letter hoping I would see her perspective and change my mind. I could become a lady of society and join her ladies' group.

I received my acceptance into a three-year training course to be a nurse at a voluntary hospital called, St. Angela's in London.

Voluntary or teaching hospitals were thought of as superior to the infirmaries, as studying at them was almost the same as studying at a university for they were privately run. They ran on donations and the patients were almost always privately paying. Whereas the infirmaries were public and were open to anyone. Unfortunately, at the time a good health care system was not in place in the country. Most infirmaries were built near cemeteries where most patients went on a one-way trip when they entered.

The neighbouring St. Angela's Convent ran the St. Angela's Voluntary Hospital. Both civilian and sister nurses worked there. The hospital was prestigious and well-respected. Queen Elizabeth, consort of King George VI, came to the hospital and opened a new training wing. It was then named after her. The training wing was supplied with the top of the range medical instruments of the time and was superbly decorated. The hospital also held a unit of Queen Alexandria's Imperial Military Nursing Service, which meant I would be able to become a military nurse if war broke out.

I was beyond proud to say that I studied there.

On a Saturday afternoon in September 1937, our family driver Beatty drove me to the convent. Beatty was a quiet middle-aged man who dedicated his life to our family and the estate. I liked being in his company as he saw me for me, not who I could be or how he wanted me to be. Beatty looked upon me and my brothers as his kin.

We arrived at St. Angela's, and I was in awe of the old, gothic building. My Grandfather Webley donated a large sum of money to this convent many years ago and in honour of this the nuns dedicated a section of the garden to him, called the *Allister Webley Walled Garden* and a small ward was dedicated to my grandmother, called the *Adelaide Webley Ward*.

Upon seeing the walled garden, I began to bite my nails. I wanted to leave behind the Webley name, or the connotations that came with it, even for a short while. But alas, it was not to be. The name followed me everywhere, or so it appeared.

A small old nun stood at the door of the convent waiting for me. Beatty got out of the car, opened my door, and handed me my suitcase.

"Will you be okay Miss?" Beatty whispered.

"Yes, thank you Beatty," I smiled at him. "Safe trip back home."

Part of me wanted to get back into the car with Beatty and go back to what was familiar. But I walked towards the nun with my suitcase in hand.

I could see she was observing me, the car, my driver, my clothes, and my suitcase. I wore my new lilac metropolitan dress, since I was in London, and paired it with my white and brown cut-out Oxford walking shoes, silk stockings, white crotchet-lace gloves, and my new Slouch hat. My suitcase had my initials in gold-plated letters on the side of it, and on each of the locks it had a 'W' for Webley carved into it.

I had never felt more aware of my upbringing, my background, and my clothes before this, as the way the nun looked at me made me feel insecure. I was aware of my life and my family's wealth. I expected to be met with more similar looks inside by the other girls.

"Good afternoon and welcome to St. Angela's. I am Sister Dominic, and you must be?"

"Lucy Annabelle Webley," I shyly replied.

"Webley?" Sr Dominic slowly nodded to herself as she looked towards the walled garden. "Very good, Miss Webley, you are most welcome here. Our convent and way of life is very modest...might be a shock for you," she laughed. "Nonetheless, follow me."

The magnificent wooden doors opened onto the hallway, revealing a mosaic tiled floor, carved oak staircase, and a long stain-glass window at the top of the stairs which beamed down onto the floor, igniting the colours of the mosaic. I stood in awe looking around the room until I saw Sr Dominic staring at me with a smile.

"That was exactly my reaction when I walked through those doors for the first time," she joyfully recalled.

Sister Dominic took in the room and breathed deeply, as if sparking old memories. I followed her example and took in a deep breath. It smelled of polished wooden floors, with blossoming lilies on the end table, carbolic soap and polish used daily on the stairs.

"Make sure you take it all in, you won't be allowed on this side of the convent once you begin your training," Sister Dominic's voice broke my trance. "The others are in this room through here."

I began to wonder about my time spent here. Would I only be surrounded by nuns and not with other girls like me? Is this why my parents let me go – so that I would be monitored and surrounded by nuns?

"Sister?" I called. "Are all the girls that I am to train with nuns like you?"

"No there will be other girls like you – civilians. Some of the nurses that will train you will be nuns, but not all of them," she answered. "We wear the habit, and you wear the uniform, Miss Webley, that's the only real difference. We are first and foremost nurses, and we are united through that." Sister Dominic reassuringly smiled as she opened the door for me and then left me to walk into the room alone.

I shyly glanced at the unfamiliar faces as the girls looked out the long sash window at my family's automobile. They quickly turned their gaze to me and I moved my eyes back to the floor. They took their turn to slowly look me up and down. The room was unbearably quiet.

Sr Dominic had officially left me, so I tried to break the silence.

I shyly waved. "Hello, I'm Lucy."

More silence. Why did I wave? I must have looked ridiculous to them.

They heard my accent, saw my clothes and that I had a family automobile, and they immediately made their mind up about me – that I was an idiotic rich girl.

One of the girls evaluated me in disgust while creeping towards me.

"What's a girl like you doing here?" She turned to the group and smirked. "Did you take a wrong turn coming out of Selfridges? Did you tire of your servants feeding you from silver spoons?"

Her words felt like she was spitting venom at me. A circle formed around me as sniggers erupted from the group. I realised I had left Madam Speirs and quickly found myself another.

I could see most of the girls feared the outspoken one and only nodded along in fear. A bully always seems to have that ability as their only tool is fear.

The outspoken girl was taller than me by an inch which she enjoyed as she peered down at me. If she were not so angry, rude, and insulting, she would be a pretty girl. But negativity always has a way of destroying people's natural beauty.

She stood closer to me and continued to peer down, ensuring I knew who was in charge. I annoyed myself with my inability to stand taller. I hated myself for being affected by their dislike of me. But I desperately wanted a friend.

I never had one.

"Enough! What is it to you where she comes from? That does not matter here, we are all at the same level – trainee nurses. Class, our upbringing, or how much money we own means nothing in here," a kind dark haired girl spoke from the front of the group. She outstretched her hand to me with a smile. "I'm Lilian Comerford by the way."

Lilian had a warm and gentle glow to her despite her being so pale that the sun would reflect off her skin. She reminded me of *Snow White,* which happened to be my favourite fairy-tale. Her oval blue eyes were a welcoming sight and I instantly felt connected to her.

"And I'm Beatrice Howard," the outspoken girl tried to imitate Lilian's Irish accent. She turned to me with the same venom in her voice, "But why should we bother to learn your name? I bet you won't last the day. You won't be able to live without your servants waiting on you hand and foot, doing every little thing for you. Your kind of people are pathetic."

Beatrice abruptly walked past me, making sure to hit my shoulder on her way and kick my suitcase.

"Quiet!" a firm voice from behind me shouted.

I turned around and saw an old nurse standing tall. Her eyes immediately fell on me and she saw the circle of girls surrounding me. I could tell she was thinking the same things as the other girls – silly rich girl.

She looked straight in my eyes and barked, "Name?"

The other girls smugly giggled.

"Lucy," I replied with my eyes glued to the floor.

"Full name."

"Lucy Annabelle."

"In here, you go by your surname, not your first name."

I bit the side of my nail and kept my eyes glued on the floor. "Well, I shall go by Nurse Anna. That way it will keep my first name private."

The nurse glanced at the list of names on her clipboard, sighed and made a note in pencil. With a firm full stop, she stared back at me.

"Fine. Nurse Anna it is. Let us see how long you last here, Nurse Anna." She sounded out my name as though it was the title of a children's book. But I was glad to have the attention move away from me. I refused to give my surname. I did not want any more attention drawn to my background. I wanted a clean slate, to be known for me and not for my family name. Now was my chance to step away from that life.

"Right, form a line in front of me. My name is Matron Jones, and I am here to turn you girls into nurses. From now on you will no longer go by your first name. You do not have an identity once you wear your training nurse's uniform. You are representing an establishment, not yourself. Until you become a fully trained nurse, you are a number. Outside of these walls, you can be whoever you want to be and call yourself whatever name you want. Is that understood?"

Matron Claudia Jones was a harsh strong woman. Her presence alone demanded respect. She had been a nurse for over thirty years and not much surprised her. Her job was her family and home. Everyone desperately wanted to be on her good side. Matron Jones could make life hell for those that did not impress her.

I made it my mission to earn her respect. She did not need to like me, but her respect was the utmost importance to me.

Matron Jones and Sister Dominic led us to our living quarters. The nurse-quarters were three large connecting rooms. The second room was mine to share with 10 other girls. We each had a single creaky bed with a shelf above it and a bedside table. I placed my suitcase on my bed and looked around the room.

This was to be the beginning of my future in my new home. My chance to prove myself.

Lilian took the bed next to mine. The first thing we were told to learn was that a nurse should first and foremost be obedient and devoted at all times. We were told how to unpack our things and where to put them. We were handed a sheet with our weekly schedule on it and we were told that we could never be more than a second late to any of our lectures or duties.

Matron Jones told us that we needed to be broken down before we could be built up again. We needed to learn discipline and control. Matron Jones and Sr. Dominic walked through the three rooms watching each of us settle in, practically judging who would make it to the finish line and who would fail.

We began to settle into our new living quarters, and I tried to learn everyone's name but was quickly overwhelmed as most of the girls sniggered at me making Beatrice proud.

Matron Jones blew through her whistle and the room fell silent.

"During your time here as trainee nurses, you will not be allowed leave the Convent grounds for the first two months, unless you have been given permission to do so. Once you have completed a certain level of your training and can be trusted, then you will be allowed leave the convent and go wherever you wish for the day. However, you must sign yourself in and out when doing so. Most of the nurses before you usually went into central London together for the day, but until then you are to stay here. When out and about, you are absolutely not to wear your uniform. Is that clear?"

The room fell silent.

"I believe the correct answer is 'yes, Matron Jones.'"

"Yes, Matron Jones," we echoed. She had the room's attention in a heartbeat. She looked around and glared each girl in the eye. Nobody could escape her.

"Breakfast begins at 5 am and finishes at 5.45 am. Report for duty at 6am sharp. Classes have been scheduled and will take place throughout the day. You each have a copy of the timetable but in case you are foolish enough to misplace it, a timetable is on the wall. Lunch is at noon, dinner is at 4pm, and tea is at 7pm. You are to make use of the library in the convent and study there during you free time, in-between classes and work, and each evening after dinner. Lights out at 9 pm sharp," Matron Jones continued.

Yet another timetable and schedule to live by, but this time it is for something that I picked for myself.

"You are required to pay £20 which will pay for your uniform and textbooks," Sr. Dominic softly spoke. "And your salary for first year will be £18."

"That'll be all. Now, unpack and settle in. Your timetable will officially begin tomorrow," Matron Jones commanded before leaving the room with Sr. Dominic trailing behind her.

The girls began to talk once again. I overheard one girl protest, "I didn't think we would be locked up here months on end, what will my Rodney think?" while another answered her question, "what did you expect?"

I sat on my bed and soaked in the atmosphere. Would I prove my parents wrong, or right? Or would I prove something to myself?

"Where are you from?" Lilian asked which brought me out of my daydream.

"I am from a town in Buckinghamshire. You've probably never heard of it," I shyly replied. "Your accent is lovely, but I cannot seem to place where in Ireland it's from."

"I'm from county Kilkenny," she warmly smiled.

"Oh, how lovely! I do not think I have ever met someone from Kilkenny before. I've read about the castle of Kilkenny."

"You've heard of the castle? My cousins live there."

"Really?"

"No!" Lilian chuckled. "No, nobody has lived there for years."

"If you don't mind me asking, how did you end up here?"

"Ask away! I come from a farming family of five girls, including myself, and one boy. The house was getting more and more crowded over the years, so it seemed only right to leave."

"Good heavens! Four sisters and one brother."

"Yes, and my brother Michael is in the middle with women either side of him! But, me and my sisters did more work on the farm than he ever did."

"Do you miss your family?"

"I try not to think about them too much or I will long to be at home again with them. I write to them as often as I can and that helps to minimise the longing. I had to leave home. I turned 17 last July and there was no work at home. I knew if I didn't find work soon, I would be some farmers wife by the time I was 20," Lilian rolled her eyes while sighing with a laugh.

"Why did you come to London and not Dublin?"

"My Mother has an aunt here in London, so she wrote to her and asked if I could come over and stay. Aunt June was delighted to have me. She was only too happy to have someone else around the house. Aunt June has lived in London for over 40 years, and she rarely comes home but she always wrote the most wonderful letters. She's one of my favourite people."

I suddenly felt more at ease and relaxed on my bed as I continued to talk to Lilian.

"Your aunt sounds charming!"

"Do you know, living with her was the first time that I got time to myself? It was first time that I had a whole bedroom to myself, believe it or not, and I didn't know what to do with all my free time and space."

Sharing a room seemed so foreign to me.

"What did you do before coming here to St Angela's?" I asked.

"I worked in Selfridges at one of the front counters. It was a good job with good money. I really loved being on Oxford Street."

"I always loved when my mother would bring me with her into Selfridges whenever we came to visit London. It's where she buys her perfume. She would always spray a tiny bit of it on me and I would feel all grown up for the day," I reminisced.

I stopped myself from saying any more as I was afraid that some of the other girls would overhear and spark the insults again. I knew I could not tell them about my family or my life.

"You don't need to try to diminish yourself or your upbringing for my benefit," Lilian patted my hand.

"But the other girls-"

"If the other girls have an issue that you've come from a different background to them, then that's their issue and not yours," she shrugged.

I looked around the room and felt more looks of disgust being directed at me but I turned my attention back to Lilian.

"What made you decide to become a nurse?" I asked.

"I felt I wanted to do more in life, to give back. I have heard people talks about another possible war and I decided there and then that if there is to be a war, I want to do something that helps. So, I saw an advertisement for nursing here in St. Angela's and I signed up. I told my aunt and family afterwards and they seemed incredibly happy for me, which was a relief," she happily told. "What about you?"

"I want to do something that mattered but unlike you, my

family is not so supportive of my decision. They feel I should be at home, that that is my place in society."

"Well, all you can do Lucy is live for yourself, and if being a nurse makes you happy then that's all that matters," she reassuringly smiled.

Lilian had such a simple outlook of life. Things did not stress her unless she felt them important enough to spend her time thinking about them. She viewed life as a refillable glass, neither half empty nor half full.

By the end of the night, I knew I had made a true friend.

1998

"Granny, where have you gone to?" Emmy's soft voice directs me back to the living room.

I rub my eyes and readjust the cushions around me. "Oh… my apologies Emmy. I was thinking about St. Angela's and my first few months there."

"I can tell you this much Emmy, I would never go back to nurses' training," Lilian shakes her head.

"Really?" Mae asks. "But I thought you both loved St. Angela's and your nursing days."

"Love is a strong word! We did enjoy it, don't get me wrong, but it was tough," Lilian puffs out her cheeks.

I gently smile at Lilian and turn to Emmy who eagerly waits for me to continue telling her my story.

"The training was nowhere near easy, but the reward I felt at the end of the hard work was what kept us going. As trainee nurses, we were immediately thrown into cleaning duties. We cleaned beds, washed delph, mopped the floors, and worst of all cleaned out bedpans".

Lilian recoils, making us all laugh. "The bedpans…don't get me started on the bedpans."

"We had to keep ourselves immaculately clean at all times, as there were strict hygiene rules. By the end of the first week, my hands were so dry and chapped from constantly scrubbing them clean," I continue. I look at my hands now and see how wrinkled they have become over the years. I rub them together and feel their softness, yet after all this time, I can still remember the dry stinging sensation.

"For luck, your Granny and I were paired with each other for most of our duties. Or we were paired with Betty," Lilian smiles.

"Ah yes, Betty! I adored Betty. From time to time I was paired with Beatrice, who made sure to make my time hell in her company. She often would spit "pathetic" at me, just in case I forgot she did not like me." I laugh now in spite of it all. So much changed after St Angela's.

Emmy puffs. "What a horrible woman!"

A dusty memory of Beatrice filters into my mind. I remember stocking the shelves in the storage room with Beatrice who spent the entire time passive aggressively insulting me. I had reached my breaking point and shouted back at her. I told her that I believed she was jealous woman and I did not have the faintest idea why. The other girls had moved past the petty stage of insults and sniggering. They had made the effort to start over and become a friend of mine. I demanded Beatrice tell me what I had done to offend her and how we could move past these petty and tiring insults.

Beatrice stared at me with a look of utter disgust on her face. She pushed passed me and knocked everything from the shelf that I had just stocked. I tried my best to remain calm, to understand her and make excuses for her, but it got tiring and I had to endure it.

Oh, how I can I laugh at it now. But at the time, trying to win over Beatrice became a daily struggle.

Emmy glances up at me as she turns the photo-album to more pictures of my nursing days. "What was your training like, apart from the constant cleaning? How were you treated?"

"In training, Emmy, nobody was treated nicely. Matron Jones definitely held no favourites. Sometimes, it was hard to tell the difference between those she had time for and those she despised," I tell.

Lilian adjusts the cushions around her and leans forward. "You see, the medical profession at the time was male dominated with nurses being all female. This was why Matron Jones was hard on us – she wanted us to be just as good at our job, maybe even better than some of the male doctors. She pushed us and made us work *so* hard, that we would be respected."

"I can still hear Matron Jones say, 'There is no reason why any of you girls should not be doctors. In fact, many of you are more than capable of being a doctor. Unfortunately, it must be this way, and you all must be nurses for now. But by God, am I going to make sure that all of you girls under me are the best nurses this hospital has ever seen – actually, that any hospital has ever seen. St. Angela's has a reputation for training the best nurses. So, do not let me down.'

Matron Jones was inspiring and put everything she had into giving us the best training we would ever get. I would not have gotten far in my nursing if it were not for Matron Jones."

Emmy gently smiles. "She sounds very inspiring."

"The work was truly exhausting and the days were long and hard. But every day was different and I liked that," I smile. "Everyone was dressed the same. I felt I belonged somewhere, and I was among like-minded people. Once I had my nurses' uniform on, I no longer felt like I had to carry the burden of the Webley name on my shoulders and act like an impeccable lady - I discovered myself. My parents sent me to St. Angela's to humour and occupy me. They believed I would be revolted by what I saw and come home immediately. But I loved it. I loved being a nurse and helping another."

ST ANGELA'S

My first day on duty at St. Angela's hospital always stuck with me.

I nervously walked into the hospital ward with the other girls. Part of me felt as though I was playing dress up, that I did not belong in a hospital. But seeing Matron Jones standing proudly as she inspected our uniforms infused a sense of strength within me. She reassured me that I belonged here and if I was unsure what to do, she was there.

I patted down my stiff new uniform and smiled. This moment was what I wanted, for so long. And here I was. I bashfully glanced at the other girls and smiled at our new uniforms. A pale primrose pink for junior nurses, a pastel egg-shell blue was for senior nurses, and a lime green was for sisters. All the uniforms were paired with soft, white collars and cuffs, and starched wrap-around aprons. I day-dreamed of the day that I would become a senior nurse and how proud I would feel.

Once we received our duties for the day, we started to work. I met with my leader for the day, Senior Nurse Potter, whom I would shadow. She evaluated my work and taught me the ways.

Nurse Potter brought me to our first patient. He was a man in his late thirties. I introduced myself to him and looked at his chart, but he did not turn to look at me or say a word. For a moment, I thought maybe he had not heard me. Nurse Potter observed my interaction with the patient, and she shrewdly watched how I handled him. He slowly turned his head to me and looked into my eyes with the most blank expression on his face. I tried to speak to him again, but he opened his mouth as if to say something. I bent down and leaned in closer to him to hear what he might say. He turned his head and projectile vomited on me. I froze.

"It's only a bit of vomit, you'll be alright," Nurse Potter sighed. "Clean up here and then go clean your uniform. Go on, move!"

Two minutes into the working day and my new uniform was already ruined. I wanted to cry but that would not be acceptable. I quickly cleaned the man and immediately ran to the bathroom. I desperately tried to scrub myself clean but with every whiff of the sour smell of vomit that hit my nose, a sickness within me would surface.

I could not do this. I could not live every day like this, with a stranger's vomit on me. What was I thinking?

I pushed away my intruding thoughts as Nurse Potter appeared at the bathroom door, demanding that I return to the ward and continue our ward checks.

The remainder of the day went by quickly and I began to get into the swing of things. I efficiently attended all my patients that I had been assigned to for the day. Both Nurse Potter and Matron Jones recognised this. Beatrice fell behind on her duties, which Matron Jones decided to move some of Beatrice's patients over into my care. Naturally, Beatrice did not agree with this.

As I attended to one of her patients, I realised I forgot to get new bandages. I made my way to the storage room and found the bandages. As I walked back, Beatrice was leaving the ward with an object in her hand. As she grew closer, I realised it was a bedpan. She tripped and poured the contents of the bedpan all over me, while whispering "pathetic" into my ear.

Beatrice left me standing in the corridor, with urine dripping down the front of my uniform. The harsh and bitter smell filled my nostrils, and I began to gag. I sheepishly peered down at my uniform and saw the new yellow stain running down the front as it brought out the stains from the vomit. My stomach clenched, and my eyes began to well up.

All I wanted to do was curl up in a ball and cry. Instead, I cleaned myself yet again and returned to the hospital ward.

I could see Beatrice standing in the middle of a small group with a smirk on her face, each head turned to me as I passed them by. Their sniggers sent shivers down my spine. I focused on putting one foot in front of the other and hoped they would get me to the end of the day.

In late December 1938, I went home for Christmas.

The girls and I walked out of the convent with smiles on our faces as we wore our nurse's cape and a freshly cleaned uniform. We were a united front. We chatted about our holiday plans and how we would miss each other. A car horn beeped, and I turned to see Beatty standing with a proud smile as he held the door open for me. He called out to me and came to take my bags. The girls looked from Beatty to me.

A wave of embarrassment flew over me as the girls eyed up my family's shiny car and my initialised suitcase. I desired to be like the other girls – independent – as they fetched a bus or a train home to their families. I envied them. I quickly stepped into the car and asked Beatty to go immediately to avoid the glares from the girls.

This was my first-time home since I left for St. Angela's. Home felt different. My parents were delighted to see me, and they hoped I would be in tears begging them to never let me go back there again. But I wanted to cry. They were not wrong about that.

Father grinned while twirling me around in the hallway. "My darling Belle, you look adorable in your nurse's cloak."

My parents pet name for me was 'Belle' which was short for Lucy Annabelle. Since childhood, I was referred to as 'Belle' if behaved correctly. Lucy only came out when I misbehaved. It struck me how I was called different names by so many different people.

What did I call myself?

My father smiled at my unimpressed mother who quickly turned to the maid and grunted, "Daisy, prepare the tea for us in the Green Room."

The room fell silent and father tried his best to crack a joke to lighten the mood. But mother's negative disposition would not allow it.

That afternoon, we drank tea together in the Green Room. I told them about how much I loved my nurses training and how I felt like I had a purpose, that I was doing something that mattered.

At dinner, I excitedly told them about the girls I trained with. Surely, they would remember some of the names from my letters. I told them about Matron Jones and Sister Dominic, and how I admired them both. I happily told them stories about my dormitories and the different personalities. The room fell silent and I realised I had been speaking to myself. My mother kept her eyes firmly on her empty dinner plate while my father stared at the portraits on the walls.

The maids hurriedly cleared our plates from the table and placed dessert before us. I sorrowfully glanced between my parents, hoping they would notice that I had stopped talking.

My father looked to my mother who would not return his look. He gently held my hand in his and smiled.

"They are all wonderful stories. It sounds like you have had a smashing time there in St. Angela's. Don't you agree Esme? Well Lucy…if nursing makes you happy, then I am happy for you. That is all we want for you, to be happy. Isn't it Esme?"

Mother's reply was a sip of tea and a glance into her cup.

"But…" he stared intently, "if war breaks out, you are to come home. You are absolutely not going anywhere near military hospitals, London, or even the coast of England. Is that understood? You will come home and stop nursing. There will be no need for you to nurse. Is that understood?"

"Yes Papa," I mumbled.

1939

On the 1st of September 1939, Hitler invaded Poland. Britain and France declared war on Germany a few days later. World War II had officially begun. For the first few months of the war, it was relatively quiet and was often referred to as the 'Phoney War.'

As our nurse training progressed, we spent our time at the hospital practising and improving our skills that would be needed with wounded soldiers. Our duties extended beyond the hospital to helping out with the war effort in whatever way we could.

It felt as though everyone could only talk about the war and what we thought might happen. We were all frightened. An intense rush began to arise amongst people to do something to help with the war effort.

In my family, this was true. Arthur joined the RAF and George joined the Royal Navy. I prayed that they would be kept safe. My parents ordered me to come home but I could not leave St Angela's.

The war was all anyone could talk about. It dominated everyone's conversations. My father began to accept my nursing and understood that I would not be giving it up. My mother insisted I give up nursing and come home. It seemed her ladies' groups changed their opinions on nursing.

All I thought was, "what does it matter what society thinks of me now that there is a war?"

But I never spoke out of turn. That was not how I was brought up to be like. I continued my training, but I desperately wanted to help more.

Matron Jones observed me more closely as the training progressed. She privately praised me for being a quick and keen learner. After only a year's training, she recognised I had pushed myself to excel and learn as much as I could.

She especially noticed my picking up on other's slack and working with the other nurses as an efficient team. I did not know how to react to this conversation as Matron Jones rarely complimented anyone. Everyone accepted an insult quicker from her.

Matron Jones spoke of how nurses were needed in military hospitals and in hospitals nearer the coast rather than London. She believed I was being wasted in a convalescent hospital.

Of course, I needed more training, but at least I could see a potential future where my talents would be needed. I wished Matron Jones could have wrote to my parents to tell them this.

By May 1940, Hitler had advanced in his conquering of main-land Europe. He had successfully invaded Denmark, Norway, Holland, and Belgium. News was not good for the British troops fighting in France, as they were slowly being swarmed by the German army. On the 10th of May, an announcement revealed that Winston Churchill was to be the new Prime Minister. It seemed people could once again feel a sense of hope that Churchill would get us through the war. However, not everyone agreed with this.

By the end of May, British forces were trapped on the beach of Dunkirk. Lilian's brother Michael was among them. Michael joined the British Army against his family's wishes. He believed he could help. He believed this senseless war could be understood and stopped, so more men would not have to die.

Every day that passed where Michael had not yet made it back, Lilian slowly lost hope that he would ever come back.

Many of the other nurses also had brothers, cousins, uncles, friends, and fiancés fighting in France and each day that came without news, they lost more and more hope.

Life became a waiting game. Some of the troops stuck in Belgium and Norway were evacuated by the sea. We were told to prepare for them in the hospital, and we were shocked by what we saw. Each face that I saw had sunken eyes and complete loss of hope.

Were these the same men that left our shores months ago?

Many people began to panic that we would not win the war and that Herr Hitler and his Nazi party would take over the world, just like he insisted he would. Every light of morning brought more and more uncertainty. By night fall, life as we knew it could be changed.

I could not stomach newspapers. I was too afraid to see the headlines. Bad news was all that was ever reported. But something that Matron Jones said seemed to ease my anxiety. In moments of turmoil, I often returned to her words.

"Girls gather around," Matron Jones commanded one evening after dinner. "You have probably heard about the difficult and unsuccessful time our troops are facing out in Europe. I am sure most of you are fearful of what the future may hold for us as a nation. I am not going to lie to you, it will be a bumpy road ahead. But I want you to know that you have a family, it is here in St. Angela's. We will be here to support you whenever and wherever you need us. Either singularly or collectively, we will be there to help. You are not alone, you have our family.

"All you simply have to do is write a letter or telephone us, and we will be there. I understand that many of you have brothers, fathers, uncles, cousins, and friends who are bravely fighting for their country. Unfortunately, not all of them will come back to us...But I want you to know, you have your family here to support you and care for you if the unfortunate news should come to your doorstep. We need to be here for each other now more than ever. It is our job to care for the patients that come in here, but it is also our job to care for one other. Some of you will be moved to other hospitals, some will stay here. Wherever you find a St. Angela's girl by your side, you have your family. Take care of each other."

For the first time in my life, I felt I had found a place where I could completely be myself and be accepted just as I was. I had found my family and my sisters in all the nurses. I did not have to be perfectly dressed in the new fashion, beautifully groomed with perfect hair and makeup, or eloquently spoken, always. No matter what my state, I was accepted. The girls knew exactly what I was experiencing as they themselves were in the same boat.

It was a magnificent bond, as only we could know and understand what we had been through.

JUNE 1940

In June 1940, the emergency bell shrieked throughout the halls of the hospital. British citizens across the country put together a concerted effort to bring the men stranded in Dunkirk back home. Boats of every kind were used to sail across the ocean to Dunkirk. I felt tremendously proud and humbled to witness the patriotic bond between people as everyone did their bit to help.

Once back on home soil, the soldiers were rushed to various hospitals. Truckloads of men arrived at St. Angela's. Running on adrenaline, I went outside with the other nurses to bring in the men. Smoke rose from the trucks as they parked in the yard making it hard to see. My hands were shaking and I did not know how to calm them. I reminded myself to breathe. Just breathe.

Smells of smoke, sweat, stale seawater, blood and cigarettes filled my lungs. I began to cough with the harsh scents as my stomach knotted. The rumbling of the trucks, the cries of the soldiers, and the panicking of the nurses was all that I could hear. Some of the nurses ran past me and called out for their loved ones who were trapped in Dunkirk. Unfortunately, there was not many answers to these outcries. Other nurses stumbled and staggered as their eyes adjusted to the men in front of us.

Smells of rotten cheese hit me and I held my breath. I turned to see a soldier lying against the inner wall of the army truck. With his torn blood-soaked trousers and his grey clammy face, he hollowly called out to me. Beads of sweat trickled down his face. I carefully pulled back the torn material and saw an open wound, rotting with infection. I gently pressed my finger against the wound. Pus and white slimy moving balls oozed out of the wound in chunks.

I jumped back, "Maggots."

"They told me it would clean the wound," the soldier croaked.

I held a handkerchief to my nose to conceal the smell. "Who told you that?"

A litter arrived, and the soldier was placed on it and carried inside. With my handkerchief firmly held to my nose, I squeamishly turned back to the other trucks.

A clearing in the smoke appeared and I walked towards it. Wounded soldiers were everywhere. It was chaotic. Wherever I looked, a soldier pleaded with me to help them. My hands and arms were being pulled as the men desperately tried to get my attention to help them. I saw Arthur and George in every one of them.

Many were carried into the hospital on stretchers or litters, and I helped carry a few but struggled with the weight. I looked around the hospital ward and evaluated who was a priority. Training never taught me what to do when everyone was a priority.

Many of the men had been dressed using whatever was to hand on the beach, but these had to be redone. I noticed that a few of the nurses quietly retreated to an empty hallway or storage room and cried. Adrenaline seemed to be cursing through my veins. I had no time to stop and process what was happening. Until I attended to one soldier and his harrowing account of the previous days.

He kept going in and out of consciousness, but the terrors that he witnessed in Dunkirk were enough to make him stay awake. His eyes, so numb and hollow, stared blankly ahead. I wondered, did he recognise my presence beside him. I wanted to hold his hand, but I did not want to frighten him.

"They shot horses on the beach for no other reason than we had no room for them...Perfectly healthy and beautiful horses," he sobbed. "And they shot them right on the beach where we were all just waiting and waiting to go home. All we did was bloody wait...So many went mad. I went mad... I went mad. Some were out of their wits on drink and desperation...Thousands of us lining up. It felt like we were lining up to be killed, almost apocalyptic."

He reached out and grabbed my hand, squeezing it so

tightly that the blood retreated from the tips of my fingers. I carefully rubbed his hand and tried to soothe his grasp, but when his eyes found mine, he held on tighter. "I just want to go home...please let me go home."

I gently smiled at him and watched his face grey face relax. "You are home now. Don't worry, I am here. You are home and in the hospital. We will take care of you. Once you are done here, you will be looking brand new. I promise you that. Everything is going to be okay."

I could feel his body shake as he struggled to steady his breathing, yet he managed to smile at me.

"I was shot in the shoulder and twisted my left ankle. I spent my time on the beach trying to hide this as I over-heard my CO say to the man next to me, 'Good thing you're not wounded as we are leaving the wounded behind. They will weigh us down,'" he paused, catching his breath. "That's the thanks I get for fighting for my country...I was going to be left on that beach to die because I got shot."

I sat in a melancholic daze, gently rubbing his shaking hand. His breathing steadied and his body began to relax. A figure stood over us and I looked up to find Beatrice.

"Don't get attached. Just do your bloody job, you trollop," she barked before walking away.

A fire began to rise in my throat, as I watched Beatrice stare back at me, her eyes so full of hatred. But I calmed the fire, as I watched the soldier begin to fall asleep. He did not need any more fighting.

Lilian sneaked away into one of the storage rooms, clutching something in her hand. I finished patching up the soldier and followed her. I found her on the floor, curled up in a ball, sobbing into her hands. I sat down next to her and put my arms around her and she began to cry even more frantically. She held her hands to her face to muffle her screams.

Lilian outstretched her hand and placed a crumpled picture into my hands. I smoothed out the picture until the image became clear. It was her brother, Michael.

"Oh Michael...what have you done?" she sobbed into my chest. "My big brother...gone."

Lilian took the picture from me and stared heart-brokenly at it. My thoughts quickly fled to Arthur and George. I prayed that I would never know of Lilian's pain, that I would never know the devastation of losing my brothers. Lilian and I stayed like this for a few moments until Lilian gathered herself and decided to go back out and treat the men.

All she could say was, "Maybe I can save a man and spare another family the horrible news that I have just received."

Lilian walked away with her head bowed and her red eyes lowered to the floor. She placed the picture of Michael in her breast pocket and held her hand over it. I began to follow her but Matron Jones pulled me aside.

Matron Jones began to lecture me for introducing myself as 'Lucy' to the soldiers and not remaining professional and calling myself 'Nurse Anna.'

Matron Jones pointedly jabbed her finger at my uniform.

"You must remember that you have to remain professional and remove yourself from the situation and get on with your job. Otherwise, it will be a nightmare for you trying to detach yourself from each patient. When you give your first name, it becomes intimate, almost like caring for family, and that helps no-one. Remember, you are Nurse Anna when you have that uniform on."

In the moment, I did not recognise how useful this advice was nor did I heed her warnings of keeping a professional distance.

For the remainder of the day, I tried to remain professional, nurturing yet detached, supportive yet distanced, helpful yet dutiful. I tried. I really did. But every wounded soldier reminded me of the cold war that lay beyond our shores. A war that killed men I knew since girlhood. A war that was tearing this world apart. A war that changed people.

The day was long and tiring, with so many soldiers to treat. But I knew I was making a difference. At first, the chaotic scene in front of me frightened me. Most of the girls felt the same.

But as I looked around and saw how scared the men were, the only thing I felt was a need to help.

Many soldiers had an empty look in their eyes, almost as

if they were already dead inside. Maybe they were. Dried blood stains, sand, mud, sweat, and tears lingered on almost every soldier's uniform. Despite this, most of the soldiers still managed to smile even after what they had saw and lived through in Dunkirk. With a cigarette in mouth, tea, and bread in hand they were simply happy to be alive and home.

Unfortunately, this was only the beginning of a long and brutal war.

News broke that Hitler continued his conquest into France and on the 14th of June, he had captured Paris. By the 21st, he had all of France. Frighteningly, he had Germany, Austria, Poland, Denmark, Norway, Holland, Belgium, and France.

All the British troops withdrew from Europe, and it began to look like we had no chance of winning the war.

HOME

At the end of June, I went home for a short visit.

"A girl of your upbringing does not go near war or battlefields Lucy," my mother huffed as she rubbed her temples. We were yet again discussing my nursing and how inconvenient it was to the family.

"I don't understand why we keep having the same conversation. You can take care of the valiant men when they come to your convalescent hospital. They need you more there than at a general hospital or infirmary where you would witness terrible things. Whereas in a convalescent, you will be taking care of men who look like men, and not savages covered in blood."

I sat deflated on the couch as my mother roamed up and down the room naming off the many terrible qualities of being a nurse that she could think of and added in qualities of my own that were a disappointment to her.

My mother turned to me, flustered by my ignorance and lack of common sense. "Honestly, what will people think of a Webley girl covered in blood, near a warzone? I still have to conceal the fact that you are nursing to many of our friends and neighbours. You are being so inconsiderate of our family's reputation. What an idiotic girl you are! Might I add, you will be left a spinster. You too will look just as haggard as the men who fought. I do not understand why you want to do this job and sacrifice the life you have here to be practically a servant to those soldiers."

The drawing door opened with Daisy carrying a tray of tea. Daisy lowered her eyes to the floor as the word 'servant' hung in the air.

"You do understand, Mama, that there is a difference between a servant and serving others," I looked her straight in the eye. "Serving others is not degrading but rewarding.

You should try doing something for someone else once in a while."

I understood that my parents were from a different generation than me and that they did not understand my wishes, but I felt trapped. Utterly trapped. Yet, I felt guilty obligated to please my parents and my family, as though it was my duty.

The hospital staff encouraged me to do more and to strive to be more, but I was being punctured by my own parents. My parents wanted me to stay at home, to marry as soon as possible so that my husband would have a wife to come home to after the war. But I could not do this. I needed to decide - was I going to live my life the way I wanted or was I going to continue to be told how to live it?

I returned to St. Angela's and searched for the answer to my questions. Of course, the other girls had their own problems and challenges. But I wished I were more like them. I craved and envied their freedom.

The girls and I were allowed a night off for completing another part of our training. Matron Jones permitted us to celebrate in our nursing quarters and we were even allocated time to play music on the small radio.

Betty and Dorothy successfully tuned the new-fangled radio to the BBC. All we could hear at first was static and faint music until the enchanting voice of Charles Trenet, singing '*Boum!*' suddenly blared through the speakers and the room instantly lit up.

It was the first night that we were allowed to be together and not worry about the hospital. Some of the girls danced to the wonderful music, while others sat around and chatted. Lilian arrived back from her visit to Aunt June and she smiled again. It was a lovely sight to see. The grief of losing Michael had changed her, but as always, Lilian was still Lady Optimism.

I could always count on Lilian to see the best in dark and tricky situations and to believe there was a light at the end of the tunnel when all anyone else could see was darkness. Lilian's belief in a better future kept many of us going. It was as though Lilian radiated an infectious sense of optimistic strength. I admired her so much for this rare ability.

The music grew louder and Lilian's smile slowly expanded across her face. I pulled out my trunk from underneath my bed and grabbed two bottles of Webley Whiskey which I snuck from my visit home. All the girls chuckled when they saw what I had.

Betty playfully hit my arm, "You actually managed to smuggle in whiskey to a convent! Lucy you are going to hell for this."

"Who cares aren't we all! Pass it around," howled Joan over the music.

Lilian proudly held a bottle in the air as the girls cheered again. "I've got some wine."

Some whiskey, wine, music, and great company made it a memorable night. The nurse's quarters filled with laughter and made my heart boom with happiness to hear these lovely sounds after the constant bustle and straining atmosphere in the hospital that we faced every day.

We collectively decided to make this type of night into a tradition of ours whenever we could. If there was no music - we sang. If there was no more alcohol – we found some more. Cigarettes were passed around, the conversation was always in full-swing and most importantly, there was laughter.

Some of the girls sat on the window seat and looked onto the street below, watching who passed by.

Whilma excitedly placed her empty cup of wine onto a bedside table and squealed as she leaned out the window.

"Quick! Come here! Look who was on a date and is sneaking in after curfew."

We all loved a bit of gossip so, naturally we ran over to the window and desperately tried to get a glance at who it was. But with over 30 mildly sober girls trying to have a look at the same time, it was merely impossible.

A few moments later, the door burst open and Beatrice proudly walked in. The girls instantly started to cheer and tease Beatrice. We each found a place to sit on random beds to ensure we had the best view of the room before us.

"Would you look who it is! Sneaking in after curfew," Betty called out from across the room.

Beatrice's cheeks burned red. She peered around the room until her eyes fell onto the bottles of whiskey and wine. The music continued to boom over us and she angrily glared at the radio. Whilma turned the music up louder, almost challenging Beatrice to get angry. Beatrice knew she could not report any one of us as that would mean she would have to admit to sneaking in after curfew and spending an evening with a soldier.

"So, who's your beau?" piped up Joan, while we made ourselves comfortable on the beds.

Beatrice searched the room for Joan. "Shut up and mind your own business the lot of ye."

"Ah go on, tell us," Lilian shouted over the laughing.

Whilma held out her empty cup as Betty filled it up with more wine. "He looked a bit diseased with all those freckles across his face, but I suppose it's a good thing you only see him at night."

Beatrice's cheeks became a deeper shade of red. Small strands of hair fell from under hat and stuck to her sticky forehead. She forcefully pushed the strands of hair away from her face and pulled her hat from her head, throwing it at Whilma. The hat hit the window and the girls laughter grew louder. It was in that moment that we realised the one thing Beatrice wants is control, and when she did not have it, she lashed out.

"What's it to you Whilma? It's not as if a girl like you will ever find a man with that ugly face of yours," Beatrice snapped.

The girls booed Beatrice. Circles of sweat formed under her armpits.

"Well how did you find one then Beatrice?" Betty mocked.

Rita wiggled her legs free from underneath her and swung them over the side of the bed. She playfully tapped along to the music. "I wonder what Matron Jones will have to say about you dating a soldier?"

"Shut up!" Beatrice barked. "Yes, I went on a date, so what? How many of you can say that? It's not exactly written in the rules that we can't date, it's only warned against and frowned upon. The rules are that we are not allowed *marry*, while in training, that doesn't mean we can't date and have a bit of fun...And don't tell me that all of you are so innocent that you don't chase after the soldiers that come in here every day."

Beatrice's breathing began to hasten. She clenched her hands into a fist as the laughter grew louder. As she stood in the centre of the room, she looked around and began to pick out random girls to try and tease. But she knew that the rooms attention would not leave her.

"At least I'm not like you Rita, desperately running after each man that walks in the door...Or like you Betty, throwing myself at anything that has a heartbeat. Or you Joan-"

"Come on Beatrice! We are just having a bit of fun," Whilma quickly interrupted with a smile. "Please tell us about your date. What is his name?"

Beatrice clenched her fists and twirled on her heal. She stormed into the bathroom and began shouting her complaints about the lack of privacy and the right to a personal life. She yelled insults in-between these complaints but they only added to the hysterical laughing. Some of the girls bravely followed Beatrice into the bathroom to cheer her up, but she practically chased them away.

I think it was this night that we fully bonded and became good friends. We began to look out for each other instead of trying to get ahead and only think of ourselves. We were individuals, but we were also a team. A family. We were and always would be the St. Angela girls.

People spoke about the 'brotherly bond' that men formed when they became soldiers in the war, but nobody ever spoke about the sisterly bond made between the women that nursed during the war. Every one of us cared for each other as though we were family. It made a lot of the girls feel less homesick, as they had found family within their friends.

Whilma always used to say, "If you're homesick, don't be ashamed. That is a good thing. It means you came from a happy home. But we will do our best to make here home for now."

And we did just that.

1998

"Granny, where have you gone to now?" Emmy asks with a caring smile.

How long was I gone for now?

"I was just thinking of the women that I used to work with," I smile to myself.

"Anybody in particular?" Mae lifts her head from the photo-albums.

I turn to Lilian who is looking through another photo-album with a smile on her face.

"I was remembering five girls...Without them, I don't know how I would have made it through nursing! Do you remember Whilma, Lil?"

"Whilma Stewart!" Lilian lovingly says. "Of course, I do! I may be old, but I could never forget Whilma. She was such a mother-hen, always caring for and looking after everyone...and you can't forget Betty."

"Ah yes, Betty Smith! The jokester of the group, making everyone laugh especially on days that no-one could even bare to smile," I chuckle as I think of her side-splitting jokes.

"And Dottie!", Lilian adds. "She was the sweetest person I have ever known, not a mean bone in her body."

"Then there was Rita who was a hot mess, she had a head like a sieve! But she was the most genuine person you could ever come across," I chuckle.

"That's only four, who is the fifth?" Emmy eagerly asks.

Lilian and I turn to each other and smile.

"Joan!" we howl together making Emmy and Mae laugh.

"Joan Miller was well..." I begin.

Lilian tilts her head and laughs. "Joan was Joan! There is no other way of describing her."

"She was the rebel of the group, always ready for the next adventure and wherever it took her. Joan always looked picture-ready, even in her nightgown, she had a face full of make-up, with red lipstick being essential," I reminisce. "Of course, everyone that met her instantly fell in love with her."

Lilian happily adds, "Joan loved wearing rouge and walking through the corridors of the convent and hospital with a cigarette in hand!"

"But Joan was never dismissed as she was an incredible nurse and we desperately needed her. She was also very charming which got her out of many sticky situations that she put herself in. I think Matron Jones kept her around because Joan was something that she could talk about with the other senior nurses and sisters," I tell.

Lilian smiles while admiring the picture of Joan. "She was certainly an interesting topic of conversation!"

Emmy hands me a picture. "Are these the women that you have named?"

I smile at the young women, smartly dressed in their nurses' uniform standing in a line outside St Angela's.

Joan stood at the end of the row with her long legs pointing forward and her hand on her hip, staring straight down the camera lens. Betty stood slightly behind her with the same pose. Dorothy, Whilma, and Rita followed next with me and Lilian at the end of the row.

I lean over and hand the picture to Lilian who takes a moment to look at each of the faces. For some time, these wonderful women were our life.

JULY 1940

July 1940 arrived, and the Battle of Britain began. The Luftwaffe consistently bombed England and the sound of the air raid siren became a daily sound to us all. RAF fields, channel ports and shipping docks were mainly bombed at first, but soon cities and towns across the country experienced the blasts. The RAF worked day and night to stop the Luftwaffe. As the air raids and military campaigns intensified, our nursing duties began to expand.

In St. Angela's, we cared for recovering patients rather than receiving them immediately from an attack. But we were often called upon to help in other hospitals nearby.

The German's mistakenly bombed London in late August and began to make it a frequent occurrence. The horrific Blitz had begun. It was one of the most traumatic sights I had unfortunately witnessed in my lifetime.

Fires still burned days after the bombing and rubble littered everywhere with dust still lingering in the air. Sometimes we as nurses would be on fire-watching duties during the air-raids as many buildings around us went up in flames.

When I walked through the streets, I saw children playing in the rubble and it made me smile. Even with a war going on, the children still managed to carry on as normal and use their imagination to take them away from this dreadful sight. I wished I could go with them.

One thing that Hitler failed to do was to crush our spirits. He in fact made everyone come together, made the nation stand as one. It was amazing to see that each time we were bombed, people got out every day and began to try build the country again. Men, women, and children picked up rubble, swept the streets, and cleared away broken furniture and objects. It showed me that there still was hope. Hope could not be crushed that easily. People still believed in a brighter future and were not going to let our country fall apart. It was inspiring.

There were many days where I helped clear the streets after an attack and offered my assistance to anyone that needed it. Sometimes I helped families reunite after a bombing.

After Hitler ordered the Luftwaffe to bomb London, the RAF soon got their revenge and bombed Berlin. By September, Hitler postponed his invasion of Britain. News came that Germany had allied with Italy and Japan. This became despairing more than ever for Britain. It began to feel like we were alone in this war. But if we were to be alone, we would be alone together.

The evacuation of children from the cities into the countryside began during the Blitz. It went against the natural instinct to protect the young. Why must we separate children from their own flesh and blood, and send them to strangers in the hopes that they will be protected? Unfortunately, the city was no place for a child and the countryside became the only place for their safety.

My mother wrote to tell me that she had decided to take in four children, all from the one family. They were called the Radley's.

Webley Hazelton Manor,
30th August 1940

My dearest Belle,

I hope you are well and taking good care of yourself, especially with these dreadful air-raids occurring almost weekly now. Your father and I always worry about your safety. Have you considered coming home to us to get away from the city? Maybe you could come home for good? Your father and I think you should. It would be the honourable and wise thing to do.

I have some news for you – your father and I have taken in four charming children from London, for safety and respite from the bombing. They are the Radley family from Whitechapel. Their names are Russell (13), Sally (11), Tim (8) and Edward (7). They are the most lovely and polite children that I have ever come across! However, I believe they are deeply homesick.

Maybe you could come home and help ease their homesickness? You could act as a governess to them.

When I heard that Frannie Wincup volunteered to take children from London, I thought to myself, 'Well if Frannie Wincup is housing children, I must do my part.' One must stay on top of things, even if there is a war. Rumours are in circulation in the village that Frannie received three rude children, whereas I got four darlings! Absolute darlings.

The Radley children's mother is still residing in London. As you know only children are being evacuated. But she works in a little shop which I am sure is keeping her occupied. I am certain it is not doing much to distract her from worrying about her children and husband. A mother always worries, it is part of their job! I try to write to her to inform her of her children's safety.

The children's father is in the RAF and has been working tremendously fighting off the Luftwaffe, just like our Arthur is. I am always frightened each morning when I wake that I might have some dreadful news for them regarding their parents, but so far there has been none. It is nice having children in the house again, making noise. I missed that when you and your brothers left, as the house was so empty and sad. Your father says I nearly became a hysterical woman with the silence. Let me assure you, I have not and never will be hysterical.

Every Sunday at Church, a new list of local deaths is placed on the rear wall. The list is becoming longer each time I check it. I checked it last week and unfortunately, I recognised many of the names on it. Our old stable boys were on it. I have sympathised with their families, but things will never be the same for them.

Your father gives his best. Take care of yourself, my sweetheart, and come home soon for a visit, we miss you terribly.

Love always,
Mama.

When Arthur died in February 1941, I was allocated a week's leave from St Angela's. The house was not the same.

My mother stayed in her bed for days and refused to leave the house. My father threw himself completely into estate affairs. I could find him in the Stud bossing around the staff, at the whiskey distillery demanding more from the workers, or at home buried under books in his study. He could barely talk to me.

I do not think he knew how to anymore.

George was away with the Navy fighting in North Africa and the Mediterranean Sea and news of Arthur did not reach him for a long time. But when he found out, there was nothing he could do. He could not come home, he just persevered.

When I left for nursing, my mother returned to her bed and stayed there while father buried himself under more work.

We were heartbroken and we no longer knew how to talk to each other. Just like Nell's death, Arthur was no longer spoken about.

Arthur's death made me more determined to help-out with the war. I knew that if I stayed where I was, I would instantly be reminded and attacked by memories of Arthur and maybe even George one day if he too died. Even walking around the village was too painful as everyone was struck by a death from the war. So many boys that were my age, dead.

I could not bear hearing another person utter the words, "Another young man gone too soon. How terrible!"

Being at home meant I spent my days waiting and worrying that I might hear of another loved one being killed, and I could not do that anymore. Yet again, I tried to bring up the topic of moving to another hospital to my mother, but she was adamant more than ever that I could not leave. The thought of something happening to me was unbearable for her.

More than ever, I felt trapped. I needed to move. I needed to get away. Further than London.

St. Angela's was a good hospital, and I was never out of a job to do, but I was not satisfied. I mainly cared for elderly patients or soldiers who had been treated at another hospital who were then sent to St. Angela's to recover. The war was not going well for Britain and its allies, which meant there were often more of our soldiers coming back in Hospital Ships than we were sending out to fight. Lots of RAF planes were being shot down and the bombing intensified.

The work was tough in St. Angela's and my days were long. But I felt a calling to be in a hospital that was busier. A hospital on the coast receiving soldiers from Europe and North Africa, that was where I was really needed. I wanted to be at the front-line.

I wanted to take care of the wounded men, help them recover, give them the chance to live or even give them a smiling face in their last few moments. I wanted to help with surgeries, rather than just handing out medicine, tea or plumping pillows.

The country faced food shortages and many people were on the brink of starvation. People were trying to survive on tea and bread. Many of the ships carrying food and raw materials to Britain were targeted by German U-Boats.

My mother's letters began to only talk about rationing and the food shortages. Everyone had their own Ration Book, which included coupons or units for food and clothes that they wished to purchase. Only a certain amount could be bought each week and people were forced to take whatever they were offered. Nobody could afford to be picky.

One was now considered to be lucky if one had butter. Sweets, sugar, flour, bread, and cake were treated like gold dust. If women in my village heard about hard boiled sweets in the shops, they walked a mile into town to try and get the sweets just so they could sweeten up their tea. Even tea was rationed. Eggs and milk came in a powdered substance unless one could get it from a local farm. Meat also became severely rationed.

Everyone was on alert for extras that were being offered, such as flour or sugar. Some of the local farmers sold some of their extra produce, which was only told about through word of mouth. People were ordered to grow vegetable plots in their gardens instead of flowers.

In early April 1941, I went home for a weekend break. I had not been home in a while, as it was becoming harder and harder for me to walk through the house and know that Arthur would never roam these halls again.

The patch of gravel at the front door forever reminded me of the black telegram. I found it hard to walk over it. Arthur's portrait still hung in the main hall and I could not look at it. The door of his bedroom always remained closed and I was glad of it. My parents never spoke about Arthur, nor did the staff or neighbours. It was as though he never existed.

I both longed to hear his name and dreaded the mention of it. Would it ever become easier to talk about Arthur? Would Arthur's memory cease to exist?

Being at home reminded me of how enormous the house was. How unnecessarily big the house was with just my parents living in it. At least now the four Radley children occupied some rooms, but this still meant that only half of the house was in daily use. My mind circulated with thoughts of how unnecessarily rich my family were and that no amount of money could ever bring Arthur back. Money had no real value to me anymore.

My family house was beautiful, and I could appreciate this, but it felt wrong for me to call it my family home. Almost embarrassing.

I could not stand the theatrical way of living in this house. The idiotic rules and requirements of being a lady. I could not stand having a butler and maids, having my bags packed and unpacked as though I was a child. Having a maid dress and undress me. I did not want to spend my days drinking tea in the Green Room while men died out in Europe, North Africa, and the Pacific for me to drink that tea. The war was happening, and it was changing people and our ways of living.

My family's way of life seemed outdated and wrong to me. As though that time had forever passed, and the world would have no use for it again.

I stood in my bedroom, a beautiful powder-blue wallpapered room with a four-poster bed. Everything was so ostentatious and it repulsed me. From my window, green fields rolled into the horizon. I took a moment to enjoy the view before opening my bag. I took out paper documents and signed the bottom of them.

One was a document agreeing to go out to Europe when the time came. The other was a document requesting to move to another hospital where I was needed more.

I was almost 21 years old, I needed to make up my own mind and take charge of my life.

MAY 1941

In May 1941, my parents drove with me to the local train station. The ride was spent in silence. My parents were not angry with me but were worried about my safety and what I would have to endure in Portsmouth. Being so close to the coast brought many dangers. More attacks, more bombings, more challenges. London was being destroyed by the bombing but the coast took harder hits.

In the car, my mother could not look at me because each time she did she started to cry. I gently rubbed and held her hand in mine but she pushed me away. Arthur's death was still a fresh wound on us all. Three months had almost passed since his death. My parents faced losing yet another child.

A few days before, we heard the news of two British Hospital Ships being bombed by German Stuker planes while loading wounded soldiers aboard. This made my parents more reluctant to let me go and wanted nothing more than to wrap me up and lock me away until the war was over.

Hospital ships played a vital role in evacuating patients from overseas to England, and they were supposed to offer maximum safety, comfort, and medical care as they were protected by the Geneva Convention. A red cross was painted on the sides and tops of the ships to prevent bombing or being fired upon. We were told in the hospital that the red cross ensured safety. Because the red cross on our uniforms was our own safety, we wore it with pride. Unfortunately, this made the hospital ships and our nurses a target.

The ships were manned by civilian crews alongside military personnel and medical staff. Most of the ships were converted passenger liners and cargo ships. Now that the war was here, everyone and everything was used and converted into some military operation.

Everyone had a job to do - be that the troops out on the frontline fighting, sailing ships full of equipment, nursing the soldiers back to health, or even sitting at home supporting the troops – nobody escaped it.

My parents hoped I could have been one of the people who stayed in the comfort of their home, supporting the troops.

We arrived at the train station and the platform was consumed by nurses and soldiers, all heading to the coast of England. Getting closer to war-ridden Europe. There was both excitement and sadness in the air. To my dismay, I saw Beatrice among the many faces in the crowd. I spotted Lilian saying goodbye to her Aunt June, and I turned to do the same with my family.

My mother smiled through her tearing eyes. "This isn't goodbye my darling, but only a see you soon, yes?"

Father grabbed me and hugged me tightly as his voice was sprinkled with emotion. "Yes, only a see you soon." Seeing my father being anything but strong was strange sight to see.

We smiled at each other for a moment, until the train whistle reminded us of where we were. My mother pulled me in for one last hug before I got on to the train. Her voice softly whispered in my ear, begging me to stay.

I gave my final goodbyes and kissed my mother and father on the cheek. I found Lilian and we made our way towards the nurse's carriage. We sat by the platform side window and I found my parents faces among the crowd. My mother held back her tears while my father did his best to look strong. I locked eyes with my mother who gave me a warm smile.

As the train began to leave the station, I watched all the family members and loved one's wave goodbye to the soldiers and nurses. Each one tried to keep a smile on their face and not show their sorrow. Everyone was trying to be brave for each other. It was all we could do.

The train whistle pierced through the station and smoke rose from its chimney and I realised that I was leaving my cocoon. Leaving behind all that I knew. I frantically searched for my mother's face yet again but this time she had sunken eyes with tears streaming down her cheeks. My father held his arm around her waist, and he too had sunken eyes. I noticed his cheeks were glistening with fresh tears. I turned away to stop myself from crying and put my focus on the tracks ahead of us.

This was what I wanted, was it not?

We arrived late in the evening at Portsmouth as the sun set on the horizon with its colours leaking into the sea. The outline of the Navy ships and the hospital casted shadows along the port. The ships were ready to set sail.

I watched them be stocked with food, medical supplies, litters, and artillery. The ships were also filled with 'new' soldiers or replacements, with gleaming buttons and pressed shirts, yet untorn.

When we arrived at the hospital, a lone figure waited outside for us.

"Welcome to Portsmouth, I am Matron Burke, and I will be your supervisor. You will be working in wings 3 to 5 of the hospital", she tiredly spoke.

Matron Cynthia Burke's eyes were hidden by the purple circles underneath them. Two dimples appeared at the corners of her mouth whenever she spoke which added a sense of charm to her face. She was a young woman, possibly in her early thirties yet she appeared much older. She looked like she desperately needed food and sleep. I wondered how I would look in a month's time.

Matron Burke led us to our damp and small living quarters. We were put into rooms with three to five beds. It was more breathable than being in a room with 10 other girls like in St. Angela's, but I began to miss the warmth and cleanliness of the convent.

I shared a room with Lilian, Joan, Whilma, and Betty. But everyone was in and out of each other rooms, with conversations echoing out onto the hallways.

Tired from our journey, we began to settle into sleep. News came that an air-raid was to be expected. We quickly got dressed and made our way to the hospital. We moved patients already there into other areas, clearing out two wards for expected casualties.

A little after midnight, the emergency bell shrieked throughout the hallways. The Luftwaffe planes frantically flew overhead. The sharp screeches of the planes echoed above us. The vibrations of the bombs dropping could be felt all over my body. Each thud made the building shake, and dust creaked out of every nook and cranny. I looked outside and all that could be seen was blackness. Everybody did their best to block out their lights as to avoid drawing attention when the Luftwaffe were flying overhead. But it never stopped them from finding us.

Lilian was sent to help with the rescue teams and ambulances, whereas my duty for the night was to stay in the wards and treat the casualties. Soon enough, the doors flew open, and casualties came flooding in. Blood, dirt, and dust was on every one of them. They all had a frightened look on their faces. Everyone wanted an answer as to why this was happening to them. I wanted to the know the answer too. I refused to let anyone see that I was scared or upset. It was the only way to get by.

Being true to my Webley name, I persevered.

By morning light, we treated almost every casualty. It was a long night. Everyone was exhausted. I looked down at my hands and saw dried blood under each of my fingernails. I was not recoiled but familiar with this sight. No longer would I admire my manicured nails and soft delicate hands fit for a lady.

When my shift ended, I collapsed onto my bed. I did not have the energy to change out of my uniform. Yet, I was too tired to sleep. Images of the horrific casualties that I had treated crept into my mind each time that I closed my eyes. I lay on my lumpy bed listening to the sounds of the other girls sleeping, wondering did I make the right decision.

Maybe my parents were right. Maybe I was not capable of doing this job.

PORTSMOUTH, 1941

The following day, I woke and was informed that a hospital ship from North Africa was due to arrive in the afternoon and more throughout the week. We were to expect many casualties. Many of the soldiers had gangrene due to the slow journey back to England and the lack of facilities and supplies on the ships. Again, wards were cleared and ready for them.

The morning newspaper headline stated that from September 1940 to May 1941, almost 40,000 British civilians were killed by German bombing. It made me sick to think of all those innocent civilians dying. Many of them were the elderly and children. But what the newspapers failed to write was how many German civilians were killed by RAF bombing. Like us, they were innocent civilians. I began to wonder what was it that they were dying for?

More importantly, who were they dying for?

Nothing was right or fair in this war.

I tried my best to settle into my new living quarters in Portsmouth. I unpacked the few things that I owned into a small wooden wardrobe that was shared by all of us in the room. Once unpacked, I debated putting it all back into my suitcase and going home. But I took a deep breath and stood back.

Walking to the hospital, I looked around at the scenery that lay before me. Rubble lay everywhere with buildings half collapsing. It was a horrific sight, much worse than what I had witnessed in London. Yet, I knew that things were only beginning. I feared what the country would look like when the war ended.

The hospital was no longer as chaotic as it was when I left it. Now that things had calmed down, I looked around for the first time and I could see that everyone was exhausted.

People could no longer see a light at the end of this dark tunnel. Morale was at its lowest. The wards had been changed so that civilians were in a separate ward to military patients. Civilians were not to see how wounded the soldiers looked. It would lower their hopes ever more.

As the military campaigns and air-raids became a common occurrence, we often had to set up emergency units. It became necessary to evacuate some patients in the hospital on short notice from some wards to make room for the emergency casualties. The local people in the area around the hospital opened their homes to accommodate evacuated patients. Small cottage homes and convalescent hospitals also did their best to help us with the exceeding amounts of casualties.

Some nights, the casualties that we received exceeded our capacity and we were forced to put them on stretchers in corridors. Around every corner was a bleeding patient, pleading for help. I barely remembered to breathe.

In 1942, news from the warfront became even more discouraging. Britain continued to take heavy losses. In Singapore, approximately 130,000 British soldiers became prisoners of the Japanese. We knew that we would not see many of those men again. Four of those men were my cousins. News of what occurred in those POW camps spoke of unimaginable things.

By May, Germany tried to encircle advancing Russian soldiers. Throughout July and August, British troops focused their defence on North Africa. The Battle at El Alamein took place from the 1st to the 27th of July, and a second battle took place in late August. By November, German and Italian troops retreated from North Africa. On the fourth of November, British troops took over 30,000 prisoners and many were brought back to England. By the 8th of November, British and American forces landed at Casablanca, Oran, and Algiers. The Allies now had naval superiority in the Mediterranean – things were beginning to look up.

George was among those who were positioned in the Mediterranean. I had not seen my brother in over two years. I wondered when I would ever see him again.

A ward in the hospital was sectioned off for the German and Italian Prisoners of War captured in North Africa. Nurses who spoke German or Italian were drafted to work there. I was among those drafted to work on this ward.

The ward was guarded by Military Police and like the prisoners, we were being watched to make sure we were not conspiring with the enemy. I had never felt more watched and uneasy in all my life.

I mainly walked around the ward monitoring the patients, checking to see if my assistance was needed. We were told we could not speak to the patients unless it was medical. The ward was so quiet except for some coughing, sniffling, or breathing. It was eerie. We were instructed to not show any sense of compassion towards them. We were to provide medical assistance without the care.

"Kranchenswester?" a German soldier whispered in my direction.

He looked so young, barely eighteen years of age. A look of terror lingered in his eyes, like an animal being brought to the slaughterhouse.

"Ich habe ein Problem. Die Wunde an meinem Bein schmerzt mich. Ich habe große Schmerzen. Können sie mir helfen, bitte?"

He held his left leg in his hands and his face scrunched up in pain.

As I came closer, I could smell the infected wound.

I removed the bandage and saw the gaping wound across his upper right thigh. Some of the bandage clung to his wound as I gently peeled it off, part of his skin came with it. Green and yellow pus oozed out. The soldier scrunched his face and breathed slowly through his mouth.

The horrendous smell of decaying skin hit my nose. I tried not to show my physical disgust. It embarrassed me that I was not used to this smell by now nor could I control my sense of disgust. The soldier began to gag with the smell, so I distracted him with questions.

"Wo kommen Sie aus?" I asked.

I quickly glanced over at Corporal Rayne, the military police on duty, who watched me. Corporal Rayne looked at me as though I were the most disgusting thing he had ever laid eyes on. I felt unclean. I lowered my eyes to the infected wound.

"Ich komme aus Stuttgart," the German soldier breathed heavily as I continued to extract the pus from the wound. "Wo hassen Sie Deutsch gelernt?"

"Meine Gouvernante hat mich Deutsch bei gebracht."

As we talked, I began to see him as a person, not an enemy. I wrongly judged him because of his uniform. I reminded myself that he was only doing what every other soldier was doing – following orders.

Many of these men probably did not want to fight in this war yet had to due to 'patriotic duty.'

I looked at these soldiers around me and I saw Arthur and George in all of them. I hoped that if in an unfortunate circumstance George was a POW, that he would have a nice nurse attending to him, who treated him like a normal man and would not judge him based on the uniform he wore.

The German soldier laughed at my struggle to remember my German and how I tried to get the grammar and accent just right. It was as painful for him to listen to me stutter as it was for me to remember. He had a wonderful smile and laugh, the kind that completely transformed the face when it appeared.

Unfortunately, his laugh drew attention to us. Corporal Rayne stormed over and shouted at us to be quiet.

The German soldier lowered his head in defeat. All traces of the smile were now gone. Corporal Rayne turned to me and signalled me to come forward to him as if I were a child who severely misbehaved. I expected Madame Speirs to appear from behind him with her splintered wooden ruler and await my punishment.

Corporal Rayne glared at me. "What in god's name do you think you are doing?"

"Treating an infected wound."

"Don't be smart with me. I just saw you over there laughing with the enemy when you should be doing your job," he spat.

I wiped his spit from my eye and sharply glared at him.

"That is exactly what I am doing, Corporal Rayne, caring

for my patient. Part of my job includes me talking to my patients to distract them from their pain."

Corporal Rayne jabbed his stumpy finger into my shoulder, pushing me back.

"Your job is to provide medical assistance not to care for them like a lover. He deserves to suffer from the pain of his pathetic wounds for what he did to our men. The bastard got off lucky with only a little scratch on his leg."

"I am sure you'd know all about pain, Corporal, when you spend your days running errands in an office or standing stiffly at ward doors watching everyone walk by. Gosh, you must be so exhausted."

The leering smile quickly fell from Corporal Rayne's smug face. He stood closer so that he peered down at me, his body completely stiff. I could almost hear his pulse quicken.

Corporal Rayne's low voice shivered past my ears. "Your job is to treat patients, that's it. Not to flirt and make friends with the bloody enemy, you disloyal cow."

I stood tall, returning his glare. "Well, if you had not rudely interrupted me, you would have seen I was doing exactly just that – treating a patient. Now run along Corporal Rayne, for you are wasting my valuable time. Unlike you, I have a job to do."

"I am going to report you for this."

"What are you going to say?" I chuckled. "Are you going to tell your Commanding Officer that you saw a nurse laughing with a soldier? I am sure he will have more important things to worry about than a nurse and soldier talking. Now corporal, you have wasted enough of my time and for some of us around here, we have a job to do. So, why don't you go back to your little door and focus on your job, and I'll do mine," I glared back at him.

Corporal Rayne looked me up and down before walking back to the ward door. I turned my attention back to the soldier that I was treating, and his smile had returned.

1998

"I worked day and night in that hospital in Portsmouth and witnessed the most terrible side of humanity," I lament. "I wouldn't wish it on anyone."

Emmy and Mae shake their heads in disbelief while Lilian sadly nods in agreement.

"It seemed there was a never-ending stream of wounded men coming in. I witnessed too many men crying out for their mothers in their final moments. I never want to hear a sound like that ever again. Home felt like a thousand miles away. Luckily for me I had Lil," I playfully hit Lilian's hand and smile at her, "and the girls from St. Angela's working alongside me. Like Matron Jones said, I had my family and knew that I could face anything with them by my side."

"We often worked with maybe two or three-hours rest. We were never not on duty," Lilian sighs. "But with the girls there, we all took care of each other."

I take in a deep breath to push the memories back into their box.

"Memories of some of the horrendous cases that I dealt with will always remain with me. Even at this age, sometimes when I close my eyes, I can still see these men's faces and…I feel as if I am back there again."

Mae holds her steaming mug of tea in her hands and kindly smiles at me.

"That sounds very traumatic Mam, I don't know how you and Lilian ever got through that."

"It's surreal to think that I was about Emmy's age when I started nursing and was only a few years older when I officially became a military nurse. If that were today, I would not let Emmy go at all. I have no idea how I persuaded my parents to let me do so," I quietly say.

Lilian leans against the edge of her armchair. "Even though it was hard work, and we witnessed such awful things, things that man did to man, I would not change a thing. I am where I am today because of it."

"I agree, Lil, I would not change a thing. It's nice to know that that unpleasantness is all tidied away in the past."

Lilian softly looks to the photo-albums.

"We saw so many heart-breaking things, terrifying things, but we survived it. Many soldiers and nurses did not get the time together with their loved one's that they so desperately longed for and deserved. But we were one of the lucky ones who did. We got even more than that. We survived, made a family, and saw them grow up!"

We sit in silence for a few moments taking in Lilian's words and I take this time to appreciate my daughter and granddaughter. I watch Emmy as she continues to look through the photo-album but pauses and shyly looks up at me.

"Yes Emmy?"

"Granny," Emmy hesitates, "there's an old photograph that is not in any of the photo-albums but is in your room. I found it with Nell on the ground beside your bed."

I close my eyes and nod to myself. I knew there would come a day that I would be asked this question.

Emmy places the photo-album in her lap onto the table. "I promise you I wasn't snooping. I just passed your room earlier with Nell and we saw it on the ground. It is a young soldier. He does not look like any of the men in these albums. The back of the photograph has an 'A' on it. I was just wondering, who is the man? I wasn't going through your things, I promise."

Mae looks to me. "What photo are you talking about Emmy? The young soldier is probably your Grandad Will."

"But that's the thing Mam. It is not Grandad, Arthur, or Uncle George. I've never seen this man before."

Lilian holds out her hand to me and I squeeze it as I look to Emmy.

"Go and fetch the photo please, Emmy."

As Emmy leaves the room, Mae continues to stare at me.

"Mam?"

Lilian leans closer to me. "Are you sure you want to tell this Lucy?"

"Yes Lil. I think it's time...his memory deserves it."

"Okay. I think we'll need more tea then," Lilian tries to joke.

"Mam? You don't look well."

I begin rearranging the cushions on my armchair to distract myself so that I do not cry. One of the cushions catches my attention. My daisy print cushion. I pick up the cushion, place it on my lap and hold onto it, running my wrinkled hand over it.

"Mae please don't think any differently of me when you hear this story. Please..."

Mae hesitantly smiles at me and moves over to the edge of the couch to hold my hand.

"Mam, you are worrying me. What is this about?"

"I have never told anyone this story despite it being over 50 years ago. Just know that that does not make it any easier."

Mae slowly nods her head trying to understand me.

"You don't have to tell the story tonight. We can leave it for another day. You look tired and it has been a long day for you. I can bring your cup of tea up to bed for you and you can relax and-"

"-Thank you, Mae. But I feel now is the time for me to tell this story."

"Are you sure we can't leave it for another day? I will explain it to Emmy. She will understand that you are tired. It has been a long day for you."

"No, there is no other day better than today to tell it."

"Okay," Mae whispers.

Emmy re-enters the heavy room and hands me the old, frail picture. I hold it in my hand as if it is the most precious thing I own. The only thing I see is those big, beautiful chocolate brown eyes staring back at me from the photo. As always, everything fades away when I look at them.

"Can I see the picture?" Mae holds out her hand but drops it as she watches me hold onto it even more.

Emmy joins Mae on the couch, eager to hear the next story. They settle onto the couch waiting for me to begin telling them about the man in the picture. I continue to stare at the photo until Lilian comes in with another tray full of tea and biscuits. She sits onto the couch and worryingly looks at me. She holds out her hand to me and I gently grab it.

"Are you sure you're ready, Lucy?"

"Yes Lil. It is time…It is time to tell that chapter of my life that I have carefully packed away for too long, it needs to be told."

I take a deep breath before I begin, still looking at his eyes.

'A'

"His name was Adam Carow…" I begin, "and he was my first love. I believed at the time that he was the love of my life. I suppose he was for some time."

Hearing his name fall from my lips feels strange. A name that I have not uttered for so long. It is a simple name, only two syllables with four letters, but it is the hardest thing for me to say.

I look at his photo once again and a smile slowly spreads across my face.

"Adam was a true gentleman. He was someone who taught me so much about myself. I loved him with every fibre of my being, and he showed me that I could be loved. We used to say to each other 'my one and only.'"

"I thought you always said that Dad was your one and only love," Mae interrupts.

"Your father was the love of my life, Mae, but Adam was my first great love. There are some people who are lucky enough to experience the two," I simply reply, "but there is a difference. People can love more than one person in their lifetime."

I look at the wall of hanging photo frames beside me. My eyes fall on Will's smile. What must he think of me?

Emmy grabs her mug of tea and holds it close to her. "How did you meet him? Adam, I mean."

"I met Adam while nursing in St. Angela's. It was the 11th of July 1940, I have always remembered that date. I think it is engrained in my head and I can still remember -"

"- Wait, you met him in 1940?" Emmy interrupts.

"You failed to mention that earlier. So, I take it that there are a lot of gaps you left in your stories?" Mae grunts. "Why have you never spoke of this man before, I don't understand this? In all my life, not once has there ever been an opportunity for you to tell me about this man? When I experienced my first love and heartbreak, you never spoke of yours. Why? And why now tell us?"

"Indeed Mae, there is a lot that I left out and have done so for 50 years. Nobody other than Lilian and some of the St. Angela girls knew about him. Even your father did not know about him. I could never bring myself to tell you about him, or anyone about him for that matter. I just…I just couldn't."

Mae furiously shakes her head as I speak, her furrowed eyebrows crinkle across her forehead. I watch her emotions begin to brew under the surface. I take in a deep breath, preparing myself for more outbursts to come.

"Your father asked me one day had I ever loved another man before him, and I didn't lie. I told him I had and that was it. We never discussed it again. There was no need to," I explain.

I look at Mae and Emmy and watch their faces as they listen to me speak.

I know that this story is going to be hard for me to tell them, but it is just as hard for them to listen and understand. They are so used to me reminiscing about Will and how much I adored and loved him.

Especially today on Will's 80th birthday, I have spent so much of my time telling my family how great my life was because of Will. To now hear that I have loved another man, and kept it a secret, is not going to be easy for them. I feel I am betraying their memory of Will or their memory of me.

"You will understand why your mother has never talked of him before now when you hear her story. Just listen and please try not to judge, Mae. I am lucky enough to know this story, but it is only because I lived through it with her and was there every step of the way. In all the years that I have known my Luc," Lilian picks up my hand and gently squeezes it, "now is the only time that I have seen her want to acknowledge Adam and is able to say his name without crying."

Lilian smiles at me through already tearing eyes.

"You don't know, you couldn't possibly know, how broken Lucy became. For a long time, I thought I lost her and would never get her back. But she came back, in her own time. So please, Mae, don't be haste to jump to conclusions or anger when your mother tells her story. There are reasons why she never told it before."

Lilian gives me the nod of encouragement that I need to continue telling the story. I look down at my shaking hands holding Adam's picture and I try to remember the sound of his voice or his laugh.

Unfortunately, those sounds have faded with time. I take a deep breath to steady my voice.

Emmy leans forward and smiles at me.

"Please tell us your story, Granny. We would love to hear about Adam, wouldn't we Mam?"

Mae folds her arms. "Yes. Please do go on."

I let out a deep sigh as I watch Mae stare out the window behind me. Her eyes will not meet mine. I turn to the picture once more.

"Adam was a British soldier. He helped with the rescue teams and ambulances at the hospital when I worked at St. Angela's. He was just a regular soldier, but he was far from any regular man that I knew or ever have known," I begin.

"Adam was based in London as part of a patrol. He was in the 'B Company, 1st Battalion of the Royal Sussex Regiment…I always remember writing that on his letters. Unfortunately, I lost all the letters he wrote to me during the war as they were destroyed in a fire from a bomb. I would love nothing more than to have just an envelope of one of those letters that he sent me, so that I could look at his writing."

I have always believed a person's handwriting is the written form of their voice, that is why handwritten letters are so intimate and personal. A part of the person is almost within the lines of the page. You can practically see their thought process, hear their voice in their words and know that what they have to say is just for you.

I take a deep breath to stop myself from wavering as the memories of Adam suddenly flood into my mind. I can still see his melting chocolate eyes gazing at me from across a room with a smile only for me. Those smiles made me feel as though I was the most important person in the world. I meant something to another. My presence eased their mind and made them happy. I felt loved.

I never tired of looking into his eyes. Forever lived in those moments, yet never long enough, in the way his head tilted back as he laughed like a little child, and how his cheeks softly blushed when he smiled brightening up his face. These were among my favourite things about him. I admired how he treated everyone with respect regardless of their status, how he could speak to anyone and make them feel like their words were the only ones he wanted to hear. He possessed a gentle soul, a rare find. Adam was tall with strong broad shoulders, and wonderful dark brown curly hair. He could never hide in a crowd with his signature curly hair.

"Can I look at the picture?" Mae asks.

I carefully hand it to her, watching her as she looks at him with curious eyes.

"Oh yes, he was very handsome wasn't he. No wonder you fell for him." But Mae's smile quickly fades as she scrutinises the man in the picture once more.

"Very handsome indeed!" Emmy encouragingly smiles at me. "How did you two officially meet?"

I pause as the image of Adam dressed in his clean, soldier's uniform walking proudly through the ward doors enters my mind.

"We met in St Angela's hospital. I was attending to a Sergeant, named Roger, who was recovering from his injuries that he received in Dunkirk. A young soldier walked over to us and I realised he was visiting Roger…"

I smile to myself as I have not thought of this day in an exceedingly long time.

"I remember looking up and being met with these amazing brown eyes looking back at me. It was the strangest thing, as if I were looking into my own eyes, despite my eyes being green…I cannot explain it, but it felt invasive yet magnetic… I felt I knew him before, that we had met before – and I was coming home, as though home was a person…There was something so familiar about him. Yet at the same time his features were completely foreign to me. Oh, I probably sound ridiculous. But that was how I felt."

My smile grows as I remember the encounter. I can still smell the fresh paint from the hospital corridor, the starch from the bed linen, and see the bandage on Roger's wounds. I can faintly hear the bustle of the busy ward around me.

"We both stood staring at each other, and the room just seemed to fade out," I chuckle. "I had never experienced anything like that before but only read about it in books. For a while, I questioned did it ever happen or was it sleep deprivation."

"It was love at first sight! So romantic," Emmy whispers as she leans forward in her seat, eager to hear more.

Lilian grins at Emmy. "It surely was! I remember finishing up on a patient and I turned to say something to your Granny, but she was staring at a soldier with her mouth open wide."

"I was not!" I laugh.

Emmy chuckles as she adjusts the cushions around her, moving closer to Lilian and me.

"I looked from Lucy to Adam and Adam to Lucy. Even waved my hands at them but nothing would break their gaze! It was as if they could have conversations with each other, just by looking into their eyes. I have to admit, it was funny to watch! Even poor Roger just sat back and laughed."

A wave of embarrassment flows over me and I try to hide my blushing cheeks. I feel a laugh bubbling within me.

"Oh wow, it still makes you blush even today!" Emmy admires.

I begin to let my laugh escape. It is ridiculous to be laughing like this at my age. I try to stop myself from blushing and giggling like a schoolgirl, but it is no use.

I tilt my head, leaning into my hand, to conceal my blushed cheeks.

"Yes, I believed it was love at first sight for both of us. There was such a magnetic attraction between us from the beginning. It was truly an incredible experience, something that has always stayed with me. I realised after some time that I was staring and stopped, suddenly becoming embarrassed. I had never done anything like that before. My mother surely would have shouted at me for looking like a codfish. Roger introduced Adam and I and everything seemed to change for me."

"I finished bandaging Roger and I moved onto other patients. But I found myself constantly looking over at Adam, and to my delight he would be already looking at me!"

I can still feel my cheeks blushing at Adam when he caught me looking at him. It seems as if the butterflies in my stomach have been re-awakened.

"Every so often Roger would call me over and say his bandage was too tight and would I fix it for him. Any excuse like this just so Adam and I could talk."

"You say any excuse, but really you loved it as it meant you were back over chatting to Adam, well, staring at him!" Lilian continues to tease. "If I remember correctly, you had developed a sudden muteness when near Adam, as if you had undertaken a vow of silence."

I playfully sigh while rolling my eyes at Lilian.

"Adam was a great friend to Roger and came to visit him every day to see how he was doing," I try to continue.

Emmy sniggers. "Oh yes, I am sure it was Roger he was coming to see!"

"I remember many a day Emmy, where I would be walking along the corridors, and I would catch Adam wandering aimlessly. He was always looking out for your Granny and he would become embarrassed when he saw me. Listening to how he 'got lost' despite him coming to the hospital every day, made me laugh. That was a thing Adam did quite a lot – 'get lost.' But I knew, it was all just to get a glimpse of your Granny." Lilian laughs.

Emmy's face melts with a smile. "That is so sweet! All he wanted was just a glimpse."

I have forgotten these little things about Adam, yet they still make me laugh as if it just happened.

Lilian lovingly smiles, "To Adam's dismay, Roger was unfortunately recovering surprisingly fast, and he was dismissed from the hospital. Your Granny was of course very sad on Roger's last day as Adam was not there. She was all down and out about not being able to see Adam again and she cried about not having an address for him," Lilian reveals.

"You see, this was the first time that your Granny ever

showed an interest in a soldier. There were soldier's coming in and out every day at the hospital and many were desperately trying to win her over, she was never interested. But Adam, he was different."

I begin to fall further into my memories, making Lilian's voice drift away from me.

I have opened a dusty, old box that has been tightly shut for many years. Like Pandora's box, once opened, it cannot be closed...

DAISIES

I had not seen Adam for a few days, and I found myself pinning for him, which made me annoyed with myself – pinning for a man that I only casually talked with. Absolute nonsense. I should have my head checked.

As the days passed by, I grew sadder thinking about what could have been. It was silly of me to get attached to a soldier. I should have learned my lesson not to be known on a first name basis and to stick to 'Nurse Anna.'

As I sluggishly tended to an older soldier, I heard my name echoing from behind me. I turned around and there Adam stood, proud and tall. I shyly made my way over to him, unsure as to what to say. His smile grew bigger with each step that I took and I felt more at ease.

"When are you off for lunch?" Adam asked.

"In an hour. Why?" I eagerly replied.

Adam began to rub the back of his neck as he stared at the ground, carefully picking out his next words. "Would you maybe...possibly...like to have tea...with me...that is tea with me alongside of you, well to drink the tea with you while you are on your break? Or maybe we could have some lunch, some food if you are hungry or if you are not hungry, then no food it is. But that is not to say you cannot have food, you can -"

"-Yes! I'd love to," I beamed.

"Brilliant. I'll meet you out front in an hour." Adam began to walk away but quickly turned before leaving. "I forgot to say, you look lovely today. Well, you always look lovely, but today you are particularly lovely."

A giggle escaped my mouth and I looked away to hide my reddening cheeks. He happily walked out of the ward with a new spring in his step. I turned back to the soldier that I was attending and found him smiling at me.

"The poor lad could barely get his words out, hopefully he will be better with some tea and food."

I laughed to myself, gently patted his shoulder, and continued bandaging his leg.

The hour could not come quick enough. I spent the whole time looking back and forth at the slow ticking clock, hanging above the ward door.

As soon as my shift was over, I made a beeline for the front doors. Adam stood there waiting for me. It felt so surreal to see him standing there *for me.* He had his back to the door and watched the people pass him by, not a care in the world.

My footsteps echoed on the stairs, and he turned to greet me. I saw he had small bunch of daisies in his hand which he bashfully handed to me.

"These are for you! Daisies are such a friendly flower, don't you think? I thought of you when I saw them."

I had never received flowers from a man before and I did not know how to contain my excitement or the need to place them in a vase of water. I watched as he stared at his now empty hands, unsure as to what to do with them. I held out my arm to him and he graciously took it.

"M'lady," he playfully bowed.

Adam and I went for tea on our first date. The conversation never stopped flowing. He was so nervous at first, afraid that he would say or do something wrong, but what he did not know was I too was panicking inside.

1998

Emmy's laugh gently pulls me from of my memories, and I return to the room. Lilian has a playful smirk on her face and Emmy is recovering from a bellyful laugh. They turn their attention to me. I quickly smile at them to hide my previous absence from the conversation.

Emmy leans forward to catch my hand. "Are you okay Granny?"

I squeeze her hand and smile. I turn my attention back to the cushion on my lap and rub the daisies.

"Do you know, every time that Adam and I met he had daisies for me? Sometimes it would be the small daisies, other times it would be marguerites and sometimes a mix of both. He always made sure he had at least one daisy for me when he came to see me. It was a small tradition of ours."

Mae tightly folds her arms across her chest.

"Is that why you have always had daisies in the house? So, that it reminds you of *him*?"

"Yes, it's a reminder of Adam, Mae, as I don't have many things to remind me of him other than my memories and this photograph," I calmly answer.

"Well, I think that was a lovely tradition you two had," Emmy nods at me to continue.

I watch Mae bite her bottom lip while she shakes her head yet again. She turns her attention to the photo of Will beside her.

Since she was a child, Mae has always been a person who hates any form of change unless she herself was making the change happen. Some would say she is a control freak, others would say she is simply organised.

Mae likes things to occur in stages, like the seasons, so

113

that she has time to adjust. Slow and steady have always been her pace. Yet, Mae hates people who are stuck in their ways but refuses to budge an inch if someone tries to move her.

Will was always the one to try and coax her into accepting change. He was among those who believed Mae was just organised and needed everything in its rightful place, for that is where it belongs.

Adam does not fit into a neat box for Mae. He does not fit into her timeline for me. Adam does not fit into this day, Will's birthday.

I watch as Mae looks around the room picking out the various daisy patterns. I try to catch her eye but she will not look at me.

"But Mae dear, it's also because I love daisies. They are a lovely flower, my favourite flower. Sometimes I have questioned getting rid of daisies altogether in my life as it can be too painful looking at them and being reminded of Adam. But that is exactly what I want – to remember him in a way that only the two of us knew," I try to win her over.

"And daisies are a friendly flower, they are welcoming and classically beautiful…I don't have to explain myself. If I want daisies in my house, I will have them here."

"But I thought daisies were your favourite flower because you just liked them. I didn't know you had a man in mind when looking at them," Mae grunts like a child.

I lean forward and stare at Mae, even if she will not look at me.

"How many objects and things remind us of other people when we look at them, Mae? How many songs, books, and films remind us of people when we hear them? Yet do we simply stop having those reminders around us for the simple fact that they remind us of people from our past? This entire house reminds me of your father. Everywhere I look, I see Will. I am reminded of the day we found this house, of the day we painted this room, of the day we bought these couches that we are sitting on and all the conversations we have had in here. Every time I reach for a cup, I must stop myself from calling out, 'Do you want a cup of tea too?' Every time I lie in bed at night, I still find myself saying, 'goodnight' to Will. But do I just drop all those memories, leave this house, get rid of all my possessions because they remind me of your father?"

The room falls heavy and silent. The only sound is Mae's tapping foot.

"But…" Mae sighs, "to place a vase of daisies beside a picture of Dad in the hallway makes me wonder who you really pinning for…Who are you remembering? When you look at that hall table, who are you remembering? Because, under no circumstances, would I have a reminder of my ex beside a picture of my husband…So Mam, who is taking centre stage of your memories? Who are you trying to remember?"

"Well, I think it's very romantic of Granny-" Emmy begins.

"-Let her answer the question Emmy," Mae interrupts. "Who are you remembering Mam?"

"I am remembering *me*. I am remembering all the different parts of myself, all the various phases of my life, all the ways that I have looked and acted. I am wholeheartedly remembering me and who I was when I was with loved ones of my past. I am remembering how I was in these phases of my life and how I have since changed. I look at that picture of your father and I, and I remember who I was then and how I felt. And when I look at the daisies, I remember so many memories of who I was when daisies became an integral part of my being. And when I look at both the picture and the daisies, I am reminded of how much my life has changed. How I have overcome every difficulty in my life, how I am still alive and how I have grown. I remember me every time, Mae. If you only look at objects and think of other people and never who you were, then I ask you to start doing it."

The room falls silent as I stare at Mae who bows her head.

"I personally think it is a lovely idea that you have daisies all around the house. Even the cushions on the couch and your bed quilt have daisies on them. I think it's nice because when daisies are not in bloom you still have some around the house," Emmy reassuringly smiles at me.

"Yes, that's right Emmy. The daisies Adam brought me used to brighten up my day and ever since then they still do." I pause remembering the many moments that he handed me a daisy.

Lilian holds her warm mug between her hands and smiles at me to continue.

"So...if you two had worked out, would you have married him and had a family with him instead of Dad?" Mae challenges.

"Yes. I would have, Mae," I calmly reply. "That was the original plan."

"But how could you marry Dad if you still loved another man?"

"Well, if you listen to the story Mae, you'll understand why we didn't work out," I warn her.

Mae glares at me before continuing.

"Were you still seeing this man when you met Dad? It just makes me question did you really love Dad, since you are here giggling about another man? Dad is only dead two months and today is his 80th birthday...I wonder would you have rather married Adam instead?"

"Maybe Mae and then I wouldn't have a little brat like you giving me grief!" I snap.

"There's my Lucy! I wondered where she had gone," Lilian chuckles. "Honestly, Mae, you ought to listen to the full story before you make a comment. Your behaviour is absolutely ridiculous."

I look at Lilian and give a nod in gratitude to her. She always has my back. That is something I never have to question.

Mae sits back into the couch and crosses both her legs and arms as I continue to tell them about Adam.

APRIL 1941

Adam and I many dates and soon enough we were an item. We kept it private at first, with only our closest friends knowing. We were both very quick to say the words 'I love you' to each other and we genuinely meant it with all our hearts.

In early October 1940, I went home for a weekend. I wanted nothing more than to tell my parents all about Adam. But my father was only just accepting my nursing and my mother was still not onboard. I knew that if I told them about Adam, I would be brought straight home. They were extremely strict on things like that.

My parents always told me that they would pick who I was to court and who I was to marry. According to my parents, the man I was to be with would be more of a business deal than love. Since I would not be inheriting the estate or hold any shares in Webley establishments, my parents wanted to marry me into a wealthy family where I could be 'taken care of.'

Adam and I continued to see each other as much as we could, and we wrote to each other when we could not be together. His letters were my opium. It was hard trying to quietly get away from the nursing quarters after my shifts and see him. As always, the other nurses were on the look-out for some gossip or scandal! But they soon found out that we were together and teased me mercilessly. They liked him and approved of him, which was a great relief. Yet I still could not pluck up the courage to tell my parents about him.

When Adam could, he took me dancing, bought me dinner, or brought me to the pictures. I always had a wonderful time with him, wherever we were. I did not want to be anywhere else when I was with him. We always made the most of our time together.

In April 1941, I had a weekend off and stayed at the family house in Cornwall Terrace. Adam came to visit me. He told me his news while we strolled around Regent's Park. His battalion was moving to the coastal hospitals where their next step would one day soon be Europe. We found a bench under a Willow tree and set up our small picnic while looking out at the park, watching the world go by.

"I will write to you every chance that I get. I promise you that," Adam assured.

I lovingly smiled at him as I leaned into his chest with his arm around me.

"And I'll eagerly wait for your letters and write back as soon as I have read the last word."

Adam tightly hugged me. His breath tickling my ear as he softly spoke. "This isn't goodbye you know that?"

I clutched onto him tighter. "I know that. I don't want to ever say goodbye to you Adam. I suppose we shouldn't feel so sad...we are very lucky that we've had this amount of time together, considering that many people don't get this these days."

He solemnly nodded and held me closer.

I cuddled my head into his shoulder and we watched the people stroll by. I wanted to look at him, but I could not get myself to do so. If I started to cry, would I ever stop? We sat like this for a few moments, lost in our own thoughts.

"Could you..." he hesitated, "spray your letters with your perfume? It will feel like you're there with me."

I watched as his cheeks reddened and I smiled, loving him even more in that moment.

"Of course! Don't you worry, I will write to you so much that you'll be sick of me."

Adam picked up my hand and gently placed a kiss on it. I knew he was scared but desperately tried to hide it. But he could never fool me. It was as if I could feel his every emotion like my own.

Adam dreaded the intense bombing occurring in the coastal areas and being put into a plane or shipped off to North Africa. He feared losing more friends like he already had. But the thing that scared him the most was receiving a

'Dear John' letter from me.

No matter how much I tried to assure him that that would not happen, he never fully believed me. Adam always had a nagging feeling that he would lose me. I on the other hand, always had the nagging feeling that I would be the one to lose him.

There were many stories of soldier's being promised by their girl that she would wait for him but did not. The war infected every aspect of life, it brought people together and drove them apart. It infected everyone's minds and nobody was immune to it.

We spent all our time that we could together before Adam had to go. Around the same time, I signed the papers to move to another hospital. I wrote a letter to him telling him of my news.

I was not following Adam. I was following my own path. I often reminded myself of this.

I was following my own path.

I felt I was needed in a busier hospital, that I was meant to be out on the frontlines and my move to Portsmouth confirmed this. I did not realise that I would move so soon but I felt ready for it. More ready than I had ever been.

When I arrived at the train station on that May afternoon in 1941, I said my goodbyes to my parents and turned to get onto the train. Something caught my eye in the crowd. I saw familiar brown eyes staring back at me. Adam's eyes.

I wanted nothing more than to run over to him, but I could not as my parents were present and still did not know of him. My mind and body froze. I could not move towards Adam nor turn to my parents. I was nothing but a coward.

I could not make myself introduce Adam to my parents and I hated myself for that. I tried to open my mouth and call my parents but forgot how to speak. I tried to grab hold of Adam and bring him to my parents, but my body would not do what I wanted. I was not embarrassed by Adam, I loved him. Wholeheartedly.

Yet telling my parents about him was something I could not do, and I never knew why.

My parents would never approve of Adam. He was not up to

'Webley standard.' Adam came from a lower-class family. His father was a cobbler, and one day Adam would be a cobbler. A cobbler was someone the family hired. A cobbler was staff. A cobbler could never be a son-in-law.

I hated when I looked at Adam, that these thoughts lingered in the back of my mind. I hated that I measured him on the scale of Webley family standards. I loved him. I *loved* him. Adam was exactly what I wanted and wished for all my young life. Adam was what I wanted. He wanted me.

But he would never be what my parents wanted.

My parents would never accept love as being a reason to marry someone, even though they married for love. Love was a shameful word in my family's circle.

I felt taking charge of my life should include putting my foot down about who I loved. But instead, I continued to act like my parents wanted me to. I should have run to Adam like I wanted to, if not that, I should have openly recognised him. But I did not, and I hated myself for it.

I expected Adam to hate me too, but he never did. He was always a better person than me. Adam happily told his family about me and they were more than welcoming. He never pressured me into telling my parents or tried to shove his way into the life that I had grown up in.

We had our own space carved out for the two of us.

As we began to board the train, Adam subtly made his way over to me. We continued to look forward. He gently touched my hand and wrapped his little finger around mine. The queue began to move and I let go of his hand. I walked onto the train acting as if nothing had happened.

I made my way to the nurse's carriage and took my seat. The train began to leave the station and I told Lilian that I had saw Adam. Lilian questioned me on what I had seen and tried to reassure me that I was missing Adam so much, my mind made me think I saw him. But I was one hundred percent positive.

As I uttered these words, the carriage door slid open and Adam walked in. All the nurses turned at once to look at him.

Adam smirked, "Sorry, I seem to be lost."

The girls began to chuckle and they each tapped him as he

passed by. Adam made his way over to me and bent down so that we were eye to eye.

We both looked at each other questioning if it was real what we were seeing. And, happily, it was.

"What on earth are you doing here?" he whispered.

"I have been moved to a hospital in Portsmouth," I whispered back. "I wrote to tell you but it must not have got to you on time."

Adam reached into his shirt pocket and pulled out the handkerchief that I gave him. I had sprayed it with my perfume. He opened it out and revealed two pressed, small daisies inside. He placed one in my hand. I opened my small gold locket hanging around my neck which held pictures of Nell and Arthur, and carefully placed the daisy within.

"You still manage to bring me daisies," I replied while trying to hold back tears of joy.

I was overcome with the feeling of being loved – that amazing feeling that warms you inside when you are loved back, by a friend, family member or romantically. That my existence meant something to another. It filled me up and made me think I could burst with happiness at any moment.

I knew going to the coast was where I was meant to be, but Adam confirmed it for me. He squeezed my hand and stood up to leave.

Adam walked away looking back every few steps to smile at me.

"Oh, you two are such a mouth-watering couple!" Dorothy sighed.

Dorothy's daze broke with our laughter and my cheeks turned a burning red as I watched all the faces in the carriage look at me.

When we arrived in Portsmouth, Adam's platoon was based nearby the general hospital, which meant we could see each other for a little while at least. We were incredibly lucky to be so near each other. Many of my fellow nurses had not seen their beau in a long time and were eagerly waiting on the soldiers' letters. Sadly, some of the nurse's realised that their man had died when the letter's stopped coming.

Some of nurses felt reassured, even lucky, that they were not madly in love with their corresponding soldier that died. Others were not so lucky.

THE CHOICE

Adam's platoon came and went from the army base near the hospital for various missions that needed to be carried out. He worked alongside the rescue teams and helped with the ambulance calls.

Every time that Adam left, he would say to me, 'until next time, my sweetheart.'

I hung onto those words with all my might.

When Adam was away at his army base, he would write little notes to me and often a daisy would be attached to his letters. Sometimes, Adam would go to the nearest infirmary and leave a small note or letter there for me, which was an easier and quicker way of getting a letter back to me. I would watch the days fall away on the calendar waiting to receive his letters.

The moment I saw his writing, I felt as if he was right beside me. I felt more homesick waiting for his letters to come.

I frequently dreamt of Adam. We would meet in my dreams and have long, warm conversations. But each time I would wake up to an empty, cold bed. I hated this part of myself where I pined for him, but I could do nothing about it. The more I tried to not think of him, the more I thought of him.

When Adam returned, we found a quiet place to spend a few moments together, to get away from the chaotic bustle of the war around us, and just be together. He would hug me so tightly for a few minutes, and yet it was never long enough.

One foggy night, I was working in the hospital when a flood of soldiers rushed in after an air-raid. It was chaotic. So many screaming, 'NURSE,' 'MEDIC' and 'HELP' simultaneously, with each one covered in blood. I looked around the room and to my horror, I instantly recognised some of the men – they were from Adam's battalion.

My stomach dropped with every muscle in my core clenching. The room turned blurry and I held my hand to my mouth to stop myself from vomiting. I feared seeing Adam and not seeing him. But as he walked through the door carrying a stretcher with another soldier, I breathed a heavy sigh of relief.

Adam had a minor wound on his forehead, but he was okay. He was okay. I had to repeat this to myself until my breathing calmed.

This was the first time that I officially realised I could lose him. It terrified me. There was nothing I could do but live with this constant fear. It was a dangerous thing to be in love with a soldier. Every time Adam walked away from me, I feared it was the last time that I would see him.

Adam walked towards me and repeatedly told me that he was okay, he was fine, he was not going anywhere. And I wanted to believe him, I really wanted to believe him. But an agonising pain inside told me otherwise.

I was not alone in this feeling.

Many soldiers and nurses during wartime mistook lust for love. They mistook adrenaline for love butterflies in their stomach. An atmosphere of now-or-never overcame everyone.

The hospital was not exempt from this now-or-never feeling. Countless times I had spoken to a soldier or a civilian, to only hear that they had died five minutes later. It was a strange time and I tried not to think too much about it. People were alive one second and dead the next. The realisation that I could lose someone close to me, only occurred to me when the actual event happened.

I blindly thought that it was only soldiers and civilians that died. People I did not know. I never thought it could happen to one of our own. But it did.

Betty was caught in an air-raid on her walk home after her shift and died in the rubble. Betty was not found until the following morning. When the news broke in the nursing quarters, there was an agonising silence. Nobody knew what to say or do. We all looked at each other, utterly helpless.

We stared at Betty's empty bed and the wardrobe with

her clothes. Her prayer book sat by her lamp and unopened letters from her family sat on her bed. Never to be read by her eyes.

The nursing quarters changed after Betty's death. It was quieter. Heavier.

Dorothy, Whilma, Rita, Joan, Beatrice, Lilian, and I held onto each other. Our family was becoming smaller, but we had each other. We always had each other.

Adam and I continued to see each other. We tried to keep our relationship somewhat private. I worked under an incredibly strict Matron, especially when it came to relationships. Even the word 'relationship' angered Matron Burke.

If one of the nurses became engaged, they were no longer a person in her eyes. And we worked alongside even stricter nuns who did not approve of romancing with soldiers. Matron Burke did not believe a nurse could do her job properly if she were in a relationship with a soldier.

If a nurse and soldier married, Matron Burke believed the nurses job was no longer available. If a nurse married a soldier, she must become a 'wife.'

I wanted to be with Adam, I loved him with all my being. But I did not know who I would be if I could not nurse. All that was certain in my life was that I was a nurse. Who was Lucy? Lucy Webley was foreign to me.

If our relationship were known, Adam would be re-located to another area, and I would be moved to another hospital. Our relationship compromised our job performances. I knew I would lose the respect that I worked so hard to get.

In October 1942, Adam and I celebrated our second anniversary. He asked me to marry him and I happily said yes. British soldiers did not earn a lot of money, but he had saved up for months to buy me a small diamond ring on a simple gold band. I adored the rings simplicity.

We talked about our future together as a way to forget about the war surrounding us. Adam dreamily spoke of how we would get married and when the war was over we would settle down. We would find a nice cottage overlooking the ocean, or maybe a cottage near a lake. Just, someplace where we could finally get some peace and quiet. Our own peaceful corner of the world. I desperately desired a simple, peaceful life in a small house. To me, small houses held more love and support than big ostentatious houses.

We had so many plans together. So many wonderful plans. We knew we would never complete them all, but we could dream.

Soon after Adam proposed, I discovered I was pregnant. A dilemma overwhelmed me. I could not keep the baby. If I had a baby, I would immediately be sent home. I did not want to bring a child into this senseless war.

The images of this kept me awake at night.

I knew my parents could be outraged if I came home with a baby. They would never support me. The Webley name would be shamed forever. If I stayed where I was, I would be surrounded by war. If I went home to my parents, I would be surrounded by a raging war with my family.

Yet Adam continued to beg me to keep our baby. It was all we talked about. He believed marriage and having the baby would solve everything. We wanted our own family, why was I rejecting that dream now that it was here?

I wanted to scream. I wanted these things, these dreams, but not now. Adam could not fully understand my inner turmoil. To him, the decision was simple.

"You do not understand the burden of carrying the Webley name on your shoulders. You could never know. I will bring complete and utter shame onto my family. I have worked so hard to become a nurse and to get to where I am…to throw it all away…If I have this baby, I will all lose everything. And for what?"

The air became heavy around us. I immediately regretted what I said. Adam's eyes were glued to the floor. If he could just look at me, he would see my regret. He would see that he was worth everything in my life.

"I know that I don't know what it is like to be in a family like yours or to carry a family name like that. But I know, however simple my family may be, they accept me for all that I am…" Adam trailed off.

"This is the first piece of good news that I have heard in

such a long time. I hear news of death every single day...To now hear of a birth and a new life just makes me so happy. I thought when you said yes to marrying me, it meant you wanted a family with me as well. Now might not be the time we planned to have a family, but it is the beginning of our family nonetheless...I want you to know though," he pulled me to him so that I was standing directly in front of him, "that I will support you no matter what...If they send you home, you go to my family who will take good care of you. Or we will find a temporary flat in London, we will figure it out together. You are not alone in this. This is our baby after all. I am here. If your family rejects you well then that is on them, not you. You have a family here too that will support you no matter what. Please just think about things and rest up."

Adam kissed my forehead and left the room. I watched his back as he walked away. Life seemed so simple to him and I wondered what that felt like.

An unopened letter sat on my bed. I recognised my mother's handwriting which caused another ball of nerves to curl up inside me. I still had not told my parents about Adam. We were engaged now. They would accept him, wouldn't they?

They would have to.

Webley Hazelton Manor,
2 November 1942

My dear Belle,

I regret to inform you of the horrendous news that your father and I have recently received. George has married. He has married a German woman of all people. A Nazi German woman. Her name is Margot Von Adler, and she will never be a Webley woman. I will make sure of it.

Her father is a Nazi, but George assures us that her family have morals and her father only joined the Nazi party to survive and protect his family. Nonsense I say! If Mr Von Adler had morals and principles, he would have done everything in his power to take his family out of that country and away from the Nazi regime. But he did not. Therefore, he is just as bad as the Nazi party and Herr Hitler himself. Your father and I would never stand for such a thing.

When I first read George's letter, I immediately had to lie down. I was so faint. Your father ordered Dr Fernsby to come to the house and see to me. Fernsby ordered me to stay in bed for a week.

Not only has George married a Nazi's daughter, but they have welcomed a baby girl into the world so soon after marrying. It makes us question did he marry this woman for honourable reasons? George claims he married Margot for love. George does not have the faintest idea what love is.

To think the estate is going to be left in George's hands frightens me. This would never have happened if things had worked out the way they were always planned to be. George was never to be the heir and for good reason.

The baby's name is Adelaide after Charles's mother – I think George did this for your father and me. It is a disgrace on our family. George wants to bring Margot and Adelaide to England to stay with us until he returns home from war. Certainly not! I have ordered the maids to make every room unavailable to guests unless you come home of course.

Oh Lucy, my dearest Belle, I cannot begin to imagine what people will say. Rumours will circulate that we are now in contact with Nazis. George did not think about the consequences of marrying this woman, he only thought of himself and his needs. If he continues like this when he takes over the estate, it will be in ruins.

My dear Arthur would never have done such a thing as this. He always thought of his family and the family name first and foremost. Arthur knew what was best for the family. He understood the responsibility of being the heir to this family. George has always been reckless and ignorant to responsibility. Your father is beside himself trying to think of how we can improve this situation. With any luck, the marriage can be annulled.

To think I had set-up a list of perfect, young, English ladies for George to consider marrying when he returned home. Now, I will have to explain to them all why it cannot happen. Some of those families might not want to be associated with us anymore. We may very well lose old family friends and business clientele. But *this of course means nothing to George. George never thinks of his dear parents and the burden they carry.*

Your father and I are disappointed in George. Your father said he is most upset that George's first born is a girl, but I know he does not mean this. He is only hurting. Your poor father is considering signing the estate over to you now. It may be our last resort to restore order to the family name.

I wish you would come home so we could talk to you in person about the needs of the estate and this family. This is an urgent matter.

I hope you are well my darling. The weather is dreadfully cold here, so I hope you are wrapped up well in Portsmouth. It is naturally colder by the coast. I have heard great things about the nurses, and I want you to know that your father and I are so enormously proud of you. We hope that you could come home, just a quick visit. We have not seen you in over a year. We miss you terribly every day. The house is so empty and sad without you.

Maybe you could join us this year for Christmas, since you sadly missed last years? It would mean the world to your father and I if you could come home for it.

Take care my darling Belle. Love always,
Mama.

I read my mother's letter four times, questioning how to answer her. I wondered would she be so proud of me if she knew what dilemma I was currently in.

I put the letter away and grabbed a fresh sheet of paper and began writing a letter to congratulate George on his new wife and child. Once the letter was signed, sealed, and addressed, I stared at my pen and thought of my mother.

I found Lilian and told her I was two months pregnant. I needed her advice. I wanted to be told what to do. Could someone make this all go away?

A metal clothes-hanger hung on the bathroom door. I ran to the toilet at the sight of it. Lilian held back my hair and rubbed my back as I vomited. I cried out 'no' in-between each mouthful of vomit.

Memories of last month surfaced to my mind.

Lilian and I had reluctantly performed an abortion on Beatrice only a month previous. Beatrice begged us to do it. Lilian silently prayed to herself, begging for forgiveness and absolution for what Beatrice was asking us to do.

Beatrice was raped by a drunken soldier and fell pregnant. The soldier had died shortly afterwards, and Beatrice was left with a heavy responsibility to bear.

Beatrice cried in my arms, and I tried my best to comfort her as much as I could. But nothing that I said could make her better. I had never seen Beatrice cry. Lilian and I sat either side of her and cried with her. We could not take her pain away, but she was not alone in it.

After that night, Beatrice changed. Something had broken within her. We could all see it. But she never let anyone close enough to help her. Rum was the only thing that she allowed in.

DECEMBER 1942

In late December 1942, Adam went on a rescue-run. I was three months pregnant and still had not decided what to do. Adam promised me that he would return as soon as he could and urged me not worry about our future. He reassured me that we would start to plan our wedding upon his return.

Maybe we could have a simple Christmas wedding with only a few witnesses. We would tell our parents afterwards and we would deal with their reactions together when it came to it. Adam wanted me to take as much time as I needed to decide what to do. And I knew that whatever I decided, he would be there to support me no matter what.

A Christmas wedding would be nice. Our baby would be born in June. But was it the right time for me to get married and start a family? I was twenty-two after all.

Adam kissed my cheek and left. I decided before he walked out the door that I wanted to marry him and to tell the world about us. If I could scream it from the rooftops, I would. I smiled thinking about marrying Adam and revealing the news to everyone. I let the anxiousness fade away as I focused on what our new life would look like together.

Many of the nurses began to comment on how I was often sick. I could no longer use the excuse of the vomiting bug that was present in the hospital as it had passed. Even though I was three months pregnant, I hid my bump with lots of Winter layers. Thus far, no one was the wiser.

I knew I was desperately needed as a nurse, but I was now to become a mother. I oversaw a small group of nurses as their authority figure, and I wanted to set a good example for them. I wanted to have this child with Adam, but I did not want to stop being a nurse. I put my dilemma to the back of my mind and focused on the patients in front of me as I began my shift.

Late that night, soldiers rushed into the hospital as the ambulance sirens wailed. Screams of agony and pain, all pleading with me to help them, jolted me awake but one voice stood out. It was Lilian's as she said, "Lucy come here."

As I ran over to her, Lilian stepped aside and I saw Adam limply lying on a bed. He was covered in blood, this time his own. He was shot in many places and I began to frantically try and stop the bleeding, but he weakly caught my hand. All the colour had drained from his face, I barely recognised him.

"There's no use," Adam spluttered.

I wiped the blood from Adams mouth and fell onto the side of his bed, holding his cold hands in mine. Maybe my hands could bring back the warmth in his. Lilian, Dorothy, and Adam's two friends, Jim, and Frank, tried to give us some privacy and block off the chaotic scene around us.

I could not cry as it would draw attention to us. I tried my best to hold in my tears. I wanted to remain strong for him. Adam needed me to be strong.

"I've been thinking about when we should get married and I think we should not waste any more time. You were right. Why not get married next week, I can arrange it? I can arrange the whole thing, you do not need to worry about anything. We can spend Christmas together as a married couple and our little baby will be born in June and…and we will have our cottage by then. What do you think? We can get away from all of this. Leave it all behind."

Adam smiled at me as tears slid down his cheeks.

"I think we should start thinking of names for our baby. We haven't talked of names…If it's a boy what shall we call him?"

Beads of sweat formed on Adam's forehead and his eyes drooped more and more with each blink. He looked at me with a dreamy smile.

"I always liked Jonathon, after my father. Maybe Margaret for a girl, after my mother?"

"They are beautiful names." I kept a smile on my face and rubbed his cold hands. Why were they so cold?

Tears began to trickle down his cheeks as he whispered, "My one and only."

"My one and only," I answered.

I stroked his cheek, catching his tears as they fell. Adam stared into my eyes as he contently smiled. Those beautiful chocolate eyes. My favourite sight in the whole world.

More blood seeped out from the corner of his mouth and he began to cough. I wiped the blood away as quickly as it came.

"You just need to rest up and get better. We can talk about our future when you are feeling better. We are going to have so many more great times together Adam, you just have to rest. You will be back on your feet in no time. You'll see...We are going to have our little wedding and you are going to be there when our first baby is born. You'll see. Adam?"

Adam closed his eyes as tears ran down his cheeks. I picked up his hand and placed a kiss on it.

"We are going to a find a cottage and... Remember we said this? Remember?" I choked. "Adam...remember? And we are going to start our little family and live in our small corner of the world...Remember you said this? We have so many plans, so many. And we will do them all...you just...you just need to rest. You need to rest and regain your strength. Just rest, my darling."

Adam smiled at me but did not say a single word. I held his hands in mind, pressing my lips against his cold hands. We stayed like that for a few precious moments until he drew his last breath.

"My one and only," I whispered as I kissed his lips for the last time and pulled the white sheet over him.

I would never see those beautiful eyes again or kiss his sweet lips.

I walked out into the corridor, completely lost in a haze. I walked until I found an empty little room. I heard someone call after me to see where I was going and I weakly replied, "just getting more bandages."

I entered the empty, dark room and I felt someone place their arms around me. I turned to find Lilian and I immediately began to wail. I fell to the ground as I felt my heart shatter into a million pieces. My mouth hung open as each agonising scream escaped my hold. Lilian held me closer and rocked me back and forth as the muscles in my stomach clenched with each sob. My chest was so heavy, I could barely breathe, I thought I would choke on my own breath.

Lilian's voice tickled my ear but I could not hear a word she uttered. I was consumed by a cloud of nothingness.

I looked down at my hands and saw Adams blood on them. Lilian sat next me and stroked my hair. I was so empty, yet I felt I needed to open the top of my head and release these agonising emotions. How could I be both shattered and hollow?

How could this happen to me? How? Why?

We had so many plans. We were the lucky ones.

How could this happen? Why me? Why did I have to lose Adam?

This was all just a horrible dream. Why could I not wake up?

Dorothy and Rita found us sitting on the floor and tried to console me, but it was no use. Jim and Frank followed and joined us on the ground. I could hear their tears in their voices as they tried to remain strong for me. They tried to console me, but they too could not understand how this could have happened. Jim and Frank questioned what they could have done differently, but it was no use.

Jim handed me something that they had found beside Adam when he was shot. It was my handkerchief that I gave him with his daisy inside.

I clutched the handkerchief, refusing to let another thing of Adam leave me. I could no longer control my body.

Frank and Jim stayed with me until I could stand on my feet. They reluctantly said their goodbyes and I wondered when I would see them again. Would I lose them too?

I took a few moments to gather myself before I went back out and continued my job. Lilian, Dorothy, and Rita begged me to end my shift early, but I could not face being alone with my thoughts.

That night, I saved 23 men and lost one. I would have given everything just to save that one.

I vowed that night that I would never love another man again. Especially a soldier. I could not bear losing another person that I loved and watching them die before my eyes.

I did not mourn or grieve Adam properly as I would not allow myself to do so. I threw myself completely into work. I did my best to hide the pregnancy and tried to carry on as normal.

Persevering was all that I knew how to do. After all, I was a Webley and Webley's don't cry.

JANUARY 1943

The year turned to 1943 and it was far from happy and bright. I was 4 months pregnant, and my bump was growing bigger by the day. Nobody but Lilian and I knew about the pregnancy. I entered the new year as a shell of a person that I once was. I barely recognised myself anymore. I decided to block out the memories of Adam as best as I could and tried to continue as if nothing life changing happened.

His name became a word that I banned from use. I thought that I could block out losing him and the memories of him for a while until I was able to deal with them. But once tidied away into a delicate box, I was too scared to ever dare to open it.

Instead, I put my focus onto exactly the moment I was in, as then and only then, I would think of just that moment and nothing else.

For a short time, I only focused on my growing bump. I decided wholeheartedly that this baby was what I wanted. I would care for it, love it, and watch it grow. I felt ready for my life to become completely wrapped up in a small bundle of joy, my baby.

It would give me a new purpose, set me on a new path. I accepted this unplanned surprise. I had saved up money since I started nursing, it was not much, but I knew it would be enough for me to rent a flat somewhere in London.

After Adam's death I decided to take a long hard look at my life.

For so long, I had been living in almost a dream state. Just floating about aimlessly. I knew nursing was where I was supposed to be, but I took it for granted. Adam and I had made so many plans, and I took them for granted too. I had no back-up plan. I did not think I needed one.

I knew that Lucy from four years ago would be appalled to

see where she had ended up. With a fiancé dead, pregnant out of wedlock, surrounded by rubble, dirt and blood, a broken spirit, and a raging war inside her head.

What had I become? What had I done with my life? I was an embarrassment. I was a disgrace.

Every man that I looked at, Adam's face would immediately consume my mind and I could not look at them. I accepted the decision I made that I would never marry or be with another man. I was not scared of dying or being injured from a war attack, I would have welcomed that ending.

But I was terrified of loving another human being. I was scared to death of being vulnerable and giving someone else the power to utterly destroy me.

Adam's death was not something that he planned or did to destroy or hurt me. But by loving him so much more than I loved myself and my own life, my heart and soul died with him. I no longer knew who I was. I decided I would raise my child alone and if I could, I would continue to nurse. My child would become my everything.

I had taken full responsibility for where I was, as it was me who put myself there. I had not been home since the day I left to get on the train for Portsmouth. It was not as if I was thousands of miles away, but it might as well have been. I was not sure where home was anymore.

As I walked to the nurse's quarters after my shift, these thoughts ran through my mind. But they were quickly interrupted when I felt something move within me. I felt my baby kick for the first time. A smile appeared on my face as I felt this new life growing within me. That my body was capable of such a thing.

Despite my surroundings being covered in rubble and dust, this brief little moment of happiness made me block everything out. Everywhere was slowing falling apart after the constant bombing, yet I clutched my bump and smiled as I felt the baby kick again.

I felt a small sense of life growing slowly within me, reminding me that I too am alive. It was as if my baby was breathing life back into me. I smiled and rubbed my hand over my bump as the baby kicked again. My heart lightened. I had never felt such a feeling as this.

A deafening bang arose from behind me, and my body was thrown into the air. I crashed into a pile of rubble and I tried to catch my breath. A sickening pain shot up my back and into my chest. My whole body cried out in agony, and I could not stop shaking. A thunderous ring echoed throughout my ears. Dust clung to the air. I coughed and spluttered as the dust held a firm grasp over my throat.

Another crash came from behind me. The smell of burning choked my throat and made my eyes sting. I placed my hand on my bump but as I took it away, my hand was covered in blood.

A figure came towards me and took the form of Beatrice. She looked at me, her face turning pale. She turned around to call for help but stumbled on the rubble. She crawled towards me and held out her hand.

"Everything is going to be okay. We have to get you back to the hospital. Where the bloody hell is everyone? HELP! OVER HERE!"

Beatrice stood up and waved her arms but the dust concealed us like a grave.

"Where are you hurt? I can't tell where the blood is coming from. Oh god, Lucy, you are losing a lot of blood. Don't worry, everything is going to be alright. We need to get you out of here....Stay right there and I will call for help."

"No," I protested. "Please take me home."

"You are covered in blood, Lucy, you have to go to the hospital. Don't argue with me."

"NO!" I shouted with all my might. An anger grew within me and I held out my hand to her. "Just help me up and bring me back home...And Lilian, get Lilian."

Beatrice agreed to do as I asked. We staggered back to our house through the dust as I clutched my bump and only saw red ahead of me. More thunderous vibrations randomly arrived, causing us to fall and stumble. We somehow made it back and Beatrice lifted me onto my bed. She ran with all her might to the hospital.

I lay on my bed endlessly waiting for Beatrice to come back with Lilian. Severe cramps agonisingly stabbed me, radiating through my back and abdomen. I wanted to vomit. I needed to get this pain out of my body. I wanted to scream and shout.

Beads of sweat formed on my skin, like little islands of pain. The cramps came in waves but I could not move an inch. I shivered with the cold, as if I were covered in snow. I pressed my palm to my forehead, and I began to think Beatrice placed me near a fire. I tried to move away from the burning fire, but it was no use. It grew hotter each way I moved. My room must be on fire. I needed to get out of here. Why won't my legs do as I tell them? Move!

I peered down at my small bump and could see more blood forming on my uniform. The blood slowly leaked onto my bed, staining the old quilts. What if I bled to death?

The door flew open and Lilian ran in with Beatrice behind her. I held out my hand to Lilian as I cried out her name. Beatrice swung my legs back onto the bed and pushed my shoulders back into the pillows. I cried that the room was on fire but they wouldn't listen.

Beatrice placed a cool damp cloth onto my forehead as Lilian assessed me. Lilian began to move about the room, gathering material, a basin of water and her medical bag. Beatrice solemnly stayed by my side and held my hand. She stroked my hair while she whispered sweet encouragements into my ear. Her voice was so sweet. So warm.

Lilian returned to my side and whispered incoherent words to Beatrice, who nodded an understanding. I tried to speak and sit up, but Lilian pushed me back onto my bed.

"It's okay. Don't worry, I'm here now," Lilian spoke to me in a calm soothing tone. "Everything is going to be alright. Don't worry…Me and Beatrice are with you."

Lilian repeated this over and over until a warm blackness came over me and I could hear no more.

Labour arrived and I delivered my baby, as if my baby were ready to come into this world. I lost my baby that night. I named him Jonathon Carow, not that he knew that was his name. But he was my little Jonathon none the less.

Beatrice and Lilian cried with me. They placed Jonathon in a blanket with Adam's pressed daisy, my handkerchief, and my engagement ring. They buried Jonathon for me before the other girls returned. I could not bring myself to go with them when they buried him.

My body ached all over, I thought I was paralysed.

As I lay in that bed, staring at the damp ceiling I believed it was karma that I miscarried Jonathon for not wanting him. I told myself repeatedly that it was my fault until I no longer had to repeat the words, they were doing the repeating for me. I placed my hand on my bump and felt nothing. I could not feel my heartbeat and I prayed I was dead. Maybe I was.

That night, Lilian lay with me and Beatrice made a small bed on the floor beside me. I cried into Lilian until my body could cry no longer. I eventually fell asleep.

The following morning, I tried to get of my bed but fell onto the carpeted floor. It was as though all the muscles in my legs had wasted away. I sat on the floor and cried until I could not see, hear, or feel anything else. Only tears. Beatrice wrapped her arms around me and cried with me. She helped me back into bed and tucked me in.

I could not stop crying. All that I had blocked out came flooding back in and I could not stop the tears from flowing. Would they ever stop? What was I going to do?

Beatrice had to leave to start her shift. I told her to leave me and she reluctantly did. Lilian and Whilma found me curled into a ball in my bed. They tucked me in and stayed by my side until I fell asleep. I lay in bed for a few days.

Each of the girls took turns staying by my side. Sometimes they read the paper to me or told me a funny story. Other times they held my hand and cried with me. They did not know what they were crying for, but nonetheless, they cried for me.

I tried to recover from my physical injuries but I wondered would I ever be able to leave this bed and walk out the door. The girls, bar Lilian and Beatrice, thought the grief of losing Adam was only beginning to affect me. They tried to cheer me up by talking about their memories of Adam, hoping it would make me smile. But I could not make them stop. I begged them to stop, to leave me be. But they never left me. They were always there.

I shamefully felt relief after the miscarriage, as it meant

I would not have to bring a baby into war. Jonathon was an innocent baby, and he did not deserve any of this. When I could walk again, Lilian and Beatrice brought me to Jonathon's grave and I placed some flowers on it. They had placed him in the Cypress Cemetery beside Adam. At their graves, I could not cry, and I never knew why. I felt that by burying Jonathon and Adam, I was trying to remove the memory of them. But I could never remove the memory of them despite how much I tried.

I wanted to go to my bed, fall asleep and wake in the morning to a different world. A world where Adam and Jonathon never existed. Maybe if I stayed in bed long enough, wasted away my life, the world would believe it never knew me and I never existed.

1998

I sit in my armchair, with tears silently trickling down my cheeks. Lilian holds my hand while she delicately dabs her eyes with her handkerchief. Mae and Emmy sit like statues, as the room becomes achingly silent.

Mae slowly stands up and makes her way over to me. I see she too has tears in her eyes.

"I am so sorry," Mae blubbers. "I am sorry... I had no idea..."

Mae bends down and gives me a warm, tight hug. I hold her in my arms. My baby. My baby girl that I carried full term. I got to watch her take her first steps and say her first words. I watched her educate herself and become the woman she is today. I watched her live her life to the fullest and loved her every step of the way. My dear Mae. I may have lost Jonathon, but I gained a wonderful son in Teddy and a wonderful daughter in Mae.

I hold onto Mae tightly and feel her warmth in my arms. Emmy joins us and I hold onto her even tighter.

"I can't believe you kept something like this hidden all these years," Mae shakes her head.

Lilian snivels and blows her nose into her handkerchief.

"We all have our secrets, Mae. We keep things hidden, because keeping them to ourselves is how we survive. We are not keeping secrets to hide from other people - we are keeping them to protect them. Your mother kept this hidden to protect her family, her job, Adam's name, her position of authority in the hospital, and most importantly herself. It was different times back then and there were so many pressures on her."

"I think we should do something nice to remember Adam and Jonathon, to give them the proper send-off that they never got," Emmy suggests.

"That would be lovely sweetheart," I weep. "To this day, they never received the send-off that they deserved. I have always regretted that. They should have been grieved. They deserved so much more." I bow my head and rub my hand over the daisy cushion.

Mae places her hand over mine, admiring the daisies.

"And nobody else in the family ever knew, did they?"

"No, you two are the first to know," I quietly answer. "I never told George or my parents about Adam, even when we got engaged or when he died. I do not know why I did that. I could not bring myself to write his name, or even say it. So instead, I refused to ever talk about it. And he did not deserve that. Adam's memory deserved to be remembered and for stories of him to be passed on, not forgotten. His name needs to be remembered and talked about. Adam loved me with all his heart, and I loved him. But look at the thanks I gave him – I miscarried our child and I refused to talk about them for over 50 years."

"Do not be hard on yourself at all Mam," Mae kindly says. "Those were traumatic experiences, and I will never know how you got through it. You are incredible." Mae hugs me again.

"I'll tell you how I got through it, Mae. She's sitting right here," I smile at Lilian.

"And I'll always be here, Luc." Lilian clutches my hand and dabs her eyes yet again to catch the falling tears. "Like I always say, anything that we lose will always be replaced with something better."

"And I surely did get something better, didn't I? I got Will, Teddy and Mae. And then I got an even greater present – my grandchildren," I smile.

Mae returns to her seat on the couch and picks up the picture of Adam. "So, what happened afterwards?"

"Well," I take a deep breath, "I just kept moving forward as best as I could."

My chest is heavy, and I have suddenly become aware of my heartbeat. A faint scent passes my nose and I try to search for it. Daisies.

My vision becomes hazy, and I let my memories take me away as the voices around me slowly decrescendo.

WEBLEY'S DON'T CRY

The evening that I miscarried, I planned on writing a long letter home telling my parents about my current situation. I wanted to write a similar letter to George, hoping he might understand me better.

But when I lost Jonathon, I lost more than just my baby. I lost more plans that I had made. I no longer could see or think of my future. My mind became blank on who I was supposed to be, where I wanted to go, what I wanted to do. Making plans somewhat frightened me. So, I only ever thought about making it to the end of each day.

I never wrote those letters. Instead, I tried to act as if none of it ever happened. I refused to let anyone see I was hurting. But as always, Lilian was there for me and could see right through my pretence.

My father's voice saying, "Webleys don't cry," always seemed to be on repeat in my head.

Oh, how I wished I could have silenced that phrase.

Beatrice and Lilian told the hospital that I was injured in a bomb explosion and needed time to recover, which both the hospital and staff were supportive of.

I stayed curled up in my bed for a week, not moving an inch. Lilian and Beatrice brought me some food. The sight of it was enough to make me vomit. But they stayed with me until I ate a portion of it.

Every night I dreamt happily about Adam, Jonathan, and me. We were together in our white cottage. Jonathon was growing bigger and more beautiful every time I looked at him and Adam had the biggest smile on his face. We were happy, so happy.

Each morning my heart would re-break when I realised it was only ever a dream.

In my emotionally numb periods, I feared that I had moved

into a lesser state of grief, and I frantically wanted the pain to come back. Just so I could feel something. The pain would always come back, and it consumed me. It was all I could think of.

Matron Burke began to worry that I might have the Winter blues or was homesick. She thought I should go home for a while. I overheard her sharing her concerns with Lilian and I was determined to prove them wrong.

The next morning, I woke up early, washed my deflated body, got dressed and headed for the hospital. When I walked into the ward, the nurses and staff were shocked to see me. Everybody seemed to move out of my way. I wondered did they know. Surely, they were disgusted with me as much as I was.

I threw myself into work and acted as though the baby and Adam never existed. If I told myself enough times that I was fine, maybe I would believe it and it would come true. But Matron Burke pulled me aside as soon as she came into the ward.

"You should be in bed resting. I heard you got a pretty bad knock to your head after the explosion, but I didn't think it knocked all the sense out of you," was all that she seemed to say to me. It was all anyone could say to me.

Matron Burke sympathetically smiled at me. A smile that I hated with all my being. Do not pity me, hate me. I pleaded with her to let me work. I was able to stand and move about the ward, wasn't I? What use would I be lying in that stained bed and staring at the four walls around me?

I kept my head bowed so that nobody could look into my eyes. If they took one look at me, I knew I would begin to cry. And how would I ever stop?

But all Matron Burke asked of me was to take care of myself. Betty's death was still fresh on everyone's mind and I knew the ward could not face losing another nurse. More than anything, I wanted everyone to stop looking at me the way they did. The soldiers seemed to pity me as well.

Every eye monitored me. Every action was judged as a cry for help. I forced my face into a smile when I could still remember how to do that.

Lilian stormed into the ward and found me. I heavily sighed, awaiting the lecture.

"There you are. I woke up this morning and your bed was empty and I couldn't find you anywhere. You are supposed to be resting in bed, Lucy."

I pinched the bridge of my nose.

"Lilian don't do this. Please. I can't bear to sit in that horrible room, lie in the most uncomfortable bed and do nothing all day when I know I am needed here. I can be useful here. I feel useless in bed."

"You're not well Lucy and you need to take care of yourself, not throw yourself into work. That will only make things worse."

I refused to look at her.

"I know you're hurting and what you went through is traumatic, but you can't just lock it in a box and hope that it goes away by itself."

"Who hasn't been through something traumatising, Lil? This is war. Look around you," I blurted out. "There are people who have had it worse than me. Just look!"

"I know there are people who have had it worse, but that doesn't lessen what you've gone through. And you shouldn't lessen it either."

Some of the other nurses began to watch us and I could feel my cheeks redden. I tried to walk away but Lilian grabbed my arm and pulled me back. A new strength emerged in Lilian that I had never witnessed before, a protective strength.

"What you have just gone through is the worst thing that has happened to you, and I hope, will ever happen to you. I hope that you will never experience that type of pain ever again, physically, and mentally. But you need to take some time out and deal with what you have gone through," Lilian said.

I sneaked a look at Lilian and saw the tears in her eyes. If I could take away her pain and add it to my pile, I would. I did not want people to be looking after me and worrying about me - to be looked at as a wounded, fragile thing. It did not feel right to me. I wanted everyone to carry on as normal and treat me as a whole being, not like a shattered girl who would break at a moment's notice.

Lilian caught me by my arms and turned me so that I was facing her.

"Lucy, I only want you to be happy. And I know that happiness looks like an impossible dream right now, but I want you to know I am here...I always will be. I will be here to look after you, even if you won't look after yourself. And that is non-negotiable."

I shrugged Lilian off, but she did not flinch. She caringly rubbed my shoulder and worked alongside me for the remainder of the day. Every time I looked up, Lilian was only steps away from me.

From that day on, Lilian kept her eye on me. Lilian ordered the other nurses to do the same.

During the day, she would come at random intervals with food. I could not stomach it, but I did not want to disappoint Lilian, so I took it and waited for her to leave before I gave it to one of the patients or children outside. This did not last long.

Lilian began to wait and stay beside me until I had eaten all the food. If she could not be there watching me, Beatrice, Rita, Dorothy, Joan, or Whilma took up post. My St Angela's family surrounded me, and I felt stronger because of them.

After weeks of pushing myself to work harder, the girls were concerned for me and the weight I was shedding.

I no longer recognised my own reflection. I stayed away from mirrors because of this.

I no longer recognised the woman looking back at me. I tried to reassure the girls that I was perfectly okay, and that it was nothing that a good night's rest could not solve. I was not sure if I was trying to convince them or myself.

I tried to carry on as normal in the hospital and work my normal shifts. But I found that the night shifts always brought me back to the night that I lost Adam. Every time I looked up to the door, I would see his body being carried in on a stretcher.

I asked Matron Burke to be put on a rescue-team helping with the ambulances on emergency calls. It got me out of the hospital and out of my head and own thoughts. The adrenaline of being on the rescue teams successfully distracted me for some time. It was that sense of excitement that I needed. I felt alive.

For once, I could feel something other than pain.

MARCH 1943

In March 1943, I received yet another letter from my mother. In the past few months, I had opened all her letters but never replied. I would read them and throw them into a box and shut them tight. I felt so ashamed when she would write to me, to the Lucy she knew. I could not bear to think what she would say about me now.

I picked up the letter and quickly read it before I started a night shift with the rescue-team.

Webley Hazelton Manor,
20th March 1943

My darling Belle,

It is with my deepest regret that I inform you of your dear father. He suffered a stroke last night.

Fortunately, Doctor Fernsby came as soon as he could and was able to help him. He is currently lying-in bed as I sorrowfully write this letter, watching his chest rise and fall. I am terrified to look at him and not see him breathing or moving. It is so strange to see him lying here in the middle of the day. Your dear father was always a man that never stopped moving. Always stimulating his mind.

For the past two weeks he has been complaining about his poor health, but his stubborn old self would not visit the doctor. Fernsby assures me that nothing could have prevented this stroke. I beg to differ.

For the past few weeks, I noticed your father acting contrary, more so than usual. He would question everything and anything. The servants and I dreaded seeing him as he would make everything difficult and unnecessarily complicated, but they did their best to please him. As they always do.

On Wednesday, as I sat in the Green Room with your father drinking tea he said, 'The weather is nice.' I nodded in agreement. But because he did not get the answer he desired, he repeated this phrase three more times until he got another answer. Even then, he still fought with me about whether I really thought the weather was nice. I can safely say I was exhausted with this constant questioning. But I would give anything, do anything, to have his contrary old self back instead of his current state.

Last night, after we finished our evening meal, he retired as usual to his armchair by the fire. Since it was a Friday night, I joined him. I have become accustomed to retiring to the drawing room to read as of late, but on Fridays it has become our new tradition to sit together after dinner. Daisy had poured him a glass of whiskey and left the room.

I was reading my book and he was reading his. I heard glass shatter on the floor and it frightened me. I looked up and saw it was your father's glass and that he was making a strange face. I quickly called the maids to come at once and told Mary to run to Fernsbys' house. My dear Charles was mumbling something to me, but he made no sense. I had never felt more frightened in my life.

What if I had not been there with him, Lucy?

Your father has been asleep all night and the majority of today. But when he woke, he was suddenly fluent in cursing! It seems all he can say is curse words, and he shouts them at everyone. I fear we will not be able to bring him anywhere or have any visitors, because it is utterly shocking what he says. Hopefully, this is only a temporary thing and our dear Charles will soon be his normal self again. But Fernsby thinks not…

Fernsby spoke of how victims of stroke can often undergo a personality change and it cannot be undone. I fear I may be losing Charles forever.

I am feeling dreadfully hopeless, Lucy. I wish you would come home for a visit, even if it were for a few days. I miss you terribly and I think the visit would do a world of good for your father. A familiar old face would brighten our recently dark days.

We missed you at Christmas and it will be Easter soon – maybe you could come home for Easter? You have not been home since

May 1941, the day you left on the train. How awfully long ago
that was. I have also written to George, but he will not be able to
come home as he is in the middle of the ocean somewhere. He is
very secretive with his whereabouts.

As always, take care my sweetheart and please
come home soon. I beg of you. We miss you.
Mama.

I fell onto my bed when I read the first line of the letter.
Lilian saw me and ran over, always prepared to take care of
me. I hated that Lilian felt obliged to take care of me, but I
needed her. I feared what I would do if she were not there.
Lilian's strength was the among the few things keeping me
upright.

Lilian tried her best to comfort me, but I was emotionless. I
could not feel anything, just a gaping emptiness inside. I had
become so accustomed to loss that I did not know how to
react anymore. Lilian looked at me and shook me, but it was
no use, I was not there. She called my name over and over
again but it was as though she was calling another. I did not
know who Lucy was.

I handed her the letter and watched her eyes move back
and forth across the page, taking in every word.

"Oh Lucy, I am so sorry," Lilian sympathised.

I shrugged my shoulders at her as if it meant nothing to
me.

"Lucy, just cry. It is okay. You do not have to be pretend to be
strong for me. It's me, for God's sake!"

"I can't, Lilian. My body won't let me. My father always used
to say that 'Webley's don't cry. They stand tall and proud.'
And that is exactly what he would want me to do. He would
be ashamed to see me cry," I blankly replied. "I am ashamed
to see me cry."

"But you need to cry, Lucy. You need to let it out, stop
holding everything in. You'll only burst and that will not be
anyway helpful to you." She sadly stared into my eyes and
sighed. "Just cry!"

"I don't feel a thing. I don't think I am capable of feeling anymore. You don't understand, I can't explain what the bloody hell is going on inside me and my head if I don't understand it myself."

Lilian caringly smiled at me and held my hand. I could feel her strength radiating into my hands.

"It'll be okay…We'll figure it out together."

I left the letter and Lilian on my bed and walked to the hospital.

A call came to the hospital for an ambulance to rescue soldiers from a site nearby during an air-raid. I quickly ran towards the ambulance, glad to be running away and doing something other than thinking. Oh, if I could stop my mind from thinking. Maybe there was a medicine for that or a quick procedure to rip out the pain and bad memories and throw them away.

For now, I could pray that hard work would silence my mind.

Bombs exploded in the surrounding areas as we desperately tried to drive as quickly as we could to the wounded soldiers. We got out of the ambulance and ran to the bodies on the ground trying to assess as quickly as possible who was priority. But it became too dangerous to try and drive back to the hospital. We found a vacant, crumbling building and brought the men into it. Those that could walk, helped carry the wounded. Everywhere was black with the only light coming from the fires ignited by the bombs.

One soldier bled profusely. His fellow men from his platoon placed their hands on his wounds, applying pressure to stop the bleeding. Their faces desperately followed the rescue team, pleading with them to help. We hastily placed him onto the dusty table in the middle of the room. We found some oil lamps and candles and lit them low. The light allowed us to see the frightening amount of blood loss from the soldiers' wounds. He needed surgery or else he would bleed to death.

I looked at Dr Noone as he quickly assessed the scene. We needed to perform surgery right now with the limited equipment that we had.

"Do you have any morphine on you?" Dr Noone impatiently

asked.

"No, it's in the ambulance," I shakily replied.

I looked around the room and saw some shattered glass on the floor in the back corner. I walked over to it and found two bottles still intact. One was a clear bottle of vodka, and the other was a familiar dark green bottle.

Webley's Whiskey.

The last night I was home, I sat at the dining room table with my parents joyfully laughing and smiling at each other as my father cracked yet another joke. He poured whiskey into my mother's crystal glass and a generous amount for me too.

I had always dreamed of the day that I would sit at the table and join my father in a glass of whiskey. Since, we were celebrating my twenty-first birthday, a glass of Webley's whiskey marked my new position as an adult in the family. Pride bubbled within me.

Dinner had just finished, and the staff cleared away the beautifully dressed table. All the fine China was out, just for me. I was getting the train to Portsmouth the following morning and my parents wanted to give me a memorable send-off. Mother tipsily swung her glass of whiskey as she hiccupped her way through a story about the Royal family and their war effort.

My mother rarely drank as the smell of alcohol alone was enough to make her tipsy. But when she did, this wonderful, vibrant, funny character came out that she rarely showed. I wondered was this the woman that my father had fallen in love with.

"You know Lucy," my mother turned to me, "when you first started nursing, I wasn't sure of it. But I hid it well and you never knew that."

I heartily laughed. "I knew you didn't approve."

"No, you didn't know because I hid it well," she hiccupped again. "A lady always knows how to hide her true emotions."

My father sarcastically nodded in agreement while winking at me. I laughed again and turned to my mother.

"But I just want you to know that I am so proud of you. Always have been and always will be. I love you so much, my darling, so much. I was really onboard with the whole thing when Frannie Wincup told me about how many girls from families, like ours, are only sitting in their comfortable homes barely recognising that there is a war and I thought-"

"-Frannie Wincup", father interrupted as he rolled his eyes and laughed.

"Yes Charles, Frannie Wincup. She keeps me with up to date with everything" she replied while looking him straight in the eye. "Where was I, oh yes...I thought that my Lucy wanted to help with the war before the war even came. She was ahead of most Charles, in her thoughts and actions. And I just want you to know, Lucy dear, that I think what you are doing is wonderful. You have worked so hard and studied so hard to get where you are. Even Madam Speirs would be impressed!"

My father leaned forward and placed his hand on my mother's hand.

"I think what your poor mother is trying to say is that we are very proud of you and we are going to miss you terribly."

"I know you are only going to Portsmouth, it's not as if you will be million miles away, but war always makes home feel a million miles away doesn't it, Charles? Just know we are always here to welcome you home."

Both of my parents hugged me tightly and it felt bittersweet. I had never experienced a night like this before and I wished that we had.

My father held his glass proudly in the air as my mother and I chinked his glass with ours. My mother accidently spilled some of her whiskey on me and the carpet. But instead of flustering around frantically like she normally would, she laughed, and it was the most beautiful sound to hear.

Another blast vibrated through me and I realised I had been standing in the corner staring at the bottle of whiskey in my hand.

"Nurse?" Noone shouted over to me. "Have you found anything that we can use?"

"Here, we can use these."

The wounded soldier eagerly drank some of the whiskey

while Noone began to treat the wound.

The soldier screamed out in agony but luckily for us, his screams were masked by the bombing and planes overhead. Noone successfully stopped the bleeding and we moved onto the other soldiers and citizens that were there.

The shooting stopped after 3am. We loaded up the ambulance and made our way back to the hospital. I hid the bottle of whiskey in my first aid bag, before we left the desolate scene.

When I finished my shift, I went back to the nurses' quarters. My room was empty, but I knew the girls would be back soon. I opened my bag and took out the bottle of whiskey and began to drink it straight from the bottle - something I had never done before.

I hoped the whiskey would numb me, make me forget what I desperately wanted to forget. I sat on my bed and took short sips. I began to feel dizzy and knew that the whiskey was working. I had barely eaten all day, so I knew the alcohol would be a shock to the system. Maybe a shock well needed. I wanted to numb my mind but feel something at the same time.

The door opened, and Joan walked in.

"You can't have a party by yourself. Give us a drink!"

I handed her the bottle and watched as she took a large swig.

"Ah! That hit the spot!" Joan bounced over to her bed and pulled out her trunk from underneath. "You know, we haven't had one of these nights in a long time...and we desperately need one. I never thought I'd say it but, I think I miss St. Angela's."

Joan excitedly walked back over to my bed with two bottles of red wine in her hands. The door burst open and Beatrice, Rita, Whilma, and Dorothy walked in. They happily joined us when they saw the bottles. They were exhausted after their shift, but they put on a smile, and I envied their ability to do that. Beatrice joined me on my bed and pulled a hipflask out of her pocket.

Everybody, including me for some time, failed to see that Beatrice was deeply hurting inside. I watched her as she drank from her hipflask and saw her eyes were already red from crying and drinking. But she hid it so well. This was one of her many talents.

Beatrice sadly grinned at her flask. "My medicine."

I could smell rum from her sour breath as she spoke.

"Does it work?"

"If you drink enough of it, it does."

Beatrice took another swig and realised she was at the end of her flask. I handed her my bottle of whiskey, and she eagerly took a gulp of it before handing it back to me. Meanwhile, the other girls talked and laughed with each other.

Beatrice and I watched from my bed and continued to drink. It felt as if we were watching a scene play out in front of us. I felt both there with them yet on the outside looking in.

By the time Lilian arrived, the sun began to rise. Dorothy returned to her room. Joan and Rita reminisced and laughed with each other. Beatrice stumbled around the room, swinging a bottle of wine, and singing to herself while Whilma sat on Betty's old bed, silently crying.

Since Betty's death, none of us could talk about her without one of us crying. But Whilma took it the hardest.

Lilian found me cradling my body on the floor with tears streaming down my face. She kneeled in front of me and took the bottle of whiskey from my hands. She put her arms around me and gently rubbed my hair.

"I miss him, Lil," I sobbed. "I just miss him so much. Why does it have to be this hard?" I almost choked on my words.

The other girls joined us on the floor when they heard me crying.

"Adam?" Whilma softly asked as she wiped her tears away.

I shook my head furiously at her as my insides almost repulsed at the sound of his name.

"Don't say that name, please. I can't bear to hear it."

I continued to cry into Lilian as she rubbed my hair and gently hummed.

"I will never love again. Never!"

Rita tried to calm me. "It's unfair, I know. But do not give up on love entirely."

"I will never see his face again, his smile, hear his laugh, hug him, kiss him, listen to him talk, know his family as my own...live in our cottage, get married, hold his hand... nothing. He has gone forever and I do not know what to do. What do I do?"

The girls tried to comfort me, but it was no use. I was inconsolable. We sat on the floor for some time and Lilian handed me back the bottle of whiskey. They sat in silence with me until I could cry no more.

When my body began to droop, they put me to bed. Once my heavy head hit the pillow, I instantly fell asleep.

When I woke, the sun was high in the sky and the room was back to normal. Lilian had cleaned up so that we would not be faced with a reminder of the hours before. Once she saw that I was awake, she brought me water, tea and then forced food onto me.

"Eat!" was all that she commanded.

After I unwillingly ate the food, I vomited all over myself and the bed. Lilian dragged me out of bed and placed me into the bath and poured cold water over me. I screamed, squealed, and fought with her.

"We don't have time to heat up the water on the stove. You need to sober up, Lucy, your shift starts in an hour," Lilian nagged while washing me.

Once dressed and cleaned, I looked somewhat presentable from afar. But up-close, my face and lifeless eyes told another story. I hated myself for being like this, but I couldn't find a way out of it.

I continued like this for some time, drinking after my shifts to numb the pain. But it only heightened it. I was never alone in my drinking. I could always count on Beatrice or Joan for company. Both had their own problems to deal with and I knew that if I were with them, neither one would mention Adam to me or the miscarriage.

Lilian was not impressed, but she never argued with me as she knew that would only make things worse. Instead, she was always there taking care of me, making sure I ate at least some bit of food, washed, slept, got to work on time. I was never drunk while working, as working itself drowned out my memories and thoughts. I only needed alcohol when my shifts ended, because that was when I was left alone with my aching thoughts.

Throughout March, the war was at sea in the Atlantic. The German army sank over 482,000 tons of allied shipping from the US to Britain. The hospital was constantly being swarmed with victims from these U-Boat attacks, mainly civilians. Most days, I felt as though I could not breathe. I drowned in the sea of wounded men, women, and children. How could I possibly help them? How could I possibly heal them? But I did my best. That was all anyone could do. By May, the Allies destroyed so many U-Boats that Germany had no other option but to withdraw from the Atlantic. I smiled knowing George stood among these navy men, helping to win the war. The Allies did not stop here. They also bombed two major dams in Germany. The war began to look good for Britain and its allies. A momentary victory at least. Maybe we could finally be able to fight back and end this miserable war.

JUNE 1943

By late June 1943, bottles of alcohol lay hidden under my bed. Some were empty, others were half full. I knew I had a problem when I got out of bed in the morning and tripped over empty bottles by my bedside table, waking the other girls. I looked in the mirror and hardly recognised myself.

Matron Burke gave me the day off, to put it lightly, and I did not know what to do with myself.

The evening before, I aided a soldier who returned from theatre. He lost both of his legs. Seeing him drowsily lie in the bed, still unaware that he had lost his legs, pained me. I knew there was nothing I could say to possibly comfort him. As I held a glass of water to his mouth, another young soldier ran up to me while pressing a damp cloth to his jaw.

"Are you serious?" I shouted at the young soldier. "This man just lost both of his legs and you're asking me do I have something for a little tooth ache? That you can't go on living?"

I continued to shout at him, not even remotely embarrassed that everyone in the ward had turned their attention to me. I wanted to scream and shout louder.

"Deal with the pain, it adds character!"

Matron Burke appeared in front of me. She did not once raise her voice, she did not need to. Her look alone told me everything. I followed her into her small office, and I could feel a storm brewing inside me. I had never felt so angry and annoyed at a person, and I had no idea why I felt so angry. I did not know the man, I had no reason to be so angry with him.

Yet, I hated him.

I needed to scream, and a scream would not be loud enough. I needed to get this anger out of me.

Matron Burke's expression turned serious, but her features

softened ever so slightly when she looked at me. She looked differently at me from how she looked at everyone else, and I was confused whether I liked this or not. Did she think I was different from everyone else? Did she think I was not able to handle my work? Did she think I was weak?

Matron Burke folded her arms.

"It is your duty to heal and help these men, not to shout at them. I understand that you have been working day in and day out for the past few months, and you must be tired. I appreciate that you have taken on many roles and are training in most of the new nurses, but you cannot behave like that."

I could not reply to her as I feared I might cry or burst with anger.

"How will you be any good to us if you are burnt out?"

I agreed with what she was saying, yet I still refused to stop working. She could not stop me from working. She could not do that to me. I needed to work. I needed to be busy. She needed me in this hospital.

"I also understand, Nurse Anna, that many nurses often come running to you to fix a problem, even when you are off duty. I have been told that there have been countless nights and days where you were asleep after your shift, and a nurse has come to you to deal with a patient. That should not be happening. I have been told that it was you who allowed this to happen and, in fact, encouraged it."

Matron Burke glared at me from behind her glasses until I answered.

"What you have been told is correct, Matron, but really, I do not mind working the extra hours if I am needed."

"No. You need to learn to draw a line with your trainee nurses and with other nurses when you are off duty. I will only accept you coming to help when you are off duty, if and only if, there is an emergency. The girls need to learn to solve their problems themselves, otherwise they will never be able to survive. You cannot be everywhere at once and you cannot solve everyone's problems. You have your own problems to deal with."

I shamefully looked down at the floor, watching my foot

tap slowly against the leg of the chair.

"Yes Matron."

"I know it hasn't been easy on you losing our fellow nurse, Betty Smith. And I also know that you lost a loved one, a soldier at the end of last year, was it?" Matron Burke sympathised.

I refused to look at her but kept my eyes firmly on floor.

"I just want you to know that throwing yourself into work doesn't help anything. I should know, I did it. But now, my job is my husband and family. Take a fool's advice and take tomorrow off, Nurse Anna. And I am sure a day is not even enough, so if you need more time, I will be happy to accommodate. We cannot have you shouting and tearing off in a rage in the wards. That will be all."

"Yes Matron."

I pushed the conversation with Matron Burke to the side of my mind and washed myself.

My uniform hung over the back of the chair by my bed, and I contemplated putting it on and going to the hospital. But I knew that I would be immediately sent back to my room if I did.

I looked at my single shelf in the wardrobe and tried to pick out an outfit. Every dress, top, cardigan or skirt I picked up reminded me of when I last wore them. Almost all of them had a memory of Adam attached to them.

I picked out a simple shirt dress and put it on. I had not worn the dress in a long time. I thought that this might mean the memory of Adam would have washed away with time.

As I buttoned up the dress and looked at myself in the mirror, I could see that the dress no longer fit me like it used to. The shoulders and sleeves were slipping off my bony arms, and the middle of the dress loosely hung around my waist where it once clung delicately to my skin. The fabric drowned me. I attempted to put some make-up on to cover up my tired eyes and sunken cheeks. But I looked worse. I left my room and decided to put some space between me and the hospital.

With every uncertain step that I took, I considered immediately turning around and running back to the cocoon that I had carved out for myself. But I stopped myself and turned my attention to what was in front of me – the footpath.

If I focused on this footpath, then I would be okay for at least a few moments. If I did not worry about where the footpath took me, then I could ease my mind momentarily. I looked at the buildings and how the sun fell onto the buildings and casted shadows onto the footpath.

Maybe if I took notice of what lay around me, instead of blanking out my surroundings, I could breathe.

Where had my mind been for these past few months? Had these building always stood there? Surely this was not the first time that I saw them. What had I done for the past few months? What was today's date? What was I doing with my life?

I focused so much of my energy on trying to forget Adam, my dear Jonathon, and the pain of losing both that, I could only remember them and nothing else.

Why was it that the things I desperately tried to forget were the very things that I remembered so well?

Picking roads at random, I walked aimlessly, until hunger overcame me. A small café revealed itself to me. I took a seat by the window near the back of the room, away from the preying eyes around me. When the red-haired waitress placed my cup of tea onto my table, I asked her for a pen and paper. My mind moved to thoughts of my mother. I realised that I never wrote back to my mother regarding my father's stroke.

Three months passed since his stroke, but my mother continued to keep me up to date regardless and I appreciated it. I could not begin to remember what I did in those weeks other than drink and work.

The waitress returned with a pen and a small copybook of paper. I wrote 'Dear Mama' at the top of the page. What now? I wrote the date and Portsmouth slowly at the top of the letter, hoping some words would come to mind for me to write.

I wrote 'how are you?' and then crossed it out. 'Thank you for your letters, I hope you are well.' I crossed that sentence

163

out as well. 'How is father? I am sorry I did not write sooner. I was very busy.' I moved my pen through the line until the words were illegible.

'Sorry.'

I dropped the pen onto the table, picked up my cup of tea and stared hopelessly out of the window.

A young mother with her toddler son passed by my window. The boy wobbled on the footpath. He was determined to walk by himself. But his mother impatiently pulled him along. The boy managed to sneak out of his mother's grasp and waddled over to my window. He steadied himself on the window ledge and looked through the window at me. He began to smile and wave, and I found myself smiling at him and waving back. His mother grabbed him, apologised to me through the windowpane and briskly walked on.

How long had it been since I last smiled?

My smile faded as quickly as it came as I realised that my Jonathon should have arrived this week.

Oh, I had been such a fool these past few months. I did not think much about myself, I only thought about what I had to do, which was nursing. But what I failed to realise was how selfish I had become.

I never thought about anyone else, especially those around me. Patients became numbers and charts. I no longer viewed them as people with a family or a life. I only saw them as another job to do. I had become so detached from my job and life, that I had somehow become so caught up in myself, which was what I desperately tried to get away from.

I finally wrote letters to my mother and George as I drank my tea. I made up some pathetic excuse to explain my lack of replies to their letters. I knew that there was nothing that I could say in those letters that would make their anguish and agony any better, but the letter itself might do something to help them. I posted the letters and made my way back to the living quarters.

It began to lightly rain which quickly turned into a downpour. Almost as if someone turned on the tap to its full capacity and the water came pouring down. I stopped in the street and observed everyone desperately running to get out of the rain. But I stood still, letting the rain touch every possible part of me. And for the first time in a long while, I could finally breathe.

When I got back to my room, I gladly found it empty. I looked around and saw how desolate it looked.

Bottles sneaked out from under the quilt of my unmade bed, clothes stuffed into the wardrobe, and four other unmade beds. I took all the bottles and dumped them, regardless of whether they had drink in them or not. The thought of alcohol suddenly repulsed me. I began to make the beds, rearranged the wardrobe, and cleaned anything else I could get my hands on. When there was nothing else to clean, I sat on my bed and looked around. I felt lost.

I was so weighed down with a load that I was somehow carrying on my shoulders. I did not know what I was carrying or how to unload it. What had I done with my life?

There was nobody else to blame but myself for where I was, and I fully accepted this.

I sat on my creaky bed and stared blankly at the pink floral wallpaper on the walls around me. I allowed my tears to stream down my face. But my mouth dared not let a sound escape. My walls felt as if they were beginning to cave in. I needed to allow myself to cry and to accept what I was feeling. I lay on my bed and cried until my tears burned.

I had not been there for myself. I had not supported or taken care of myself in the past few months. I neglected me and it was exactly me that I needed. A person can only accept help and be helped when they decide to help themselves. I did not want pity. I did not want sympathetic stares. I did not want desperate smiles and small talk. I wanted a helping hand. I wanted someone to help me, help me.

Once I was able to sit up again and not feel so faint from crying, I removed my damp clothes and cleaned myself.

Lilian returned later and stood in the doorframe staring in disbelief.

"My god, I almost didn't recognise you. I thought I had walked into the wrong room."

Lilian heartedly laughed as she walked towards me. Her

laugh quietened as she joined me on my bed. She gently stroked my cheek and looked at my blotchy red face.

"Matron Burke and I thought we would find you in the hospital this morning, attending patients. A few of us placed a bet on whether you would come in or not! Dottie was one of the few who thought you wouldn't come in, she believed in you."

I tried to laugh but a pathetic sound came out. I wiped away my tears and blew my nose into my handkerchief.

Lilian tilted her head and smiled, "Where did you go?"

I tried my best to smile at her, but my face pained me from the crying.

"I got dressed and went for a walk. I just kept walking. Following the footpath in front of me, it eventually led me to a small café."

Lilian warmly placed her arm around me.

"Well, I am proud of you for getting out of bed, getting dressed, putting on some make-up and going somewhere other than the hospital. You almost look like Lucy again. Did you eat anything today?"

"Yes, I did," I proudly answered.

I watched Lilian move towards the bathroom and wash her face.

"And you'll be happy to know that I have removed any trace of alcohol in this room. I cannot bear to even look at a bottle of alcohol anymore."

Lilian slowly turned to me and stood in the doorway, patting her face dry with the towel.

"I am glad to hear."

Lilians face almost seemed to melt with a sense of pride to see me doing well again. I could faintly see that her eyes were glistening with fresh tears.

"I am so sorry," I began to sob.

Lilians face crinkled and she rushed over to me, putting her warm, motherly arms around me.

"For what?"

"For the way I have behaved in the past few months. I just want you to know that I cannot thank you enough for being there for me. I don't know where I would be without you."

166

"I wouldn't be anywhere else."

CLEAN

The next day, I returned to the hospital and requested to take more time off work to go home and visit my family. Matron Burke quizzed me on how long it was since I saw my family. I tiredly admitted I had not been home since May 1941. Matron Burke insisted that it was important for nurses to get away from the hospital and to return to civilisation occasionally.

When I had time off, I used to travel to London with Adam and stay in Cornwall Terrace. I counted down the days until I could be with Adam. I created lists of things to do and see with our limited time together.

On the days that he could not get time off, I would stay with Lilian at Aunt June's house. I never went home. I did not want to be reminded of Arthur and my old life, so I refused to go home. Home became a place that I avoided with all my might.

But now that I sat on the train, I counted down the hours and minutes until I could be with my family. It felt strange to be sitting on the train and seeing civilian life again. I forgot what life used to be like.

Beatty waited for me at the train station and eagerly welcomed me into the car. His double take of me told me of more reactions to come.

I did my best to look presentable, but all my clothes no longer fit me. I knew that no amount of makeup would be able to conceal my thin, hollow, and tired face. I did my hair up in the style that my parents always liked, pinned up in the front of my face with my natural curls flowing down my back. I had not worn my hair down for so long that it felt heavy hanging over my shoulders.

On our car ride back home, Beatty happily informed me of village news and news from the estate. He talked about my parents, our neighbours and how news had spread that I was coming home. He told me about the hardships the village had suffered, the men we had lost, and the limitations placed on daily life. Beatty still held out for the day that his name would be called up to fight, but we both knew that would never happen.

I happily listened to Beatty's ramblings. It was a nice distraction from my own thoughts. Driving along the old familiar roads felt as though I no longer knew my old life. That strange feeling where I looked around, at the place where I once used to spend all my days, and nothing had changed yet everything had changed. The car turned and stopped outside the familiar big, black gates with 'Webley Hazelton Manor' shining in gold plated letters, proudly placed at the top. The gates opened and we drove up the long winding avenue. The lime trees were in full bloom and the July sun speckled through the gaps of the leaves, igniting the red bricks on the house. The house seemed to almost gleam in the summer light.

When the car halted to a stop, I sat for a moment in awe of the building, soaking in the memories and slowly remembering my old life. Two years was a long time since I had set my eyes on these bricks. I held my hand over the car handle and found I could not pull it. I could not open the door. The was nothing wrong with the door, it worked perfectly. It was me.

Beatty ran around the car and opened my door for me. He held out his hand to me and I nervously took it. My legs began to shake but I straightened my back and stood tall. Mr. Sutcliffe, the butler, proudly waited at the door and welcomed me inside.

How strange.

I needed the butler to welcome me into my own home. For I could not.

I glanced around the great hallway as though it was my first time there. But my eyes fell onto the smallest details of the room that I had forgotten and memories slowly came back to me. They were paired with new eyes.

I admired the knots in the oak flooring, the slight creases on the wallpaper, the years' worth of wax dripping down the sides of the candlesticks on the mantlepiece. Footsteps echoed on the stairs and I shyly looked up to see who it was.

"Lucy," Mama rejoiced. She pulled me into a tight hug. "I have missed you so much."

We stayed like this for some time until she let me out of her perfumed embrace and placed her hands on my cheeks, taking me all in. I pulled at my sleeves and patted down my dress, as if that would make me look better.

"You look so thin and tired. Well, we'll just have to change that, won't we! I have ordered the kitchen to make your favourite meals and desserts for the week."

I looked at my mother. Wrinkles had formed at the corners of her eyes and mouth. Lines lay ingrained on her forehead, telling stories of the years that she had lived. But time could not diminish her beauty. She was still the most beautiful woman in any room.

Her clothes were less glamourous, and it seemed she had become more reserved in her choice of fashion. Her lilac dress was faded from the many times it was washed. My mother would never dare to wear a piece of clothing repeatedly. She always bought a new wardrobe every Spring and Autumn. The only jewellery that she wore was her wedding band. She noticed me looking at her and sadly smiled.

"Rationing."

She made it sound as if this were the toughest thing she had had to deal with since war came.

My mother took me to my father who was sitting in the Green Room. He looked like his old self, sitting proudly in his armchair. Chester, loyal and caring as ever, proudly sat beside him.

As I grew closer, I saw my father's limp right arm cradled in his lap. He tried to speak but the words would not come out for him like he effortlessly used to be able to do. Father's face crumpled with frustration, and he went into a fit of cursing. I stood back in shock and looked at Mother who stood completely unfazed.

"Charles dear, take your time," she gently spoke before leaving the room to search for a maid.

After some time, he successfully said, "Belle."

I sat on the chair next to him and held his hand in mine. He squeezed my hand with all his might and stared into my eyes. It appeared as if he was desperately trying to remember every detail of my face.

I had never known my father to be anything but a strong man, walking around, busy with errands. My mother's letters could not have warned nor prepared me for how my father was in person.

As we sat together in a comfortable silence, I surveyed the room. Nothing had changed except for the people in it.

The sun shone through the long windows and casted shadows across the room, making the pictures hanging on the wall dance. The fire was lit despite it being in the middle of summer. The goose-feathered pillows were plumped on the two couches, the dust had been beaten out of the rugs earlier that day, every ornament and decoration in the room had been polished and dusted. The grand piano was opened and sitting promisingly in the small, rounded tower section of the room.

Everything was especially laid out for my visit home.

For the past two years this was all my parents have wished for. I felt my father squeezing my hand, which was his new way of getting one's attention, and he softly smiled.

"I am sorry, Papa," I whispered.

My father tried to rub my face but his hands failed him.

"I am so sorry I did not write or come home when I heard you had a stroke. I have no excuse, Papa. I am so sorry…"

"Belle."

My father did not need to say anything more. I placed my head on his shoulder and I smelt the tobacco from his pipe. I looked down at the end-table beside him and saw his black pipe, lying lonely beside his unread book.

"Do you want me to light your pipe for you?" I asked.

He eagerly nodded. I lit the pipe and carefully placed it in his mouth.

"I knew there was something missing! My father without his pipe is not my father."

He managed to laugh. "Belle?"

As I turned to him, his eyes moved from me to the piano. I walked over and sat down on the piano seat.

Since I left for Portsmouth, I had not played the piano. I wondered would my hands still remember how to move. I gently rubbed my hands along the shiny ivory keys and placed my right foot on the sustain pedal. I could hear the echo of the dampeners moving away from the strings as my foot pressed harder. I positioned my hands on the familiar keys and before I began to play, I looked over at my father whose smile lit up the room.

I began to play *Chopin Nocturne No. 2 op. 9*. I closed my eyes and let my hands move across the piano like they had done so many times before. I willingly let the sweet melody take me away.

Almost as soon as the final chord was struck, I heard clapping. I opened my eyes and saw my mother with some of the staff standing in the room. My father had his eyes closed, still smiling, and I had never seen him look so content. He opened his eyes when the clapping stopped and tried to join in, but his body failed him yet again.

He did not let this ruin his mood so instead he howled, 'Belle!'

We all laughed, especially Mother.

"I missed that sound," mother tearfully lilted.

Father gestured for her to take his handkerchief and she eagerly did. She gently dabbed her damp cheeks and eyes.

"Enough crying! Tea is ready."

For the week that I was at home, I spent most of it in my bed sleeping. I did not realise how exhausted I was. I did not know when I last slept in a room by myself. I had become so accustomed to the nurse's lifestyle, being surrounded every hour of the day by people. I had become so used to the noise and bustle that the silence seemed to scream at me.

Thoughts of Adam circulated in my mind, and I questioned ever leaving my bed. My mother never asked me any questions that would require an elaborate answer. Instead, she just let me talk whether I wanted to or not. We enjoyed each other's company.

I felt somewhat isolated when I came home as I did not

know anyone who had been through what I had or saw what I had seen. No one knew what my life had been like for the past two years, and I was going to make sure no one ever would.

I decided to visit Molly in her small cottage in the village. Arty was now two years old and looked strikingly like Arthur. It was my first time to meet my nephew. It was bittersweet as I knew I would be the only member of the Webley family to ever know him. I also craved to talk to someone who knew Arthur and could say his name.

Molly and I chatted for some time about many things, until I had to leave. As we walked out of her charming home, she grabbed my arm.

"I never got the chance to thank you for what you did for me and Arty."

"I didn't do anything."

"You did more than you could ever know. I believe the envelope with money that is posted to me every month does not come from angels or some mystical creature. Thank you for that, Lucy."

Molly squeezed Arty in her arms and a wonderful smile appeared on her face.

"I miss him every day...Arthur, I miss him. There is not a day that goes by where he does not cross my mind. Even more so now that Arty is beginning to look like him."

"I miss him too."

"Would you like me to write to you and keep you up to date with little Arty?"

"I would love nothing more. Since my brother cannot be here to see his son grow up and my family...well my parents are the way they are, I will be here. I am his aunt after all! If you need anything Molly, no matter how big or small, do not hesitate to ask."

"And same to you, Lucy. I will always be here if you need anything. You will always have a friend in me."

MOTHER

Before I returned to the estate, I walked around the grounds. I visited the stables and watched the two stable boys brushing a magnificent chestnut horse. It was Arthur's horse, Noble.

The day Arthur got Noble still lingered in my memories. Wasn't it strange the things we remembered?

I could faintly hear Arthur saying, "I named him Noble because he is such a handsome and noble looking horse. And I thought that, no name can justify his nobility other than Noble."

Arthur was so proud to show off his horse. It was all he talked about. George and I teased Arthur about how he would probably one day marry Noble instead of a woman.

Noble gently moved towards me and I lovingly rubbed her smooth, strong neck. I peered into the stable and spotted the two young stable boys teasing each other. They were brothers, remarkably close in age, like Arthur and George.

On Arthur and George's summer holidays from boarding school, their horses were often confiscated from them because they had got into mischief yet again. One was as bad as the other, but together they were dynamite. They often snuck out of the house and took their horses out for a ride, and without fail, they would always stumble upon trouble. They preferred to call this 'an adventure.'

I missed them dearly when they would return to school in the autumn. The house would become unbearably quiet and no adventures were had. I counted the days on my calendar until they would return. I should be used to not having them around, but it still hits me nonetheless.

I continued my walk around the stables, the estate grounds, and gardens before returning to the house. Hopefully answers to some of my questions would find me.

I wanted to see how the war had affected Webley Estate since I left.

Mother asked the gardeners to grow vegetables and fruit in an unused part of the garden to help with the limited food they received with rationing. When the vegetables and fruit were ripe, Mrs. Flood, the cook, took what she needed for the estate kitchen. Mother and Mrs. Flood then handed out the left-over vegetables to people around the village that were struggling, which sadly was almost everyone. They especially tried to help the staff that were let go.

Many of the staff had been reluctantly let go due to the house being quieter without Arthur, George, and me. There was a need for the staff when the Radley children were residing at the house, but the children left in February. The house became quiet again and Mother tried her best to make jobs for the maids and other staff. She reluctantly let them go because there was not much else they could do.

Letting go of the staff felt like letting go of family for my parents.

It seemed my mother had changed quite a bit in my absence. She no longer seemed to be occupied with thoughts of 'what would society say?' She was relaxed and content with what she had instead of frantically pacing around making sure that everything was perfect. A wave of calm flowed around her. There was such a subtle strength to her calmness.

I found myself occupied and wrapped up in my own thoughts when I stumbled upon a field of marguerite daisies. I stood in a melancholic daze looking out onto the field of daisies, gently blowing back and forth in the hazy summer breeze.

I climbed over the metal farm gate and made my way through the daisies. I picked a single daisy and held it in my hand for some time and I felt tears fall down my cheeks. I gently closed my eyes and listened to the sound of the wind, swishing the daisies around me.

I picked a small bunch and decided that daisies would forever be a reminder of my happier days. I would not remove daisies from my life like I had desperately tried to do with the memories of Adam. Daisies would always be our emblem. They would be my favourite flower.

I stayed in the field until my tears dried on my cheeks.

When I arrived back to the house, my mother's voice called me into the drawing room. I followed the voice to find her sitting in her armchair flicking through her fashion magazine. My mother excitedly told me that she arranged for Gladys, the local hairdresser, to come to the house and cut my hair.

That evening Gladys came. Gladys combed her willowy fingers through my scraggily hair before beginning. The slight touch of her hand on my hair reminded me of Adam's hands once running through it. I immediately wanted to chop all of it off, thinking if I cut my hair, it too would cut the memories of Adam from my mind. But unfortunately, I was learning my heart was not that simple.

I stopped myself from thinking that way, and I focused on the daisies sitting in the antique vase in front of me. I sat quietly in the stiff wooden chair as Gladys began to cut my hair.

As she worked, she revealed her most recently discovered village gossip to mother. Gladys coyly called her village gossip, "the perks of working in the local shop." I wondered what 'news' Gladys would tell the village after her visit to the estate.

Mother practically sat on the edge of her seat listening to every word that fell from Gladys's mouth. This level of attention fed Gladys's ego, making her reveal more and add flares of dramatics and outrageousness to the news.

Their chatter continued until they ran out of people to talk about. Mother then moved the conversation to my nursing.

"My Lucy has been doing some wonderful work in that hospital of hers. Did you hear, Gladys, that she now trains nurses too? Yes, our Lucy is very important in her hospital."

Gladys pretended to be intrigued, but I knew she was taking everything in and would tell everyone about it the next day in the shop. Possibly change some of the wording so that it sounded as though a scandal was occurring in the Webley Estate.

"Yes, we are immensely proud of our Lucy. Charles and I have not seen her for two years. She has only just been allowed time off now. Lucy is so important in that hospital, the soldiers depend on her. Sadly, she is only home for a week," my mother softly spoke as her smile faded.

"You know, I used to wait every morning for the post, hoping and praying that there would be a letter from Lucy or George. Most days went by and there never was. But then, the day would come, and I would have a letter sitting in my lap with the words, '*Dearest Mama*', scribbled on top. And it made my week or perhaps even made my month as sometimes I would be waiting over a month for another letter to arrive."

Gladys stopped cutting my hair as my mother began to cry. The room filled with silence. My mother stared passed us, out the window. Gladys curiously glared at me and placed the scissors onto the table.

"Oh, I lived for those days", mother sighed, "where letters from my two surviving children came to me. I would write and write to them, sometimes sending them ten-page letters detailing everything that I could think of to tell. And weeks would go by until I received a letter, and I would greedily open it to only find a single page. I told myself that they were busy. But I couldn't help but feel so alone."

I walked over to Mother and held her hand in mine as she dabbed her cheeks with her handkerchief.

"I am sorry Mama that I did not write as often as you would have liked. There is no excuse for it."

"Since Arthur's death, you and George are all your father and I live for. We don't have anything else. My job was always to care for my children and when you all grew up and no longer needed caring for, I questioned what am I here for? I am not needed anymore, and it pains me to feel like I am of no use."

I wiped away her tears with my sleeve and she began to chuckle.

"One should not use their sleeve to wipe anything," mother mocked Madam Speirs's voice.

Gladys and I joined her in laughing. Gladys softly smiled and moved closer us, "The joys of motherhood."

I ignored Gladys's stares and focused on mother.

"Mama, even though George and I are grown up and are no longer children, it does not mean we do not need you. We most certainly do need you. Unfortunately, we are both too stubborn to ask for your help. But I want you to know that George and I both understand and appreciate you and father being here and worrying about us and writing to us to tell us to 'be careful', and 'to take care of yourself.' You may not know it, but we need to be reminded of that every now and again."

Mother smiled up at me with tears in her eyes.

"Your letters have provided such comfort to me in many times of despair and darkness, and I am sorry that I could not return the kind favour to you. I only ever thought of myself and not once did I think of you and Papa. I am deeply sorry."

"Thank you," mother tearfully smiled while stroking my damp hair. "Oh, Gladys!"

Mother sprung up from her chair and ushered me to sit back down.

"I am sorry Gladys that you had to listen to us two blubbering. Please continue with Lucy's hair before she catches a cold."

Once Gladys finished cutting and styling my hair, my mother came over and stroked my glossy hair.

Mother gently held my face in her hands. "Much better! More like my Lucy again."

I smiled back at her, but I began to question myself – who was Lucy?

I desperately wanted to be my old self again, but I was still trying to find her in every little thing that I looked at and everywhere I went. Would I ever find her again? Or would I recreate myself?

After dinner that night, father went to bed, and mother and I retired to the drawing room. We sat by the fire, and she filled me in on what was happening at home while I was gone. A warm silence fell upon us as we happily sipped our nightcaps.

"Did I ever tell you that between you and George, I had a miscarriage," she slowly spoke.

"No, I never knew."

"I was only four months pregnant, but I miscarried. It was a boy. Your father and I were deeply upset. I became very distant and withdrew into myself. I slept a lot and spent most of my days in bed or busying myself with running the house. I was no longer a mother to Arthur and George, but a ghostly figure roaming the halls."

Mother stared at the glass in her hand and sighed.

"Your father worried about me, but I always insisted I was fine. I became pregnant again and I was terrified that I would miscarry. But you arrived safe and sound, a healthy baby who filled my days with happiness once more."

She reached out and held my hand as she warmly smiled deep into my eyes.

"I suppose after experiencing something like that, one recognises the signs in another. There is always light after the darkness."

She kissed me on the forehead and said her goodnight.

When I returned to the hospital, I was a rehabilitated person.

Or at least on the road to being rehabilitated. I decided that I needed a change of scenery and to get away from Portsmouth.

Portsmouth was filled with too many memories of Adam. I needed to be somewhere that Adam never went to. I asked Matron Burke to move me to another hospital. She told me that Southampton needed more nurses.

In August, Lilian and Whilma moved with me to Southampton. My St Angela's family still stood with me and I felt stronger because of them. I felt a weight lift from my chest as the train put distance between me and Portsmouth.

Part of me did not want to leave Adam and Jonathan alone, for their graves to be forgotten about. But I was alone and isolated by being in Portsmouth.

I slowly began to take back control of my life. I did not know where my life was headed, but I no longer felt completely lost or clueless. It was a fresh start that I desperately needed.

All I knew and all I ever did was survive. It was all anyone did. Before I left, I stood in the hospital ward and looked around me. I suddenly became aware of how everyone was fighting a war - a war inside their minds - and I did not feel so alone and overwhelmed in my pain.

1998

"Mam?" Mae's voice pulls me from the depths of my memories.

"Yes dear," I hollowly answer.

"You said you tried to move on as best as you could after Adam and Johnathon's deaths, but you did not say how you dealt with things?"

I let out a heavy sigh at the thought of revealing to my daughter the truth about my darkest time. I am afraid that Mae will look at me differently or be ashamed of me. That her image of me will forever change.

But this is my past and I cannot change it nor run from it. I can only remember me as I was and accept it. My past brought me to where I am now.

I huff at the thought of my old self.

"I didn't...I didn't deal with things, Mae. I began to rely heavily on alcohol, and I became a complete workaholic. I was an absolute mess for the entirety of 1943. I was deeply depressed but I refused to accept any help."

Lilian turns to me with a smile and clutches my hand.

"It was a very dark and hard time for your mother, Mae, and we were all incredibly worried about her. She no longer lived, she just seemed to exist. But she got through it and it made her so much stronger. I was so proud of her and to see her grow from her pain."

Mae compassionately shakes her head at me.

"Mam, I never knew you went through such pain and turmoil. Whenever you used to talk about your nursing years, you would only briefly talk about it. It would always be about the soldiers fighting and never about your fight. Why did you keep it locked up for so long?"

"I never knew how to talk about it, Mae. I still don't really know how to approach it."

I hang my head and stare at the daisies on the cushion in my lap. I did not realise I had been clutching it so tightly as the stuffing is now gathered in the middle of the cushion.

"It amazes me how you managed to keep it all to yourself and not fall apart," Emmy empathically adds.

"That Emmy, was because your Granny was too stubborn to ever ask for help," Lilian teases. "Even when Adam died and was buried, she never asked for help with her grief. Even when she lay in the rubble in a pool of her own blood after that bomb went off and she miscarried Jonathan, she still would not ask for the help that she needed...Even when we buried Jonathan, she never asked for anything. All those sleepless nights that she threw herself into work, nothing."

Lilian sighs and gives me a scolding look paired with a slight grin.

"I was a fool, wasn't I?" I try to joke. "What good did it do me, never asking for help?"

I look around my living room at the photos hanging on the walls. I admire the trinkets and memorabilia that I collected over my life. I begin to wonder, would I have had any of this if I continued the way I stubbornly acted in those months after Adam died?

What would have become of me if I continued drinking liquor every day and throwing myself into my work?

I would have become something that I hated. Hate, anger, and sadness would have been the only emotions that I knew. Not everyone can make it out of that type of darkness in one piece.

Many people from my generation died inside during those war years, becoming a shell of the person they once were. When I looked into their eyes, there was no longer any sign of hope, optimism, or life in them. No spark. It frightens me to think that I was at the edge of becoming one of them.

"I see many traits of myself in you, Mae, and Emmy too. Many that I am glad to see have passed on, others not so much...I have passed on my stubbornness to both of you and stubbornness can go either way for people. You can pair it with determination and a desire to achieve your goals, and you will be met with success and happiness. That is what I hope you will use it for.

"However, stubbornness can hold you back while everyone else moves forward. It can keep you stuck in one place - a dwelling that you put yourself in. Because of my stubbornness and pride over the years, I have unnecessarily caused myself heartbreak, loss, sadness, and darkness. I refused to ask for help.

"And it is exactly my own stubbornness that stopped me from helping myself. What I want you to remember, is that it takes a lot of courage to ask for help and to admit that you need it."

I emphasis my words hoping my advice will stick. I have always felt that when giving advice to someone, you are talking to your past-self. It is almost a form of memory.

"What most people do not realise is that it takes a lot of courage to be vulnerable, to cry, to express how they really feel. Many people mistake blocking all of this out as being 'courageous' and 'getting on with things.' But I in fact believe that you are weaker if you refuse to be vulnerable with yourself and others. Most importantly, with yourself. I was weak, as I refused to deal with the things that pained me, and because of this, I put myself into a dark place. But it was only when I accepted this that I could become stronger and rebuild myself."

"I do not think you were weak at all Granny," Emmy sympathises. "None of us can know how we would react to situation until we are in it. I cannot, and I dare not, judge you as I did not live through what you have lived through."

Emmy warmly smiles at me and outstretches her hand to mine. I hold her soft warm hand in mine, taking the time to remember this sweet gesture.

"I think you were very brave, Mam," Mae agrees.

"We grew up in a time where we were told to just 'carry on', to 'deal with the pain silently', to 'get on with things and don't bother anyone else.' We were told that was the only way to get by," Lilian says. "We come from a generation where we didn't talk about our hardships because everyone had hardships. That was the norm. So instead, we buried it deep down inside and motored on. Everything was always brushed under the carpet. But I knew that I always had Lucy and she always had me. And that's how we survived."

"Lilian, I think you were, and still are, an incredible friend," Emmy praises.

Lilian blushes at the compliment and waves her hand in the air at Emmy, as always, brushing off a nice compliment.

Lilian begins to gather all the mugs onto the tray. "More tea anyone?"

"Take the compliment!" I tease.

Lilian playfully sticks out her tongue at me and walks out of the room happily carrying the tray of empty mugs.

Mae holds up the old picture of the Southampton dock.

"So, what happened when you went to Southampton?"

I let out a deep breath. "Well, it was a fresh start for me."

Mae hands me the picture and I let myself almost enter it. Taking a step back through time. I can still smell the fresh, salty, sea air.

AUGUST 1943

In August 1943, Lilian, Whilma, and I moved to Southampton. It was a much-needed change of scenery for us all. Whilma was affected by Betty's death the most, they were the best of friends. Everywhere that she went reminded her of Betty.

It seemed Portsmouth had hard memories for us all.

Upon our arrival, we were informed that Southampton was the seventh most bombed city in Britain as it was Britain's number one military port and home to Spitfire productions. I wondered how everything still stood.

The place felt like a mass building graveyard. Piles of rubble everywhere, old buildings half blown to pieces. I could still see smoke and dust lingering in the air, almost acting as a reminder of the horrific bombing that occurred. As if anyone could forget.

High street was practically destroyed. Bombsites were littered and scattered across town from Millbrook to West End. You could not escape it. The medieval gatehouse and defence structure, Bargate, and many of the underground vaults were utilised as bomb shelters.

I thought moving to Southampton would be a welcome change in scenery, but it only added to the despair and turmoil inside us all.

We were placed in a small, three-storey house on a narrow residential street and shared the house with two other nurses, two typists working at the local war office, and our landlady Gretta.

Gretta was in her late fifties, of medium height, with dark grey hair and piercing pale, blue eyes. The type of eyes that could electrocute you with a single glance. Gretta wore her floral print night-gown and held a lit cigarette in her right hand, a sight that would become a daily occurrence. She held the door open as we carried our heavy trunks. Gretta puffed smoke in our faces as she took us in.

The hallway was so narrow that only one person could walk down it at a time. The staircase ended a few inches before the front door and Gretta enjoyed the spectacle of Whilma, Lilian and I tripping over each other before turning on her heal to lead us up the narrow steep stairs to our rooms.

"House rules," Gretta called out as she climbed the stairs. "Keep the house clean. I will not be cleaning up after you and your mess. Help around the house as much as possible, that means cooking, cleaning, ironing et cetera. Visitors are allowed but are not tolerated. No men allowed at all. No man is even allowed put a hair across the front gate. I despise men."

"Every single one of them?" Whilma joked.

Gretta leaned in closely to Whilma, only inches away from her face.

"Every. Single. One of them. I cannot be dealing with them. Haven't done so since 1913."

We nodded along out of fear as Gretta angrily pointed her finger at us while speaking. Whilma chortled and tried her best to cover her mouth to stop herself from laughing.

"Why 1913? If you do not mind me asking, it is very specific," Lilian bravely asked.

Whilma elbowed Lilian into the side as a warning. Gretta stopped on the bend of the narrow stairs and leaned in making us retreat and press our backs up against the damp wall to get away from her and her sour breath.

"Because in 1913, my husband of only two months, packed his bags, went to work that morning and never returned," Gretta fumed.

"I wonder why," Whilma muttered.

Gretta turned on her heel and stormed up the creaking stairs.

"And I have been angry with men ever since."

Lilian and I were allocated the attic while Whilma shared a room with another girl.

We unpacked our few belongings and tried to make the room feel homely. I placed framed photographs of my parents, Arthur, George, Arty and Adam on my chest of drawers. I sat back and looked at the photos and tried to focus on the people in them. My eyes instinctively fell on Adam.

Adam got his photo taken when we were in London, and he gave it to me as a reminder of him before he left for Portsmouth.

When he told me that he was leaving for Portsmouth, I had my photo taken in a small studio. Lilian came with me. Lilian had two photos made, one to send home to her family and one for Aunt June. I sent one to my parents and the other was hand delivered to Adam.

I picked up Adams photo and began to panic. I was beginning to forget what he looked like, how he moved, and how his voice sounded.

Adam and I happily spoke about everything and nothing all our days together, yet now, I could not remember the sound of his voice or his laugh. It frightened me that the memory of him slowly faded away from everyone's memory, but especially mine.

Lilian walked over to me and put her arm around me. She sorrowfully looked at the picture frame in my hand and gently brushed back a strand of my hair.

"Are you okay?"

"Just trying to remember him," I replied.

I moved Adams picture from my dresser to the bed-side table. He would be the first thing I would see when I woke and the last thing I would see before I slept.

Lilian and I walked back down the narrow stairs, and I almost tripped a few times along the way, which sent Lilian immediately into a fit of laughter. As we grew closer to the kitchen, conversations began to pour out of the ajar door. I sheepishly opened the door and was met with clouds of smoke and many voices shouting "hello!" and "welcome" all at once.

Gretta proudly sat on an old armchair by one of the cream kitchen cabinets smoking a cigarette.

"Sally and Nora are nurses at the hospital that you three will be joining tomorrow. And Kitty and Rosalie are typists at the local war office."

"Actually, I have recently been promoted to be *the* secretary of Lieutenant Mason's office," Rosalie bragged. "He's a big deal around here. I am sure you have heard about him?"

The other girls rolled their eyes at her and small smiles appeared on their faces.

"Who wants a cup of tea and some bread? The water is almost boiled," Gretta asked as she turned to the stove.

"Just a word of warning," Kitty said, "there has been and still is occasional small-scale attacks from the air and on the streets, especially populated areas. There can be shootings on the streets, so be careful when walking about. Other than that, I am sure you are well used to the rubble, the rationing, the wounded people. Nothing new, eh? I am sure you are used to being careful in Portsmouth, but just be extra careful here."

The kettle whistled on the stove and Gretta poured the water into the teapot as Nora cut some bread.

"Enough talk of war, welcome to Southampton," Rosalie smiled.

The air seemed to lighten when the tea was placed on the table and we spent the evening talking about harmless topics to ease our transition into this new place.

A sense of anguish began to flow over me as I thought about the next day ahead of me. I felt I was starting all over again, almost as if I were back in St. Angela's. I felt I needed to prove myself again, prove that I was good at my job and worked hard.

Lilian and I woke early and put on our new uniforms. Lilian, Whilma, and I had been upgraded to a higher status for the hard work that we endured in London and Portsmouth.

Our uniform was now a dark, royal blue with soft white collars and cuffs as usual. I felt proud to be wearing this new uniform. We met Sally in the kitchen finishing her breakfast. She was on the same shift as us and kindly offered to walk us to the hospital.

It was 6 am when we left the house and made our way to the hospital. The milkman had just arrived, and he left everyone's milk outside their door. I looked down at the broken step outside our front door and I could not see any milk bottles. As I walked down the foot path, I could see the milk bottles sitting in their metal cage, peeping out from behind the pillar.

Gretta really was serious about no man ever setting foot on her property. Not even the milkman dared to pass the gates!

Lilian, Sally, and I tiredly walked down the streets and it somewhat saddened me that I no longer reacted or took notice of the rubble lying on the ground after the bombings. I had become so accustomed to buildings crumbling around me and having a daily image of desolation, despair, and destruction.

No matter how we much we all hoped, life was never going to return to how it was.

We shortly arrived at the hospital and Sally instructed us to make our way to the Matron's office. We were quickly put to work and before we knew it, Southampton became our new home for a little while.

OCTOBER 1943

October arrived with a harsh Winter wind. The nights grew darker and longer, and I began to dread the memories that were to come with the long nights. After completing one of my night shifts, the walk back to Gretta's house brought unwelcome thoughts.

I realised that a year had passed since I discovered that I was pregnant. I wondered if I had accepted the pregnancy, would Jonathan be alive today? What if I had not fought with Adam about the pregnancy and keeping the baby? Adam might have been in a better frame of mind the night he left for that rescue call, and he might not have been shot. What if I had not been so caught up in myself and thought of someone else for once?

What if?

What if…

I stopped myself from spiralling out of control with my thoughts and tried my best to walk home. When I arrived in the door, I found three letters waiting for me on the small table by the front door. I opened the first one.

16th October 1943

Lucy Loo,

Sorry, I have not written to you in a long time. I have been preoccupied with the war and all!

How are you? How is the nurse-life treating you? I tried to ring your hospital when I was briefly near a telephone last week, and I asked for Lucy. But they had no recollection of a Lucy. Nobody seemed to know you as Lucy Webley. Then I was put through to a Matron Burke who seemed to know you. I began to wonder were you tricking us all with your nursing stories!

Matron Burke told me that you go by Nurse Anna. Why Nurse Anna? Why not Nurse Webley? Are you trying to get away from your family name? I had to describe you to Matron Burke and try name things that you like or do, and she did not recognise any of them. I thought – "does this woman know Lucy?", or "do I not know my sister anymore?"

Matron Burke also informed me that you are no longer in the Portsmouth hospital but have moved to Southampton. You should have written to save me all this embarrassment!

Despite this brief fiasco, I need your help with something. And do not begin to think that I have put myself into a spot of bother, I have not! I need your help with my lovely dear wife, Margot, and my even more so beautiful and charming daughter, Ada. I will tell you more in detail when you write back to me. I am unsure whether this address is even yours.

Please write back ASAP. Your loving brother,
Captain George Webley.

I opened the second letter, and it was from my mother. Father's health had deteriorated since I was home, and most days he rarely moved from his bed. His left side began to struggle like his right and his speech grew worse. He had been sleeping more and ate truly little food. I could almost feel Mother's agony and nerves from her words in the long letter.

I moved onto the next letter, with its unfamiliar writing. My name and address seemed to have been scribbled onto the envelope in a hurry.

Portsmouth Hospital,
20th October 1943

Dear Lucy,

It is with my deepest sympathy and regret that I write to inform you of the death of Matron Burke and Beatrice Howard. Their deaths have been a shock on us all.

Matron Burke was shot by a man, while walking home after a late shift, whom we later discovered was a German spy. He thankfully was captured at a military stop and was immediately brought in for questioning and imprisoned soon after. However, we later heard that he took a cyanide tablet poisoning himself. Matron Burke died on the 17th of October. The hospital has not been the same without her. We all learned so much from her.

As I tried to write this letter to tell you of Matron Burke, more unfortunate news found me.

Beatrice died on the 18th. It saddens me to write this Lucy but, she took her own life. Beatrice had not turned up for work and we all began to worry about her. Some of the other girls and I went to visit her, and she was in a state. Beatrice had empty bottles around her, and it seemed she had been like this for some time. The tears would not stop flowing down her face and she was not making much sense. We stayed with her until she fell asleep, and we left to go back to our rooms, thinking we had calmed her. We hoped the next morning would reveal a calmer and happier Beatrice. The next morning Rita knocked on Beatrice's door and found her... None of us could believe it.

We are so incredibly shocked. Heartbroken does not begin to explain it. It is a grief that cannot be described or explained. We are blaming ourselves for not noticing that something was wrong with Beatrice. We knew she was drinking a lot for some time, but none of us ever stopped to ask why.

Oh Lucy, what sort of family have we become? We promised each other at the beginning of this war that we would look out for each other, care for each other. We said that we were a family - we were the St. Angela girls. I fear that this death will drive us apart, but maybe it might bring us closer together. I hope it will bring us together. We need to be here for each other.

I hope you are taking good care of yourself. I have sent letters to Lilian and Whilma as well. Please look after each other.

With love, your friend,
Dottie Reed.

I sat on my bed in shock, staring at Dorothy's letter. The words of her letter circulated in my head, piercing through my skull. The bedroom door burst open as Lilian and Whilma walked in, both clutching their letters and a handkerchief. They joined me on my bed, and we shed our tears together.

"Ar dheis Dé go raibh a hanam. Codladh sámh, Beatrice," Lilian tearfully croaked.

PORTSMOUTH 1943

Lilian, Whilma, and I visited Portsmouth to be with the girls. In the brief time that we had been away, it felt as if so much had changed. The hospital felt quieter and colder since the death of Matron Burke and Beatrice. A new Matron had been appointed and many of the hospital staff and nurses were not impressed with her. Unfortunately, no one would ever be able to replace Matron Burke and that was the problem.

The girls sat in the small kitchen drinking tea. Rita and Dorothy jumped from their seats and gave us a warm, comforting hug. We all held onto each other, terrified to lose another.

"Beatrice's mother came by the other day to collect her stuff. We offered to send it to her so that she would not have to see how her daughter lived. But she insisted on coming," Rita told us.

Dorothy placed a fresh pot of tea on the table.

"It was heart-breaking to bring Mrs. Howard into Beatrice's room and she asked us was this where she died."

"Did Mrs Howard know that Beatrice took her own life?" Whilma asked.

Rita solemnly shook her head. "We decided to tell her that Beatrice died in an accident while on duty. We did not want to upset her mother any further, so instead we said she died valiantly. That is what they say for soldiers, why not say it for Beatrice."

Rita took a deep breath and busied herself by pouring the tea. I watched as she brushed away silent tears from her rosy cheeks. Rita had grown thinner since I last saw her. There was a hollowness to her cheeks and her smile. She kept her sad and colourless eyes low.

My eyes fell onto Dorothy who intently stared at her hands.

She noticed me watching her and quickly smiled before shoving her hands into her pockets.

"Dottie, what is it? What are you hiding?" Whilma questioned.

Dorothy blushed, "Nothing. Now is not the right time to tell. It is nothing. More tea anyone?"

The sound of her foot nervously tapping on the floor drew even more attention to her.

"Dorothy what is it?" Rita insisted.

Dorothy removed her hands from her pockets and revealed a small ring.

I pulled Dorothy into a tight hug.

"You are engaged! That is wonderful news," I gently took her hand and admired the ring.

The other girls crowded around Dorothy, except for Rita, who fell back into her seat, eyes welling up.

Dorothy's face beamed with a bashful smile.

"Rick proposed last week but I didn't want to say anything. We were all so upset about Beatrice and Matron Burke. It would not be right of me to push my news on everyone like that. Sorry... I didn't mean to upset anyone by not telling."

Whilma beamed as she tightly embraced Dorothy.

"This is such wonderful news, and we all desperately need some good news."

"I am so happy for you! You will make such a beautiful war bride," Lilian exclaimed.

"Will you stop nursing when you marry?" Whilma worriedly asked. "You are such a good nurse, we would hate to lose you."

"Rick and I are going to wait for a few months until we get married. He is positive this war will not last too long more. I will be able to stop nursing then. He wants me to move to Ohio with him, and I said yes."

Lilian gasped. "Ohio...so far away."

"I know...but when you come to visit me it means you will have to stay for a long time."

"Me in America – can you imagine that!" Lilian chuckled.

"I have some ideas for my wedding dress, would you like to see?"

Lilian and Whilma followed Dorothy out of the kitchen, but I remained seated as I watched Rita sink further into her seat. I walked towards her and knelt so that we were at eye level.

"Rita dear, what's the matter?"

Rita shook her head as the tears started to fall from her red eyes.

"I know it's very wrong and selfish of me for thinking this, but with Dorothy getting married, I will be left all alone. You, Whilma, and Lilian are in Southampton, Joan went back to London, Beatrice and Betty are gone and Dorothy will be leaving soon and I can't help but feel so alone."

"Oh Rita, you're not going to be alone. You have every right to be feeling this way right now. But to know that this is only a passing thing. It has not been easy losing Betty and now Beatrice. Be easy on yourself. And I know you are happy for Dorothy, you are not selfish for feeling the way you are. But dear, you are not alone. You may be lonely, but you are not alone. You will always have us girls.

"We are family after all. We will always be the St. Angela girls. You are an amazing woman, Rita, a brilliant nurse, and a wonderful friend – you could do anything, be anything you wanted. You are intelligent and beautiful. You are kind, generous, good fun and so much more! If I was to name off every great thing about you, we'd be here all night."

Rita light-heartedly laughed, "I've missed you, Lucy."

"You are not alone," I hugged her tightly.

Rita linked arms with me. "Come on, lets join the others. They'll be wondering where we've gone to."

Later that evening, the girls and I walked to Cypress Cemetery. The mournful cypress trees hung low over the boundary walls. We stood before three lonely crosses in the ground. Beatrice's body was buried near Adam and Jonathan's graves. Matron Burke's body was brought home to her family.

I brought flowers for the three graves and carefully placed them onto the raw earth. Fresh flowers lay on Beatrice's grave from Dorothy, Rita, and Mrs. Howard. Dorothy told me that she often placed flowers on Adam's grave when she had a spare moment, as she hated to see his memory forgotten or for him to be lonely.

"I also place flowers on the other grave, but I don't know who they are. I could find no name on it, just a small daisy chain around its cross. It saddens me to see a lonely grave, so I place some flowers on it to let those that have passed on know that they were loved," Dorothy softly wiped away tears on her red cheeks.

Lilian placed her arm around me to steady me and handed me her handkerchief. I gratefully took it from her, leaning my heavy head onto her welcoming shoulder. The tears silently fell from my eyes as I stared at the graves.

I should be holding my baby in my arms, not looking blankly at his grave. I should be in Adam's arms not staring vacantly at raw earth below my feet. I should be chatting and laughing with Beatrice not filling my brain with so many questions, wondering what turmoil she went through.

"I brought this," Rita held up a bottle of rum, "as a send-off for Beatrice. Maybe it might help us understand what Beatrice saw and felt."

Dorothy pulled out four small cups from her bag and handed one to each of us while Rita poured some rum into each one.

"Lil, you must know a good toast for the dead," Rita asked.

"Why, because I am Irish?" Lilian replied with a slight smile. "As it so happens, I do! We have a toast for everything."

We held our cups up as Lilian beautifully toasted Beatrice. We drank our glasses of rum and continued to solemnly look at Beatrice's grave. The bitter taste of the rum burned my mouth and throat. I had not tasted alcohol in weeks, and I pushed the lingering thought out of my mind telling me to have more.

Rita began to cry uncontrollably. Dorothy took off her coat and put it around Rita to stop her from shivering. Whilma and Dorothy led Rita back down the narrow path to the hospital. I remained staring at the graves, my eyes unable to move from them.

Lilian took a step towards me and placed her arm around me again.

"Would you sing for me? For them – Adam, Jonathon, and Beatrice."

My heart pinched as she dried her tears and graciously smiled at my request. She cleared her throat before beginning.

The wind howled around us as Lilian's soothing voice took me away into the melodic Irish Seanós. My hair frantically flew in every direction, my coat struggled to stay buttoned, and the grass swayed all around me as the wind blew stronger, removing all the cobwebs from my memories.

I turned my attention to Lilian. Her eyes shut tight, completely entranced in the song. Her head and mouth fluttered as she sang in melisma. I sat on the grass at the foot of Adam's grave and took a handful of the wet clay. I rubbed it between my fingers, sprinkling it.

As Lilian sang her last note, her voice quivered with emotion. Her pale face was damp with tears. I stood up and I pulled her into a tight embrace, cradling her head into my neck. A single raindrop fell onto my nose and slid the whole way down onto my lips. The clouds above were slowly turning a murky grey and the wind grew colder. Single raindrops fell at first, until the tap was turned on full blast and the rain turned into a waterfall. Our clothes became instantly drenched and our hair clung to our faces. Lilian began to laugh in spite of it all.

We said our goodbyes once again, which started our tears once more, wishing those that were gone might return even just for a moment.

But that's not how life works.

GEORGE

The last week of October sadly marked the end of autumn. The leaves turned magnificent shades of yellow, orange, red and brown, almost as if they were burning on the trees. While walking to the hospital, I became entranced by watching the autumn leaves fall around me, paving my way to work. The morning sun shone weakly through the leaves, further igniting the last of the Autumn colours.

The hospital was mostly quiet and calm throughout the day, which pleased me because I could attend to all the patients and spend some time with them rather than rushing onto the next.

My work became interrupted when 'Lucy Loo' echoed throughout the ward. I quickly turned around to find a silhouette of a man in the doorframe.

George proudly walked towards me, with his arms outstretched. He wore his shining Navy uniform. He looked immaculate. So much older and taller than I remembered. He looked like a man. Almost like father.

"My darling sister, I almost didn't recognise you!" George pulled me into a tight hug.

I felt as if I was little girl again being squeezed to death in a hug by George.

"It's been a long time, hasn't it?" I sighed. "What are you doing here?"

"I am based here," he smirked. "I take it you got my letter. Can we go somewhere to catch up?"

George and I sat on the edge of a wall outside the hospital, watching the world as if it were his. Many Navy sailors passed him, each one respectfully saluting him.

I could see George had successfully moved up the ranks to Captain. I felt immensely proud to watch him make a life for himself, to grow into the man he was and to be recognised for himself...to no longer be compared to Arthur every step of the way. He had officially grown into being George Webley. It suited him.

We went to a small café and drank some tea. The place was flooded with young girls courting American soldiers and British Navy personnel. People thought George and I were courting as well, but he made it his business to emphasis the word 'sister' repeatedly. It was rather amusing to watch him.

"Lucy...I need your help with something," George said as he leaned across the table.

"What is it? Are you in trouble?"

"No, no, I am not in any trouble. It's our parents that I need help with." George let out a heavy sigh before continuing. "You see, I have brought Margot and Adelaide with me and I want to bring them home, so that they can safely live there and wait for me until this bloody war is all over."

"What do you need me for?"

"Would you come with me when I bring them home? I must ship out in two days' time and will not be home for a long while. I need you to help me break the ice between Margot and Mama, as I am sure Mama has written to you about her."

George angrily took a sip of his tea. He acted as if this was hardest thing he has ever had to do. Then again, forcing the Lady Esme Webley to like someone was far from an easy task.

"You want me to try to convince Mama to let your 'Nazi Wife', as she calls her, live in the house?"

"Don't say that too loud! And Margot is not a Nazi - her father is."

I looked at George for some time, contemplating what he had asked of me.

"Please Lucy."

"It is not going to be easy, but I'll do it. I have three days off commencing tomorrow, and I will go with you then. I am quite excited to meet my niece and sister-in-law."

I watched him as his face lit up. His extraordinary George smile was still as warm and loving as always.

"How did Margot and Adelaide get here?"

George rubbed the back of his neck as he let out a laugh.

"Ahm…I smuggled them on board the ship."

"How in God's name did you manage that?"

"Well, I am Captain after all, so I pulled some strings. That reminds me, I may have also offered some of my men Webley's Whiskey to keep them quiet. So, if you could be a dear will you bring back ten bottles of Whiskey and deliver them to a man who goes by the name, Dolly."

"Dolly? A man called Dolly. George, you want me to walk into the Navy base and ask for a man called 'Dolly' while carrying a crate of whiskey?"

"Actually, make it two crates. I don't want the men thinking I am cheap."

George continued to smile at me until he broke me, and I was forced to smile back at him.

"You owe me," I warned him.

We left the café and George proudly gave me the tour of his ship. I was impressed by the respect and brotherly bonds George had formed for himself. Afterwards, he took me to a small, terraced house, secluded down a narrow side street.

The alleyway was dimly lit, and the gutters were blocked with unimaginable things. Stagnant water, urine, stale alcohol, damp, and bad hygiene reeked into my nostrils. The smell was utterly horrendous. A black, cloaked figure crouched down on the cobble-stoned alleyway and I was not sure whether they were breathing or not. I was too afraid to check.

George knocked on the small, wooden door and snorted at me as I looked around in horror.

"A friend of mine lives here. It is okay, do not be scared. You have your big brother to take care of you," George joked.

"I am not going to even ask how you know this 'friend' of yours," I whispered as I leaned closer to George, afraid that something would creep out from the shadows.

The door opened onto a dim hallway, and I hastily followed George into the house. The house smelled of damp, dust, and cigarettes. A young woman, with a baby in her arms, sat on a worn armchair by the fire. George placed his captain cap on the table, kissed the woman on the cheek and lovingly rubbed the head of the sleeping baby.

"Lucy, this is my wife Margot, and this is my dear little Adelaide."

George gently removed Adelaide from Margot's arms as she stood to greet me. George stared lovingly at his baby, rocking her back and forth. I had never seen that look on George's face before. It warmed my heart.

Margot had a perfect hour-glass figure and natural blonde hair. I was certain many women envied her. She had sparkling, warm sapphire eyes that made her even more beautiful. She had a regal air to her as she moved so effortlessly about the room, almost as if she floated on air.

Yet Margot was modest and quite shy, making her beauty feel pure and angelical.

I stayed for some time talking to Margot and George. They asked about my life over the last two years, but I was very brief. I acted as if nothing out of the ordinary happened. I wanted them to look at me as a hard-working nurse and not a wounded and heart-broken woman. I could not bear to be looked at like that anymore.

NOVEMBER 1943

The following morning, George, Margot, Adelaide, and I made our way to the Webley estate.

The train was full of American soldiers travelling to-and-fro from London and the coast. It was taking some getting used to having the American soldiers in England, but we were grateful for their ally. I prayed that their arrival meant an end to this dark tunnel and that hope was within our grasps.

For so long, the British troops were attacked and bombed across our land by the Germans. British troops were also being attacked in Europe, North Africa, the Atlantic, the Mediterranean, and the Pacific. I constantly worried about George's safety among these men. The German army also targeted the ships coming to the British shores full of food and supplies. We were almost on the brink of a famine.

But with the American troops by our side, things began to look up.

George, Margot, Adelaide, and I arrived in the early afternoon at the Station. I
had arranged with Molly to pick us up and take us to the estate. I knew Margot would need a friend once George and I left, and Molly was the perfect candidate. I could not easily count on Mother to be as kind and welcoming to Margot.

Molly eagerly waited on the platform, scanning the crowd for our faces. Her eagerness turned to shyness upon seeing George as though her memories of being a maid at the estate returned. I linked my arm around hers, steading her, as I introduced Margot and Adelaide. George stood back holding our trunks. His eyes signalled for me to come to him.

Molly showed Margot and Adelaide the car as I reassured George that Molly was somebody we could always trust and rely on. He was not immediately convinced or sure as to why

Molly and I were friends in the first place. Wasn't Molly a servant at our house?

I began to wonder would he be as difficult with our parents. Wasn't this journey supposed to be about settling in Margot, the new Mrs. Webley, and Adelaide into the Webley home? Wasn't this trip supposed to be about building bridges?

But my worries were interrupted as George thanked Molly for collecting us and that he hoped she could be a friend to Margot.

"It will be my pleasure to help the new Mrs Webley settle in," Molly bowed her head as she opened the car door for George.

George spent the ride home pointing out things to Margot, proudly presenting our village. Margot sat in wonder looking out the small car windows, eagerly following his pointing fingers and quickly moving her head from either side of the car to have a better look at the sights and landscape.

Margot stared out of the window, her face lit up with wonder. "Die Landschaft ist...wunderschön!"

"You say that as if it is surprising," George joked.

"Lucy?" Molly whispered. "I don't know a word of German. How will I be able to talk to her?"

"Don't worry, Margot can speak English. She sometimes forgets where she is and speaks German. Thanks again, Molly for doing this."

Molly patted my hand with a warm smile before returning her focus to the narrow road ahead of us.

As the car drove up the avenue, the wooden doors quickly opened, and Mr. Sutcliffe appeared with a curious look on his ageing face. Once I stepped out of the car, his worries eased.

"Miss Webley we weren't expecting you. What a lovely surprise it will be for your parents," Mr Sutcliffe warmly announced. He instructed footmen to get the bags from the car.

"It surely will be a surprise, Sutcliffe," I mumbled to myself.

George stepped out of the car, and I watched Sutcliffe's expression change to an even greater look of astonishment. George walked around to the other side of the car and held the door open for Margot, who held on tightly to Adelaide.

Mr. Sutcliffe's mouth dropped as he stared at the guests in front of him. He hurriedly ordered the footmen to manage the luggage. Mr Sutcliffe stared at Molly and half-heartedly invited her inside, but she politely refused to come in.

"Margot, if you need anything at all, just let me know. Lucy will show you where I live. My door is always open, so do not hesitate to come by," Molly waved from the car.

Mr Sutcliffe, looking like a penguin from behind, stormed ahead to inform Mother of our arrival. George and I exchanged a look, building up each other before we walked through the doors. He grabbed Margot's hand and confidently strutted into the hallway.

"I beg your pardon?" Mother's voice shrieked from above us.

High heeled shoes echoed around the impressive hallway as Mother frantically stomped down the stairs. Her glaring eyes took all of us in with her face wearing a mixture of excitement and happiness from seeing her children standing in front of her, yet utter horror at seeing Margot and Adelaide.

The room uncomfortably remained silent as we waited for Mother to collect her thoughts and say something. She opened her mouth to speak, but nothing came out.

"Ma'am, shall I have Daisy prepare tea in the Blue Room?" Mr Sutcliffe stepped forward and calmly spoke to Mother, thankfully breaking the silence. His cheeks were a burning red as he subtly dabbed his damp forehead with his handkerchief.

Mother graciously nodded at him and he marched away with his orders.

George smiling, broke the silence as he walked towards Mother and hugged her, "Mama it's so good to see you."

Mother eagerly put out her arms and welcomed him into her warm embrace. She walked towards me and pulled me to her side. I could feel her body shake.

George placed his arm around Margot, who still clung to Adelaide with all her might, and proudly introduced them to Mother.

"Welcome to Webley Hazelton Manor," Mother replied in a

monotonous voice as she forced a smile towards Margot.

Margot walked towards Mother and held out her hand. Mother repulsively gave a limp handshake to Margot while slowly completing her assessment of Margot's appearance. Her disapproving grunts made the room heavier.

Ignoring Adelaide, Mother turned from Margot and began to lead us to the Blue Room. George held Margot's hand and stood taller as she muttered her pleas into his ear, begging him to let her leave.

Daisy arrived with the tea and we sat in unbearable silence. George achingly tried to fill the silence with meaningless chatter, and I did my best to help him, but it was no use. Every time Margot contributed to the conversation, Mother would immediately attack with a snide remark or cutting comment.

Once our tea had finished and we had exhausted all conversation about the weather, Mother turned to me and gave me a stern look. A look I was familiar with and one that said, 'leave the room'.

"Lucy, will you show Ms Von Adler and her daughter to their room. I would like to talk to your brother in private," Mother ordered. "And after that, go to your father. He should be awake from his nap."

I looked to George who hung his head in defeat as he let out a heavy sigh. George helped Margot out of her seat and lovingly kissed her wet cheek before she left the room.

"It's not *her daughter* Mama. Adelaide is Margot and my daughter, *our* daughter - your grandchild. Your first grandchild. Have some respect!" George sharply corrected.

"I beg your pardon! Have some respect? Have some respect?" Mother's voice grew louder as her face melted into disgust. "You have no respect for your father and I, coming here unannounced and parading your Nazi wife in our faces. Honestly, George...have some respect for your parents and the Webley name."

George and Mother continued to shout at each other at the top of their lungs. I quickly slammed the door shut to drown out their voices as Adelaide started to cry.

I noticed Daisy and Mary sheepishly pop their heads out

from the servants' corridor, ready to run back to the servants' quarters. I signalled for them to come over and help Margot to settle into her room.

I tried to reassure Margot that everything was okay. She smiled out of curtesy, but her head hung heavy. Her eyes were ready to cry yet again.

"Daisy and Mary, Mrs. Webley will soon be Lady Webley, head of this household with her husband. Therefore, it is your duty to treat her with the upmost respect and kindness. Miss Adelaide is George's heiress to this estate. Therefore, you will treat her like royalty. I will not tolerate Mrs. Webley or Miss Webley being disrespected in their own home. Is that understood?"

"Yes, Miss," Daisy and Mary loyally bowed their heads.

"Make sure the rest of the staff understand this," I sternly commanded. "Daisy, will you please fetch Mrs Webley some food and have it brought to her room. Mary, prepare the cot for Adelaide."

Margot tried her best to speak to Daisy and Mary but found it difficult to understand their strong accents. I gave them a warning look to be patient. Once Margot was settled, I returned to the Blue Room where George and Mother still argued. Their loud voices competing to be heard.

George paced back and forth, while Mother sat proudly in her armchair, her hands outstretched on either side of the chair. Mother was the queen of this house, and she was not going to give up her throne lightly.

"If I was to tell you Mama, that Margot made me very happy and that being with her and having a family with her, fills my life with purpose and happiness – would that stretch belief?" George's voice bellowed across the room.

Mother stared at George almost amused. Her fingers slowly tapped on the chair.

"Before I left for the Navy, I had given my life to this estate and this family. All I ever wanted to do was manage this estate, but you and father always pushed me aside and gave Arthur all the things I desperately wanted. Arthur did not want anything to do with the estate, especially estate business – he despised it. And I am glad that he will not have the estate because he planned on running it to the ground the second, he got his hands on it."

"How dare you speak so unkindly about your deceased brother?" Mother fumed. "How dare you try and defile his good name?"

"It's true! He told me so...Arthur hated this house and this estate. He hated the Webley name, and he hated the burden of carrying the family name on his limp shoulders."

"How dare you!"

"Arthur was not the golden son that you imagined him to be. I was born here, and I intend to die here. You and father forced me into joining the Navy and I am glad you did as it allowed me to make my own way in this world and to find my wife. But after this war, I will claim no career beyond the management and care of this estate. I will take full responsibility for the running of it, and I have plans for it to be even more prestigious. The Webley Estate will be my second spouse and another child of mine...I promise you that, Mama. Margot desires to care for this estate and to love it as much as I do."

Mother tutted at the slight mention of Margot's name, further infuriating George.

The door suddenly opened, and father entered the room in his wheelchair. Father's face lit up as he saw George and I standing before him. George struggled to take in the sight of him.

I solemnly watched his right hand resting on his lap as he struggled to lift his left hand to us. His face had grown thinner since I last saw him, but his imperial moustache somewhat hid his sunken cheeks. His body appeared lifeless in his chair, yet his eyes and face were beaming with happiness.

Mother sent Mary to bring Adelaide back to the room. As Mary returned to the room with Adelaide, George asked Mother to hold her but she could barely look at her.

Mother's eyes slowly made their way to Adelaide's face.

"Adelaide has your eyes," I softly coaxed Mother. "Don't you agree?"

"Yes," Mother whispered, "She has George's curly hair, like

he used to have when he was a baby. It is just unfortunate she looks like that Nazi."

I shot our mother a warning look as I pulled George away, manoeuvring him to the couch.

I walked over to father and sat in the chair beside him. I held his hand as he contently watched those around, seemingly unaware as to what was happening.

"Charles dear," Mother spoke loudly and slowly. "Would you like to hold your granddaughter, Adelaide?"

George's face softened at the word 'granddaughter.' Mother gently placed Adelaide onto his lap as I protectively held out my hands to help him support her. He excitedly smiled.

"Belle!"

"No sweetheart, this is Adelaide," Mother caringly corrected him.

Father confusingly looked up at and glared at her. "Belle," he sternly insisted.

"No dear, that's Belle," Mother pointed to me. "This is Adelaide. George's daughter. In your lap, sweetheart, your grandchild."

Father turned to me and looked blankly through me before turning back to Adelaide.

"Belle...my Belle."

"Papa I'm here. Look it is me, Belle. I am right here," I tried to comfort him.

Father did not seem to hear me. He looked around the room in a devastating confusion, trying to understand where he was and who was around him. He returned his attention to Adelaide and became muddled as to who the child was on his lap. George quickly took Adelaide from him as she started to cry.

Father suddenly erupted into a fit of cursing, stunning the room. Mother tried her best to comfort and calm him, only succeeding after some time. She sat beside him which brought immediate calmness to him and brought him back to us.

"Doctor Fernsby said that your father is slowly losing his memory," Mother bowed her head. "Your father does not do well with change. We are trying our best here to make sure that every day is the same as the day before. He has his routine and is perfectly happy when everything is going according to plan. But when something different occurs, it confuses him and tires him. He becomes dreadfully agitated," Mother glared at George.

"Mama...Mama", Father proudly grinned.

"Yes dear, that's right! Adelaide was your mother's name," Mother soothingly replied. She turned back to us and said, "He comes and goes from his loss of memory. You just have to be patient with him. Be patient and calm."

George and I shared a solemn look.

Mother had failed to mention this in her letters.

PRIDE

Later that night, everyone was asleep except for Mother and me. She refused to have Margot at the dinner table and ordered food to be brought up to Margot's room instead. George and I exhaustedly tried to sway mother to let Margot eat with us, but her only reply was - "I will not dine with a Nazi."

We sat by the great open fire in the front parlour while she sipped on a glass of red wine and stared into the flames.

"Lucy?" Mother called, "I want you to move home for good and help me nurse your father. He needs you. I need you. I am just about keeping the estate afloat, but I am drowning. I cannot do it alone. I need you to come home and help me. It's your family that needs you, not the hospital."

"Mama, I can't, I am sorry."

"You can and you will."

"I cannot come home. I cannot leave the hospital. I am needed there. I have duties to carry out. Mama, I'm sorry."

"Your father is extremely sick, Lucy. If it were not for him, you wouldn't be nursing in the first place."

"Why do you say that?"

"I had three fine men, from prestigious families, lined up for you to choose from to marry. It was time you married. But it was your father who suggested letting you go do nursing. Our agreement was that if you did not like it then you would marry one of these men. Whereas he said, 'give the girl a chance to chase a petty dream.'"

"I don't believe he said that."

"He did."

"No, he would never call nursing a 'petty dream.'"

"Well, he did." Mother folded her arms and stared into the fire. "And our agreement was that we would let you nurse for a while until you were to marry. Before he had his stroke, he

211

had put plans into place for you to marry."

"I don't believe you."

"It's time, Lucy. You are twenty-three years old. Have you not any shame? It is time to marry and settle down. You've had your experience of nursing, now is your time to come home and grow up."

I shook my head trying to remain calm. "It was Papa who encouraged me to nurse, to live my life and to do what made me happy – not you. Never you."

"I encouraged and still encourage you to be happy and live your life the way you want to, Lucy. I have never once told you how to live your life...Both you and George are so ungrateful! After everything your father and I have done for you and this is the thanks we get. Hardly any letters, no visits and when you do come home, you only wish to be anywhere else than here."

She slammed her glass onto the coffee table between us.

"And today, you both arrive at the house, unannounced with no care in the world for your father's routine but instead insist on letting a stranger, a Nazi, into our house. To live here"

"She is not a Nazi, stop calling her that."

"-She is a Nazi...and her people killed Arthur. Your brother, my son. Does that not mean anything to you?"

"Margot is not a Nazi. She left Germany and her family to escape the Nazis and their ideals and she-"

"-She will always be a Nazi in my eyes," Mother interrupted. She crossed her arms and legs, refusing to look at me.

I breathed a heavy sigh, "You were neither helpful nor supportive to George this evening, when he needed you the most. For his whole life, you compared him to Arthur and instilled in him the belief that no matter what George does in life, he will never be better than Arthur. Even in death, Arthur is still better than him."

Mother furiously shook her head and tried to talk over me, but I held up my hand to stop her.

"And for me, you let another woman – a horrible woman – raise me. You encouraged her to be strict and insult me for no good reason. You approved of her punishing me for things that I never did. You, in fact, encouraged her to do this..." I took a deep breath to steady myself and to stop the tears from flowing.

"I rarely saw you because I had to spend all my days with Madam Speirs and when I did see you, you would only tolerate me for a few moments until you waved me off because you had another headache. When Madam Speirs was finished, you immediately tried to push me into marriage, to have another person take me off your hands...I was never in your care, because you always had someone else taking care of me. And when I have finally found something that I really want to do, that I love, you try your best to ruin it for me...to turn me off it because it did not suit you and your standards. Nursing makes me happy, and I won't give it up."

The room fell silent as I finished speaking. The sound of my frantically beating heartbeat and my deep breaths filled my ears. I never believed these words would ever fall from my mouth. Words that I have stored away, deep inside me.

Mother rubbed her closed eyelids, while releasing a heavy sigh.

"That is another day's conversation, Lucy. Right now, we all need to turn our focus to your father. And your duty as his daughter, is to come home and nurse him back to health."

"I thought you were proud of me for nursing, that was what you said the last time I was home. Why now have you changed? I thought you were proud to see me doing my duty as a nurse during this war."

"Well, now you can come home and take care of your father, show us why we should be proud of you," Mother's voice was clear and steady, as if nothing I said struck a chord with her.

I inhaled deeply and let out a hefty sigh before giving her my answer.

"No."

Mother angrily stood up from her chair, "Well there seems to be no talking sense into you tonight."

She slammed the door on her way out and released the long and heavy breath stuck in my throat. That was the first time

I had said no to my mother.

The following morning, Mother ordered her breakfast to be brought to her chambers. Margot, George, and I happily ate our breakfast together. George sat at the head of table eating his boiled egg and toast while reading the newspaper. As he flicked through the pages, I caught a glimpse of a young version of father.

After breakfast, George and I gave Margot and Adelaide a tour of the estate and village. We arrived home in the afternoon to find Mother gloomily waiting in the hallway. She looked between George and me and the room grew unbearably silent.

"Good afternoon, Mama," George's strong voice broke the silence, "and how are you today?"

Mother did not answer him but instead stared at her fingers, twisting her wedding band around her bony finger. She looked up and opened her mouth, but nothing came out. She closed her eyes and let out a deep sigh.

Mother walked towards Margot and shook her hand.

"I believe I have not formally introduced myself to you. I am Lady Esme Webley. You are most welcome to Webley Hazelton Manor, Ms. Von Adler."

Margot enthusiastically smiled and George and I exchanged a look of relief as we watched them begin to converse.

"Lunch is prepared in the Dining Room, if you would all care to join me," Mother continued to twist her wedding band.

George gently caught Mother's arm and pulled her towards him while I escorted Margot to the Dining Room.

"Thank you, Mama. I really appreciate you welcoming Margot in the house. But she is no longer Ms Won Adler. She is Mrs. Webley or more appropriately, Margot."

After lunch, George reluctantly had to leave to return to his Navy base. He shipped out early the next morning with the Navy and did not know when he would be back.

A melancholic haze descended onto the house. I tried my best to help Margot settle in, but a depression had overcome her.

The next day, Beatty drove me to the train station. Mother insisted on joining me yet the journey was spent in heavy silence. She walked with me to the platform and waited with me until the train arrived. I waited for her to say something to me but she stood motionless. She tightly clutched something in her gloved hands.

The train arrived and I said my goodbyes, but she would not look at me. I grabbed my trunk and went to walk away but she pulled me back and placed a soft object in my hand. She closed my hand into a fist and looked at me for the first time.

I opened my hand and found one of my Father's handkerchiefs with the initials, C. W. sewed in gold thread.

"So, you will not stay?" she whispered through tearing eyes.

"I can't."

The train whistled as the last announcement for boarding was called. Mother nodded her head in defeat, turned on her heals and walked away. She did not once look back at me but at least I felt I made the right decision.

FEBRUARY 1944

I happily welcomed 1944 while tightly closing the door shut on '43. I hoped that my darkness had ended with the end of the year and that the new year brought a new chapter. Every new year usually began with this same longing and hoping for my future. But this year, I desperately wished my prayers would be answered.

Every day I woke and found myself still alive, yet I never appreciated this. I spent my days thinking about death, sadness and darkness but failed to see that every day I was the lucky one, I was alive and breathing with blood running through my veins. I survived all my hardships that was served to me.

I spent my days feeling mostly alone when I was surrounded by a sea of people, and I needed to learn how to be alone and not be lonely. The most courageous act that I had ever done was to undertake the task of creating myself back when I thought I knew who I was.

Sometimes life presented me with a person that I could not recognise anymore. My absent-minded stares at the reflection in the mirror confirmed this. Until one day, I came to the realisation that I no longer knew who that person was anymore, that my life had carved out for me.

I needed to relearn who Lucy was. I needed to rebuild and recreate her into something better. This did not frighten me or disillusion me. The process of creating myself excited me.

In February, I took the train to London to visit Lilian. She stayed at her Aunt June's and kindly invited me to stay for a few nights. Only a few days had passed since we last were together, but I missed Lilian as though I had not seen her in months. Life was always better with Lilian in it.

Since we were in London, Lilian and I decided to visit St Angela's. The crunching gravelled avenue and the old gothic building brought a waterfall of memories. St. Angela's felt more like home than my own family abode. Sr Dominic welcomed us in with open arms and eagerly brought us to Matron Jones.

As we walked through the hallways, it struck me how when I left a place, I could never return to it as the same person I once was. I could only return with experiences and new perspectives, and I came to the realisation of how young and naïve I was. But more importantly, how much I had grown.

A look of pride spread across Matron Jones face when she lay her eyes on Lilian and me. It felt strange to be sitting with her, drinking tea, and talking to her on a such an intimate level. Lilian and I could not look at her as anything but our commanding Matron. Out of habit, we kept answering her with a "yes Matron," and a "no Matron" to which she insisted we call her Claudia. But she knew we never could.

Matron Jones proposed Lilian and I return to St. Angela's when the war was over and teach. The thought of the war ending seemed surreal to me.

Every day, I hoped and prayed that this war would end but I rarely thought what that would mean for me. What would I do once this war ended? Where would I go?

"Some of your fellow trainees are now working with the Red Cross tents across the city," Sr Dominic softly spoke, interrupting my thoughts. "I believe there is a canteen, just off Piccadilly Circus, called the 'Rainbow Corner' where some of the girls' work. They serve doughnuts and coffee. The Americans brought them over and I often hear the girls raving about them."

"About the doughnuts or the Americans?" Lilian playfully asked.

To our surprise, Sr. Dominic laughed at this and playfully tapped Lilian's arm.

We left St. Angela's and walked into the city. The more I walked through the familiar streets, the more I felt at home. I missed London.

The closer we grew to Oxford Circus, I was reminded of civilisation again. I watched how the people moved from shop to shop, carrying their bags of goods. Woman dressed nicely for a day's shopping and meetings. People poured out of cafes and restaurants. Young girls tried to catch the attention of the soldiers.

The hustle and bustle of London felt more alive than ever. The city was swarming with American soldiers. Waves of khaki green uniforms passed us by in floods, each one playfully bowing their heads to us, winking, and doing their best to charm us. The strange twang of the different American accents filled my ears as I passed by cafes and shops, hearing, and seeing snapshots of conversations.

Why did I ever leave London?

I could see the Red Cross Tent that Sr. Dominic told us about. The tent with the was a welcome sight to see in the middle of the crowds of people. Lilian and I picked our way through the crowds and tried not to lose each other.

A group of American soldiers sat at the base of the fountain in the middle of the square and played with a dog. I happily observed the young dog wagging his tail and playfully barking at the soldiers.

One soldier playfully barked at the dog while the other soldiers stood back in a small circle and laughed. Lilian and I tried our best to conceal our laughter at the barking soldier but he on the other hand enjoyed seeing us laugh and instantly smiled. We locked eyes for a brief moment and his smile grew.

His smile instinctively made me bow my head and to walk towards the Red Cross tent. Before I entered the tent, someone tapped my shoulder and I turned to see it was the soldier.

"Hello," he charmingly smiled, flashing a great mouth full of pearly white teeth.

I was overcome with shock. I did not know how to react. The American soldiers had a bold air of confidence to them. A confidence that was not British.

"Would you care to join me in a cup of coffee?" he beamed.

His accent seemed to captivate me, but I stopped myself from smiling and looked back at him completely uninterested. I began to walk away but something about him pulled me back.

He asked me the same question again with a hopeful smile, turning to Lilian for some guidance. I shuck my head and walked past him.

"Maybe try tea instead. Her name is Lucy by the way," Lilian playfully smiled at the soldier and followed me into the tent.

I quickly grabbed her arm and pulled her away from the grinning soldier.

"Lucy, I'll remember that," he shouted after me.

I shot a glance back at him and saw him grinning. I walked further away, rolling my eyes at his attempts to charm me. However, I found myself sneakily turning back to have another look at him.

"Is that a smile I see on your face?" Lilian chuckled.

I playfully smacked her hand with my purse and tried my best not to let my smile escape from my tight hold, but it was no use. Lilian's laughter grew and I felt my cheeks burn even more.

"I can't take you anywhere!" I teased. "Maybe try tea instead," I mocked her voice.

"Well, do you like coffee?" Lilian shrugged. "I know how much you love tea and was just being informative. Nothing more."

"Informative," I puffed.

"I'll go get you a cup of coffee now if you wish it, and I'll call back that lovely soldier," Lilian went to walk away but I quickly pulled her back.

Her laughter drew the St. Angela girls over to us and before we knew it, floods of emotions flowed over us. Thoughts about our days in St. Angela's took centre stage of our minds. How long had it been since we last spoke to one another?

Among the crowd in the tent, I spotted Joan surrounded by a group of American soldiers. With a cigarette in hand, red lipstick, combed back hair and a confident stance, no one could mistake Joan. Her face lit up when she saw us, which made her instantly drop her admirers, who were not so much impressed by us.

The girls and I stayed for some time reminiscing and talking about meaningless topics. Nobody wanted to talk about anything serious and ruin the flow of rare laughter.

NEW BEGINNINGS

Before we Lilian and I had to leave, Joan asked us to help her carry some large boxes of medical supplies to the hospital. The boxes were very heavy, but I was not quite struggling with the weight, just a little out of breath. An American voice appeared from behind, insisting he help me with the box.

I spun around and saw the soldier from earlier. He tipped his cap to me and took the box from my hands. I reluctantly handed him the box, if only to catch my breath again. His contagious smile entranced me and before I knew it, I was following him as he begun to walk.

"No, I'm good...It's okay. I can manage my box. Do not worry about me! Yeh that is it, walk on and do not listen to a bloody word I say! Hello?" Lilian called after me.

Another soldier walked up from behind us, laughing at Lilian. She turned to him, embarrassed, and they both began to laugh. His smile grew as she blushed and giggled uncontrollably. She willingly let him take the heavy box from her hands and walked alongside her.

"I'm Lilian Comerford by the way."

"I'm Robert, but everyone calls me Bobby."

They passed me by and I could not help but smile at how happy Lilian looked. Joan chuckled to herself as she watched Lilian and I being charmed by Americans, impressed that her trick had worked.

"I'm sorry, I realise I haven't properly introduced myself. I'm Will, Will Fraye," he tried to outstretch his hand to me from under the heavy box.

I carefully shook his hand but the box nearly fell onto me. Will quickly caught it, almost falling on top of me in the process. He apologised profusely, and I could not help but laugh at his sudden embarrassment.

"And you are Lucy, right? Is that what I heard your friend say?"

"You heard correctly. How are you finding it here in England?"

"The sun doesn't come out too much here, does it?" Will chuckled. "I've only been in England a little while now, but I like it."

I found myself leaning into him but shook away the feeling and steadied myself.

"When did you arrive here?"

My voice sounded foreign to me. A monotonous hollow sound yet tremulous at the end of every word. I could not control it as I talked to him. Regardless of this, he continued to smile and encourage me to engage in the conversation.

"I left New York in late December. We were hit with a bad winter storm while on the ship. I am sure you can imagine how nice that was! After a long while, we landed in Scotland. It was so cold there, but the views were something else. I had never seen such beautiful landscapes in my life…" Will paused with a smile, as if he were viewing the magnificent sights of rural Scotland right here in front of him.

"We then took a train south, most of the journey was spent in darkness though, since everyone blacks out their lights come curfew. So, I did not get to see much. After many hours, we reached a place near Cambridge and there were tents and cots for us all to sleep in. There was a RAF field next to us where the Lancaster bombers took off over our heads – so strange! We barely got any sleep. After that, we moved to a place in Essex. That's where I am stationed now."

Wills accent enchanted me that I could have happily walked all day with him, and it still would not have been long enough. I felt as if I had missed him all this time. I was falling for him instantly.

A wave of fear covered my body as though I was no longer in control of whether I would get hurt again. Unfortunately, when one's heart was involved in something, one lost all control of their feelings.

"Am I talking to much?" Will shyly asked.

"No, not at all. So how did you end up today in London?"

"I got a 48-hour pass and when you get those passes, you instantly get the train to London."

"Why is that?" I grinned.

"London is such a vibrant place. The people are inviting and friendly. I can jump on a bus or use the Underground and get off almost anywhere I choose – just go exploring and have a great time. I never know where I might end up or who I might meet," he smiled directly at me.

Will's smile had not once faded from his face for our entire conversation. It seemed to have grown bigger with each word. For a moment I smiled back at him, but then I quickly looked away.

We soon reached the hospital and Will walked in with me still carrying the box.

"Thank you, Private Fraye, for your help. It was lovely talking to you. Enjoy the rest of your time here in London."

My voice sounded cold and matter of fact as I spoke to him. But this did not affect Will. It just made his smile grow bigger. I took the box from him and tried to walk away.

"You can't just leave it at that. I had a great time talking to you and would very much like to talk to you again," Will called after me and gently pulled me back to face him.

"It's not as if we'll ever see each other again, so there is no point," I brushed him off. "It was lovely talking to you-"

"-I'll make sure we'll meet again."

I tried to remain imperturbable and not smile back, to not encourage his flirtatious attitude. I lowered my eyes to the ground, steadying myself.

"No," I quickly answered. "Thank you again, enjoy the rest of your stay in London. Best of luck with everything."

I could feel my body begin to shake but I successfully held myself together. I began to walk away again but something inside kept pulling me back. Like an invisible string inside me was knotted in him.

"Can I at least have your address so that I can write to you?"

"Ah go on, give the poor soldier your address!" Lilian teased.

I turned to find Lilian peeking from the door with Joan. They gave me encouraging looks but something within me said, 'this could never work, walk away.'

"Goodbye Will Fraye," I quickly said and turned on my heal and walked away.

Lilian walked past me and towards Will.

She subtly handed him a piece of paper. She tried to make it look as if she were shaking his hand, but Lilian could never do subtlety.

"Lilian!" I protested.

Lilian shrugged her shoulders. Her face beamed with mischievousness.

"I was only doing what you were too afraid to do."

"Thank you, Lilian" Will smiled. "Look out for a letter, Lucy. Until we meet again." He waved at me as he walked away, his contagious smile still on his face.

When I turned away from Will, Joan and Lilian stood side by side, with smiles on their faces. My cheeks blushed and I tried to recentre myself.

"Lilian, why did you do that? Now I will have to write back to him," I huffed.

Lilian mockingly rolled her eyes at me and let out a long sigh.

"Today I saw something in you that I have not seen in an awfully long time. I saw a spark between you and a man for the first time since Adam's death."

I winced as she said his name.

"Yes, I said the name Adam. Stop being afraid of it."

I took in a deep breath to hold myself quiet as I prepared myself for what Lilian had to say.

"For the first time since Adam, I saw a man spark your interest. Someone managed to catch your eye and make you smile. For so long, you have hidden yourself away in a self-made fortress, telling yourself that you will never love again. I knew you were not ready for a relationship."

"I'm still not ready."

Joan gently put her arm around me and comfortingly

stroked my arms, "No one is ever ready, Luc."

"I gave Will your address because he managed to bring out a smile in you that I haven't seen in a very long time," Lilian softly spoke.

"I saw it as well and it was such a wonderful sight to see. Just to see you smile again makes me so happy," Joan warmly acknowledged.

"Give him a chance is all I am asking of you," Lilian added. "And if you still don't like him, at least you know that you tried. You will know that love is not as terrifying as you believe it to be."

When I returned to Southampton, a letter from Will waited for me. I took the letter to my room and sat on my bed and stared at it for a long time. I reluctantly began to open it, but my eyes fell onto Adam's picture by my bedside. I stopped opening it and put the letter down on my bed and breathed a heavy sigh.

I continued to look at Adam and my stomach began to clench. I became irritable and I had a desperate need to apologise to Adam. A tremendous wave of guilt flowed over me. He was only dead a year and now I had another man's letter in my hand.

I looked down at the envelope beside me, which had beautiful calligraphy-style writing on it. It made my name look special and important. I decided that when I opened the letter and read it, my reaction to it would determine whether I would reply.

I slowly tore open the envelope, all the while Adam's photo glared at me. I took out the long-handwritten note and carefully unfolded it, breathing in deeply.

Essex

February 8th, 1944

Dearest Lucy,

I really hope this letter has made it safely to you and that your friend gave me the right address.

I am writing this letter as an attempt to form a bridge of sorts, where we can meet halfway and try to get to know one another. You have really struck me, and I want to get to know you more.

So, I suppose I should tell you a bit about myself - sell myself to you to show you that you are not wasting your time on a soldier like me! Just to remind you, this is William 'Will' Fraye writing to you (a woman like you seems to attract many admirers and so, I want to make myself known, to stand out from the crowd.)

I apologise if that was out of line. Again, just to clarify, this is Will.

As you may have guessed from my not-so-subtle accent, I am American. I come from a small town in Massachusetts. My parents are two of my favourite people in the world. They have given me everything that I could have possibly wished for and more. My father owns a publishing company and a small newspaper company, 'The Aurora Gazette.' Before I had to leave, I was working alongside my father learning everything I could from him about the publishing and newspaper world. When all of this is over, I am due to return to America and work at the newspaper, writing columns.

What else? I have two sisters, Vivian, and Sylvia. My younger brother, Felix, is fighting with the marines. I am the oldest. I love all my siblings equally, but if I had to choose a favourite it would be Sylvia. She has the sharpest wit and offers the best advice. Sylvia is quite possibly the smartest person I know. Do you have any siblings?

Before the war, I studied at Harvard University. I studied Journalism. I love to write, especially letters. So, if you do not reply to my letters the jokes on you because I love to write and will continue to write to you regardless of whether you reply! I will turn these letters to you into a 'dear diary' sort of thing.

On a serious note, I want you to know that I am an honest and genuine man who only wants to sit down with you over some tea. One thing that I have discovered since coming to England is that the English like their tea, so maybe we could drink some tea together? Maybe some dinner - is that pushing it? - and just talk to you. I never do this; I never run after girls, but you seem to have put some kind of spell on me, and I cannot seem to get you out of my head. I want to get to know you.

Please just consider my offer, that is all I ask.
Yours,
Will Fraye.

I held the letter in my hand and reread it three times. Each time I read it I laughed even more. Lilian read the letter and begged me to write back.

I sat on my bed staring at her grinning face as she read through the letter again and laughed at his words.

I took out my writing set and began to write. I looked at Adam's picture, took in a deep breath and let it out. I returned my focus to the blank page in front of me and wrote,

Dear Will…

1998

"I wrote to Will. But once I finished the letter, I sealed it and put it in my beside-locker. I couldn't get myself to post it," I reluctantly tell.

"Why not? He made you laugh, he made you smile – he completely charmed you. Why wouldn't you reply to his letter?" Emmy asks.

"It was exactly for those reasons, Emmy. I was terrified to write back to him…You see, when Adam died, I would not allow myself to laugh, smile, have fun, or to be young. It felt wrong to be in happy about something, as I felt I had to be mourning Adam. That if I stopped grieving, it meant I was moving on. I was forgetting him and the life we planned to have. If I was happy, I was successfully living without him. And when Will came along, he made me laugh, smile, forget my woes and sorrows and it scared me."

Mae nods her head slowly as she listens and takes in my words. Emmy sits back and leans her head onto her hand, trying to understand.

"But wasn't it a good thing, a nice thing, that he made you laugh?"

"Yes, it was nice. But I had built my walls so incredibly high. When your Grandad came into my life, he effortlessly knocked them all down. I desperately tried to rebuild them, brick by brick, but with every laugh and smile they would come crumbling down yet again. I was terrified to be vulnerable, to love, to show affection to another human being and I knew that if I were to keep in contact with Will and regularly meet him, I would have to face these fears eventually. And I was quite comfortable in my own rut!"

I feel a hard-lump rise in my throat as I speak, and my eyes begin to sting as the tears try to escape. I breathe in a long, deep breath but it is shaky and my chest aches. I place my hand on my heart and try to soothe my aches.

"It frightens me even now to think of what I was willing to throw away because of my fears. I would not have had any of this – I would not have had you two," I smile at Mae and Emmy, "I would not have had the wonderful life that I have."

I place the daisy cushion to the side of the armchair and begin to stand up. Mae and Emmy immediately jump out of their seats to help me, but I wave them off.

"I need some air," I whisper.

Lilian nods reassuringly at Mae and Emmy as she begins to refill the tray with the empty mugs of tea. Emmy sits back onto the couch and picks up another old photo album and begins to flick through the pages. I reopen the patio doors to allow the night air into the heavy room. The full moon is slowly rising in the night sky, surrounded by twinkling stars.

I walk out into the garden and stand bare foot on the cool grass. I hear footsteps behind me and turn to see Mae with a blanket in her hands. She wraps the soft, woollen blanket around me and leans her head onto my shoulder.

I hear Emmy's laugh and we instinctively turn to the house and watch Emmy and Lilian laughing together in the kitchen. I begin to remember nights where that was Mae and I enjoying each other's company.

When Mae was a child, Will and I used to put her and Teddy to bed. Every Friday night, once Will and Teddy were asleep, Mae would sneak downstairs to me. I would make us both a cup of hot chocolate, with homemade marshmallows and cookies. We would sit and chat until her eyelids began to droop. Mae would tell me about her adventures, her friends, and her dreams.

As she grew older into her teens, she did not have to sneak out of bed, but she wanted to keep up the tradition.

When Mae came home at the weekends from college, she would still wait until the house was quiet and find me sitting in the conservatory waiting for her, with a mug of hot chocolate and my homemade marshmallows.

She would tell me all about college, her new friends, dates that she went on, her lectures, and her new-found interests and passions. One thing that was constant throughout those precious years was the tales of her hopes and dreams for the future.

I catch Mae's hand and squeeze it.

"We should have had more nights like this with you and Emmy," I softly say. "We should have had more nights where we talked about the things that mattered, the big things. Not meaningless chit-chat about such-and-such. I should have talked more to you about the things that mattered, instead of leaving it all till now."

"Don't worry, Mam, this is only the beginning of more nights like this to come. I am sure after tonight Emmy will still be asking you a million and one questions, and we will happily sit here and listen to you."

I bite my lip and gently smile. Mae begins to walk back into the house, but I catch her hand and pull her back to me.

"Mae there is something that I want to say to you. I know you were upset earlier when I spoke about Adam."

"There is no need to say anymore, Mam. It was idiotic the way I behaved. I don't know what came over me."

"Just let me say what I want to say, and then we will say no more on it…I loved Adam. He was my first love. It was everything all at once and I would not change a thing. We were just children thrown into a dark, adult world where we quickly had to grow up. We both brought brightness and laughter into our dark days, and it was a wonderful relationship…But then Adam died, and I thought I could never love again. And I accepted it. My life became laid out for me. I was prepared to devote my whole life to nursing."

"I know, Mam. It's okay. I am sorry for the way I acted before. I don't know why I acted so stupidly."

I pause to push back the hard lump residing in my throat and I try to steady my breathing.

"Your father, he arrived out of nowhere. He completely swept me off my feet. And he made me smile and laugh. What I want you to know, Mae, is that – yes, I did love Adam - he was my first love and it was a desperate love - but Will," I pause and smile through my tears. "Will was the love of my life. It was a healing and rejuvenating love. And I miss him every day."

"I miss him too."

Mae pulls me into a tight hug as I begin to tear up. I can feel her body shake under my arms as she too cries. We stay like this for some time, until I hear Lilian and Emmy's voices flow out from the living room.

We both wipe away our tears and I gently place a kiss onto Mae's forehead. We link arms and return to the living room to find a fresh pot of tea and biscuits.

Emmy places a cushion on her lap and lays the photo album on top.

"You must have sent the letter since we are all here," Emmy says.

Mae helps me sit back into my armchair and lovingly tucks the blanket around my legs.

"I left Will's letter sitting in my bedside locker for three weeks. In that time, he sent me three other letters!"

Mae gently laughs, "That sounds just like Dad!"

"When I saw all the letters from Will, I thought that they were getting on so well and were writing to each other," Lilian leans forward, "I never thought to ask whether Lucy was replying to them, until the day I got a letter from Will asking about Lucy. I found her in our room with his new letter and she placed it with the rest."

"You left his letters sitting in a pile?" Emmy teasingly asks.

"Yes," I reluctantly answer.

"And his letters made you laugh, did they not?"

"Yes."

"And you still did not answer him?"

"Yes," I answer with a matter-of-fact tone.

"You make no sense!"

Lilian chuckles, "Exactly Emmy! I showed Lucy my letter and I had it out with her for not replying. So, I sat with her and made her write a letter back to him, agreeing to meet him in London. And once she finished writing it, I took it from her and posted it, because I know if I left it to her to post the letter, it would mysteriously get lost."

"Lilian, stop smiling at me like that," I chuckle.

I smile at the room but find myself slowly retreating into my memories.

MARCH 1944

In March 1944, Lilian and I went to London. Lilian arranged for Will and me to meet with her and Bobby. Lilian and Bobby kept in touch since the day they met and seemed to have really hit it off. Lilian had a constant smile stapled on her face and if someone even mentioned a word that somewhat resembled 'Bobby', she would instantly light up.

It was wonderful to see and I was beyond happy for her. Seeing her so happy would often reduce me to pride tears just watching her beautiful smile light up an entire room. Lilian, the Lady of Optimism, deserved every ounce of happiness that this life could offer.

A sense of excitement lingered in the London air. A now-or-never feeling radiated amongst the courtships, as there was a constant fear that they might not be here in the morning. London was still being bombed. People genuinely did not know if they would see tomorrow. Many did not know the difference between love and lust. But people did not have too much time to think about that sort of thing, it was now-or-never.

Lilian arranged for us to meet in a small café. When Lilian and I arrived, the café was already crowded with American soldiers courting young English girls. We could not see Bobby or Will among them and knew they must be running late. So, we got a table for four and waited.

An hour went by and there was no sign of Bobby or Will. Lilian and I had drunk a pot of tea together and I had treated her to some cake. She refused to eat the cake and kept insisting that we should save it for Bobby and Will.

Another half hour went by and Lilian sat very straight and stiff in her chair, with only her eyes moving, watching the café unfold in front of her with courting couples. The corners of her lips hung low as her lips trembled. She coughed to stop the trembling and to steady her voice and breathing.

"Typical!" I began to laugh as I crossed my arms and legs.

"Don't give me that look Lucy," Lilian huffed.

"What look?"

"That, 'I knew they wouldn't come', look," Lilian glared at me from the corners of her eyes, and I could see a hint of a smile appearing on her face.

I pushed the saucer with the still uneaten cake on it, towards Lilian. She glared at me as she rested her head on her hand. I continued to push it until it was right up against her. Thankfully, she laughed. Lilian looked around the table for a fork or spoon to eat the cake.

"Don't bother, just pick it up with your hand! You need to treat yourself, Miss Lilian Comerford. You work hard and you deserve some cake."

Lilian turned her head away from me, hiding her smile. She reluctantly picked up the cake and held it delicately in her hand, looked at it for a few moments, as if contemplating life. She let out a sigh and then stuffed the entire slice into her mouth.

She could barely close her mouth. Crumbs flew everywhere as she tried to chew down. I helped to smear the icing into her face and we both could not help but laugh.

"We should do this more often," I sat back in the chair and looked around the room, "We should take each other out and treat ourselves without any dates."

"We should be each other's dates," Lilian smiled.

We sat for some time in the café as we ordered another pot of tea and more cake. Soon enough, the sound of our laughter was all that could be heard in the café. Many of the couples stared at us as if we were clinically insane.

We took a stroll around a park nearby. Lilian linked arms with me and became suddenly quiet. Her head hung low as she watched her feet take each step-in front of her.

"I'm sorry for today. I know you really like him," I tried to comfort her.

Lilian did not answer me, but instead slowly nodded her head.

"There must be some explanation for them not turning up.

Because Bobby is the biggest fool that I know if he willingly passed off a chance in a lifetime to take *the* Lilian Comerford on a date." I elbowed her into the side and a small laugh escaped her mouth.

"Thank you," she sadly smiled. "And that Will Fraye," she paused to let out a heavy sigh, "I really thought he was different. I really thought he meant what he said in those letters. I'm sorry I pushed you into replying to them."

"If it is meant to be, it will be. But do you know what, Lil? I have you and you have me, and that's what matters the most."

We continued to walk around the park enjoying the Spring sun on our skin. By the end of the day, we were on the train back to Southampton and Lilian was full of laughter as she put Bobby to the back of her mind.

The following week, letters arrived from Bobby and Will. The letters were full of apologies as they pleaded with us to understand their reason for not coming to the date.

A soldier in their company did not complete all his duties and tried to cover it up, and so the platoons 48-hour passes were revoked, and the men received extra duties. Both Will and Bobby pleaded with us to accept their offer for another date and promised us the sun, moon, and stars that they would be there.

A few days later, we met with Will and Bobby in London. Lilian linked arms with me to make sure that I did not run away, like I kept insisting I would do.

Before we left, Lilian made me dress-up nicely for the date. She picked out my outfit and made me put make-up on. She insisted that it was to make her look good. I allowed her to dress me up as I could see it took her mind off her nerves.

As we walked up the steps from the Underground into the heart of London, the sounds of the city seemed to electrify every fibre and nerve in my body and melt away my nerves.

My eyes landed on two soldiers, kitted out in their finest gear, leaning against the railing at the entrance of the Underground. Their faces lit up when they saw us. Bobby made his way over to Lilian and exploded in apologies.

"Well, well, well, we meet again!" a familiar voice appeared from behind me.

I turned to see a grinning Will Fraye.

"Hello," I coolly replied.

Will continued to smile and I felt a bubbling sensation in my stomach, as if any moment I was going to burst into a fit of laughter. I stubbornly remained poised and stern with him, but it was no use as his smile was utterly contagious.

Will raised his eyebrows at me when he saw my smile surface on my face. I crossed my arms and turned my face away from him to not let him know that he had successfully won in making me smile.

"Shall we?" Will extended his arm for me to link with him.

I blankly looked at him, continued to keep my arms tightly crossed and walked in front of him. Will flamboyantly imitated me crossing my arms and flicking my hair. He began to curl over with laughter as I stared at him open mouthed.

Just for that, I walked ahead. Alone.

We began to walk down the street towards the Red Cross tent where Will enthusiastically pointed out where we met. I rolled my eyes and continued to walk on ahead.

"Oh, you sure are a tough nut to crack!" Will chuckled. "But I like a challenge."

As we grew closer to Hyde Park, clusters of soldiers courting English girls appeared. The Park was one of the favourite places for US troops stationed in England. Hyde Park quickly became known as the place to find someone.

At the entrance of the park, chairs could be rented so that couples could sit together under the trees and watch the world go by. I watched as couples rowed small boats across the Serpentine and I smiled at their romantic journey. A feeling of excitement hung in the air.

The smell of cologne and perfume instantly hit me as the groups floated by. The Park was filled with new couples, strolling with inter-linked arms across the park. But I kept my arms firmly crossed across my chest for fear that Will would take my hand in his.

Flocks of girls passed me by, each trying to gain the attention from groups of soldiers. To the girls' delights, hemlines were shorter due to rationing, and this helped to catch the attention of the whistling soldiers.

I could not help but laugh as I watched the scene play out in front of me. Yet again, I felt as though I was watching a play unfold before me. As if I were not there, but merely existing.

We found a spot of dry grass and sat down. Other couples sprawled flat out on blankets, enjoying a small picnic while others strolled around the park, holding hands, completely lost in their own conversations. I found myself staring at these groups to distract myself from my own group.

Lilian and Bobby had not stopped talking, it was wonderful to see. Bobby wanted to know every detail about Ireland and Lilian. Will and I sat and watched Lilian and Bobby talk, like a performance unfolding in front of us. I turned to Will who was already staring at me with a mischievous smile spread across his face.

"Hello there," Will smiled, making me move back away from him.

"Stop smiling at me like that," I chuckled.

Will moved his hand across the grass between us and found something. He told me to close my eyes and I played along expecting chocolate to be placed in my hand. But when I opened my eyes, I found a single daisy on it, as he said the words 'for you.'

I watched him softly smile and enjoy the sun on his face. I thanked him and placed the daisy in my handkerchief.

I wondered was it time to move on?

Will quickly stood up and held his hand out to me.

"Would you care to join me on one of those boats on the lake? They look like fun."

I looked around me for a moment and hesitantly outstretched my hand to him. Once my hand was in his, he playfully pulled me up and I almost fell, but he caught me saving me from embarrassment.

"Let's leave these two lovebirds," Will winked at Lilian and Bobby.

He helped me into the small boat and once he comfortably sat into it, he began to row. Since his focus was upon rowing us further out into the lake, I began to look at him and take in his features.

The sun shone on his tanned face, bringing out the golden-blond speckles in his hair. I could see he had just shaved that morning as there was a tiny nick beneath his left ear. Will caught me staring and a smirk appeared on his face.

As we got to the middle of the lake, Will stopped rowing.

"I should have packed a picnic," he said. "Next time."

We sat comfortably in the small boat, gently rocking to the rhythm of the water around us. We began to talk, and he asked me lots of questions about England and nursing, but I was curious to know about America.

The more we talked, the more I felt as if I had known him all my life. I felt the urge to tell him everything about me and he felt the same way. I found myself opening up to him – a complete stranger – yet it felt so right.

The wind around us became stronger and the boat rocked harder against the water. I looked up at the sky and could see the clouds growing heavier with rain. I picked up my silk scarf and threw it around my head and neck, but the wind caught it and took it away into the lake.

"Don't worry I'll get it."

Will tried to row the boat towards the scarf, but he was not quick enough. He took off his jacket, stood up, almost staggering as the boat uneasily rocked with both of our weights and jumped into the lake. The splash of his jump attracted attention to us.

"Will, it's okay. It's just a scarf."

"Don't you worry! I got it," Will enthusiastically shouted as he caught the floating scarf and swam back.

He leaned on the side of the boat, with his hands dripping water all over me, and handed me my drenched scarf. He put his hand out for me to help him into the boat, but instead he pulled me into the lake.

I let out a piercing scream as my body hit the freezing water. As I kicked my legs frantically to keep myself up, I could feel something move around me and I began to scream more. Will choked with laughter which made me even more mad at him. But as his laughter grew and grew into incoherent sounds, I could not help but join him.

As he got his breath back and his laughter grew softer, Will pulled himself up into the boat and helped me in. I began to shiver with the cold and watched the water droplets drip one-by-one from me onto the floor of the boat, creating a small puddle around me.

Will placed his dry coat around me and rubbed his hands up and down my arms to warm me up. He too was dripping wet, but his main priority was making me warm. A wave of warmth flew over me. I watched his lips turn purple and then blue. His body was trembling with the coldness as he tried to row back to the boat house, but he was not letting it stop him.

Lilian and Bobby stood waiting for us at the edge of the lake. Bobby placed his jacket around Will and Lilian squeezed the ends of my hair.

"Maybe it wasn't such a good idea to leave you two alone near water," Bobby said.

"I take it you are going to say no to another date with me," Will managed to say through his trembling. "I don't blame you."

Will's lips had grown bluer as he stood shaking in front of me. His head hung as he waited for my reply. Lilian and Bobby tried to hide from the awkwardness of the rejection to come.

"The first time I met you, you were barking at a dog and then you chased after me. You bombarded me with letters until I answered. You never turned up to what was supposed to be our first date and when I agreed to meet you again, you pulled me into an ice-cold lake..." I sternly looked at Will as he lowered his head. "I'll go on another date with you if you promise it will be better."

Will nodded his head gracefully accepting the rejection until my words sunk in. He turned to Bobby and the two grinned from ear to ear.

Will's letters became a frequent occurrence after our date, and I began to wait in anticipation for his next one. We went on more dates with Lilian and Bobby accompanying us. Lilian no longer had to make me dress nicely for the dates, but instead I began asking her if I looked okay. Soon, Will and I began to find time alone together. We would walk for hours and talk.

I began to feel myself fall for Will with each word of his letters and every second I spent in his company. I had never been so sure of something and someone in my life, yet simultaneously so confused about it all.

In May, we were under instructions in the hospital to prepare for the mass casualties that were expected to come from D-Day. Wards were cleared out, waiting for the casualties, and extra supplies were brought in. We were told to remain within range of a call from the hospital even if we were on holidays or off duty. We knew that it was only to get busier after this next mission.

At the same time, Will asked me to be with him but I found myself saying 'no.' He accepted my answer but asked could he still write to me. In one of his letters, before he set out for France, he asked me if he survived his next mission would I reconsider my answer. I agreed and he felt a confidence grow within him.

In the hospital, Lilian, Whilma, and I were among the nurses picked to be shipped out with the Red Cross and troops to Europe, if they were successful on D-Day. If successful, we would arrive in the days after and take care of the casualties. My body and mind were terrified of the weeks to come, but I somehow managed to keep one foot in front of the other.

JUNE 1944

On Tuesday the 6th of June 1944, D-Day commenced. The German army occupied north-western Europe and the allies had not been successful at pushing back the German army since 1940. When France surrendered, the German army quickly trampled over the land and successfully took the north-west of Europe. This ensured that they were secure in their position and were slowly gaining full reign of the continent.

On the days prior to D-Day, we hurriedly prepared for the expected casualties to come. On the early hours of the morning of D-Day, I stood with Lilian at the pier in Southampton as the sun rose. We watched the men board the ships.

Lines and lines of men, all walking in formation, boarded those death ships and I wondered how many of them would ever see these shores again. I looked at the horizon and wondered what lay beyond that sky for those men. What was this all for? What were these men risking their lives for?

There was no justice in this war, it was only a game.

24,000 American, British, and Canadian airborne troops began to fall from the sky shortly after midnight. The planes were made from thin metal and were shot at while they flew. Many men did not reach the ground as they were shot and killed inside the planes.

The wind dragged many men miles away from their landing zones, causing the troops to be spread out all over the place, but in the wrong places. Many tried their best to find their way back to their companies in the darkness without any way of contacting their commanding officers or fellow comrades. Some paratroopers landed in the trees and got their parachutes stuck on the branches. They were forced to stay there till daylight, hoping one of their own would find them.

As the sun began to rise, soldiers began to land on Utah, Omaha, Gold, Sword, and Juno beaches.

By the end of the day, the beaches had been won back and the soldiers continued on their fight.

Soon, ships full of wounded men docked in Southampton port. Soldiers flooded into the hospital, there was not a moment to think. It seemed all our training had led to this day. We quickly ran out of hospital beds and men were put on stretchers throughout the hospital. Every nurse and doctor constantly ran from one stretcher to the next, but it still did not seem to achieve anything. Outcries of help flooded the wards.

The theatres were full of operations being carried out. Most of the theatre blocks had up to three men having surgery at the same time in the one room. I walked out onto the corridor in hopes to take a breath, but I was met with more men.

It struck me how 'civilised' man did this to man. It seemed that human life had become so incredibly cheap throughout this war. Nobody batted an eye when somebody died, it had become the norm.

I worked throughout the day, into the night and onto the following morning without a moments rest. In the early hours of the next morning, I tried to nap on a hard-wooden chair but every time I closed my eyes, I saw hollow eyes crying out for my help.

So many doctors and nurses broke down in tears throughout the day and night but brushed themselves off and carried on with their job. We all reminded ourselves of the sacrifice that these men went through for us, and that we would never be able to thank them enough for what they did.

These men sacrificed their day and their future for the future of this world. They stormed onto those beaches of Normandy, for us to live yet another day in this senseless world. These men were ordinary men who achieved something extraordinary. No amount of words would ever be able to fully capture what they did.

For most of those brave men that fought on D-Day, their sad and lonely graves now lie forgotten on those shores of France. So far away from their loved ones.

These men inspired me to take control of my life and to do something with it. Something worthwhile.

I spent most of my life listening to and following everyone else's advice on what my life should be like and what I should be doing. The one voice that I should have listened to, I drowned out. That voice was mine.

I often wondered who I was living my life for and who was I proving my worth to? I realised that it was me whom I was trying to prove something to. I desperately wanted to prove to myself that I was strong and brave.

After D-Day, I wanted to go to Europe. Fear lingered in the back of my mind, a natural fear for my life. But it did not consume it. My hope for a better world and an end to this war fuelled me and I wanted to put aside all my needs and lay down my life for the men who had done so for me. I wanted courage to flow through me.

If I could be there for at least one person in their final moments, and give them some ease from their pain, I would feel like I was doing something that mattered.

I wanted to prove to myself that I was truly taking control of my life as I promised myself I would.

FRANCE

In the days following D-Day, I boarded the hospital ship with medical supplies, food, bandages, artillery, and replacements. We prayed on the ship that we would make it safely to France.

As I settled into the rocking of the waves, my mind wandered to Will. He remained there until I could not bear to think of him or wonder where he was.

By daylight, we arrived in Normandy. Once docked, we were allocated to various hospitals. Lilian and I were allocated to a field hospital in St-Mere-Egléise. We were immediately brought there without a moments rest. While driving to the field hospital, we were sometimes shot at by German soldiers. Lilian and I held onto each other for dear life.

As we arrived at the square of St-Mere-Egléise, we were rapidly met with crowds of soldiers. The men no longer looked like their shining, immaculately dressed selves like they did in England. Instead, they were covered in mud, sweat and sand. They looked utterly exhausted.

The hospital was a large tent set up in the square. Lilian and I rolled up our sleeves and got to work. I was glad to be busy as it stopped my hands from shaking. The hours began to pass by without a moments rest.

More soldiers were brought in from the other field hospitals nearby due to an overflow of patients. Above all this, I heard my name being called.

Will stood at the entrance of the tent. My prayers had been answered as I searched his face and body for injuries. The only thing I saw was that big smile on his face. My shaking returned and I could not move.

I found myself throwing my arms around his neck and wishing I could hold onto him for as long as there was air in my lungs.

"Some might say, you missed me," Will chuckled. Even though he joked, his arms grew tighter around me.

He hugged me so tightly that I felt the gaping hole inside me slowly refilling.

I stepped outside the stuffy tent with Will. We sat on a grass bank and drank tea. Everything and everyone seemed to fade out once he drew a breath. He looked the same, yet something inside him was changed.

Will took in the scene around us.

"I'll take you on a proper date, in a fancy restaurant with champagne as soon as I can. I promise you that."

I began to feel myself drop the tight reigns that I had tied around myself and my emotions. I was terrified to be losing control of them. Yet when I looked at Will and listened to him talk, I knew it was worth it.

At that moment I realised how important Will was to me and I never wanted to lose him. I could not see my future without him. His side was where I was meant to be and my side was where he was meant to be.

We survived D-Day and I knew after that we would survive anything. Before he returned to his platoon, Will handed me a letter. He insisted I wait until he left for me to read it. He squeezed my hand and left.

5ᵗʰ June 1944

Dear Lucy,

If this letter has been delivered to you, it means I have not survived. It means they found this letter on my body, deep in my pocket and was brought to you. I want you to know that you were my last thought before I died.

However, if I hand this to you, it means that the letter you hold in your hands was with me every step of the way on Utah beach. Like this letter, I survived as I promised you I would.

This letter and I survived perhaps the most dangerous military operation so far in history (hopefully without a scratch).

All jokes aside, I want you to know Lucy that I adore you and want to continue to adore you. The thought of my future with you has kept me going through so many horrendous hours.

Even in the short time that I have known you, I know that you are the One for me. I never believed I would be lucky to find someone like you. Someone who fits perfectly into my jigsaw of life.

I knew it the second I heard your laugh. I had never seen something so beautiful and perfect in my entire life. You walked amongst the crowds of people, yet you stood out a mile to me. From the way your hair fell over your shoulder, to your eyes, to the way you smiled and looked before you laughed, right down to your walk – I knew you were it! I had to have you.

I know this sounds corny, it even sounds ridiculous to me, but it is the honest truth. I have never believed in love at first sight, but you have made me see that there are some things that cannot be explained, but only felt. Words fail to explain to you what you mean to me.

I think back to the time before I knew you, where I aimlessly drifted from one thing to the next, never fully sure about anything. But when I saw you, I had never been surer of anything in my life. I knew that this war was just for now, but you are my now and my future. Everything just seemed to click into place once I met you.

I now understand what the poets have spent years trying to capture.

What I am trying to say is, I am yours Lucy. Completely. You have me. I would happily wait forever for you. I want you to know that I will wait for whenever you are ready, just know that I am here.

If I survive this next mission, I would be honoured to take you on a date if you would have me?

I look forward to the moment that I hand you this letter.

Lovingly yours,
Will

I took a moment to let his words sink in. My chest was ready to burst with each pounding thud my heart made. It seemed my heart was slowly breaking free of the cage I had entrapped it in.

I looked up and saw that Will had disappeared into the crowds of soldiers and I could not seem to find him. I stood up and tried to steady myself. I started to call out for Will, but he was nowhere to be seen. I began to lose hope that he had already left with his platoon.

A soldier called out to me and pointed towards a tent. Will walked out from the tent, confused as to what the soldier was saying to him. But his eyes soon found me.

Will tried to steer me away from the watching soldiers who began to gather around us.

"Is everything all right?"

"I read your letter."

He bit his bottom lip, took in a deep breath and I could almost hear his fast-pacing heart.

"I meant every word of it. I am not taking it back, if that is what you have come to ask."

I stared at him for a few moments, taking in his features.

"Will you be with me?"

Wills mouth opened wide into a beautiful grin. "I thought you'd never ask!"

The men around us erupted into cheers and whistling as Will pulled me into a tight hug.

I tried to hide my embarrassment, but Will pulled my face up to his so that he could see me. He began to tease me for my reddening cheeks, and I could not help but laugh. My ears were filled with more cheering and whistling from the soldiers around us.

Will gestured for me to look behind and I turned to see Lilian and some of the other nurses watching us.

"Let's give them something to cheer about," Will gently whispered into my ear.

Will caught my face in between his hands and kissed me. The group grew louder but I could not hear a thing.

WINTER 1944

By September, U.S. troops had slowly made their way onto German soil. Will was among the men who were the first of the allies to enter Germany. I knew it would be a long time before I would see Will again, but his letters assured me that this would not be forever.

By November, the bitter Winter winds were in full swing. Everywhere looked incredibly bleak and grey. It was beyond Winters doing. This bleakness was man made. This was now my fifth Winter in the war, and it seemed to be the dreariest.

Supplies and food were running low. Bandages and morphine were becoming scarce in the hospital. Linen and bed sheets were ripped to make bandages. These were then washed, cleaned, and reused. Many of the men were not remotely dressed for the Winter weather and were faced with losing toes, fingers, and in some cases, limbs. The French citizens around us were living in poor conditions as well. Many were on the brink of starvation.

When the nights of bombing would arrive, we knew the hospital would be a main target. Our red-cross flag was both a blessing and a hindrance. A flag of hope for those seeking respite and healing. A flag of doom as bomber pilots treated cross as a bullseye.

We took each day as it came and tried to remain hopeful that this war would end. In these moments, I thought of home.

I had not heard from my mother is some time. There were often delays with letters arriving to us.

When I saw her handwriting, I eagerly opened it. I thought about the warm fires lit in at home, the fresh smell of linen, warm water running through the taps, warm deep baths with aromatic soap, guaranteed meals three times day and clothes hanging in my wardrobe.

Dearest Lucy,

I know not how to begin this letter that I write to you. It is hard to believe that you are reading this in Europe, many miles away. I am afraid, no words can soften the news that I sorrowfully bear.

Your dear father passed away in his sleep. I could hear his soft breathing beside me as I went to sleep, but when I woke, his hand entangled in mine was ice-cold. I lay beside him for some time, weeping for my Charles to come back to me. But he never did. Doctor Fernsby informed me that it seemed your father suffered another stroke in his sleep.

I am sorry to give you this news, Lucy. I feel as though all the life in my body has left me. Words cannot express how much I miss him. I have been mourning for your father since his first stroke. He has not been his old self in a long time.

For so long, I have devoted my time and days completely to my darling Charles. I have not left the house in some time, and we have refused visitors as it used to upset him. Now, I do not know what to do with myself.

To my surprise, I have found comfort in Margot. Margot has become an unexpected friend to me.

I want you to know that your father never stopped calling out for you. In the end, the only word that he could speak was 'Belle'.

Forgive me, I cannot write anymore. Please take care of yourself, my sweetheart.

Mama.

1945

By February 1945, the allies had moved further into Germany. The end was almost in sight. News came to hospital on the 30th of April, that Herr Hitler had committed suicide with his newly wedded wife, Eva Braun. Hitler killed himself by gunshot in his Führerbunker in Berlin.

Both relief and outrage were felt amongst people when this news broke. We were relieved to know he was dead and that this war could end. But many were angry and outraged that Hitler would never be able to pay for what he did to this world. He would never be able to apologise or suffer for his actions.

The same questions ran through everyone's mind – why now? Why did so many men, women, and children have to die because of him?

After hearing of the news of Hitlers suicide, I was amazed to see the German people picking up rubble, already trying to rebuild their country. They picked up bricks and began to stack them up into piles, slowly categorising the ruins of a country. Little did they know, the same thing would happen with the people.

My belief in humanity and civilisation slowly returned. A peaceful life was not a distant dream that could never be grasped, but a slow approaching reality.

On the 8th of May, the hospital burst open and an out of breath young boy yelled, "THE WAR HAS ENDED! VICTORY IN EUROPE."

A short silence followed his words.

Nobody dared to believe the words until the boy shouted them again. Cheers and clapping erupted all around me.

I found a chair and fell into it, trying to slow my breathing afraid that it was a false alarm and that a bomb would drop any moment. But as I watched the men and women cheer, hug, cry and breathe in a breath of free air, I knew it was real.

It was all over.

I smiled as I watched the scene unfold in front of me, not a part of it but not outside of it, just floating above it.

It was all over. My heart sank as I the words 'what would I do now?' floated into my mind.

I would only be needed as a nurse for a short while more in Europe, then all the soldiers would go back home to where they belong. I too would go back home. Maybe I would be needed as a nurse back in England, but my job was not guaranteed.

Could we fit back into our old lives?

War was all anyone talked and thought about. What would the conversations be about now? The war gave me a purpose and a job to do – what was my purpose now?

I hated myself for thinking like this.

Why could I not celebrate and enjoy this victory like everyone else? Why could I not peacefully accept this wonderful news? It was all over. The war was finally over.

My eyes fell on Lilian across the room with the same look on her face. She made her way towards me.

"What do we do now?" I asked.

Lilian shrugged her shoulders and let out a long heavy breath.

"We live."

I mourned all the men and women who did not get this wonderful opportunity, to live another day and breathe in a deep breath of peaceful air.

HOPE

On the days following Victory in Europe Day, I continued to work in the hospital. I prepared many of the men to be moved back to England for rehabilitation. The celebrations were still ongoing in the streets around the hospital. Cheers, singing, whistling, and laughter could be heard all around.

Will appeared in the doorway of the hospital ward. I thought I had dreamt it. I had not seen him since September 1944.

I fell into his welcoming arms, and we stayed like that for some time, enjoying the feel of each other.

"So, the war is over," Will pulled me outside into the sun.

"Yes. What do we do now?"

Will stood in front of me and smiled, almost as if he were trying to remember all my features. Will put his hand into his pocket and pulled out a small box.

"I have something in mind. Lucy Annabelle Webley, will you be my Mrs. Fraye?"

I slid the ring on my finger, and I stared at my hand in complete disbelief that this was actually happening.

I felt as if I was going to burst with happiness. I jumped into his arms and he spun me around. He kissed me before placing me back down, causing an eruption of cheers to surround us.

A dizziness rushed over me as the excitement and happiness ran through my body. I had never been happier in my entire life than in this moment. Oh, how I wished this moment would never end.

A soldier holding a camera walked towards us.

"Would you mind if I take a picture to send back home to our folks, to show them how the troops are getting on in Europe?"

This was to be our very first picture together.

Every time that the photographer would begin to take the photo, Will would tickle me or make a joke and I would fly off into a fit of laughter. It was almost impossible to take a photo.

In the end, the soldier gave up and allowed us to be goofy with each other.

After the photograph was captured, we turned to see Lilian running towards us at full speed, with her hands in the air, and the biggest smile on her face.

She pulled me into hug and began to wail. I could barely make out her words, but the ring on her finger was enough to understand. Bobby proudly stood beside her and placed a kiss on her cheek. Their wedding was to be as soon as possible. These last six years had taken its toll on everyone, there was no time to waste when it came to happiness. Lilian and Bobby were to be married in Paris in the following days.

As I looked around me, I realised that I was no longer lost. I had found myself and my family. I was ready to begin living my life. I had survived the war and now it was time to honour my life by living it to its' full potential.

This was a moment that I wished I could bottle forever and revisit whenever I needed to be reminded how lucky I was.

PARIS

The streets of Paris were booming with people. Shops were fully stocked, restaurants and cafés exploded with chattering customers, with snippets of their conversations echoing around me. It was vibrant and exciting once again. I adored it.

Will and I made our way to Lilian and Bobby's small wedding ceremony. Uncertain whether Paris made me a romantic or whether I made Paris romantic, I adored the city regardless.

A few couples stood outside the small church waiting to get married. Each beheld a look of pure happiness. Genuine bliss. Honest and adoring love. As though, all these years of hardship and sacrifice made the wait worth every minute.

I glanced at my own ring, glistening in the sun, and felt a surge of 'why not now?' run through me. I watched Will laugh and talk to the couples, congratulating them on their wedding day. His voice and laugh calmed and reassured me. Peacefulness was in Will.

I thought about the remainder of my life, the many birthdays ahead of me, and I smiled knowing that I got to spend them with Will.

Let's get married today, I thought. Why did Paris have that effect on people? The whole city made me want to elope.

No. Today was Lilian and Bobby's day. For the whole day, it was theirs, and I could not be happier for them if I tried.

I found Lilian in a small room inside the Church. Aunt June designed and created Lilians dress. It was a simple white lace dress that ended just above her ankles. Irish white lace for the sleeves, tied with small pearl buttons at her wrists.

Small victory curls framed Lilians face with her shiny black hair flowing down over her shoulders and back. I could not help but stare at her. She was the most beautiful bride that I had ever seen.

Lilian twirled for me, making the dress dance in the air as the sun shone through the small window, igniting the delicate lace pattern. The more I watched her, the more the tears formed in my eyes. But today was a happy day. No tears allowed.

Well, maybe a few.

Lilian stood in front of the narrow mirror, admiring the dress.

"I wrote to Aunt June some time ago about Bobby and then again when I told her we were engaged. It turns out, she began to make the dress from the first letter I wrote about him! Typical Aunt June, she spots these things a mile off. I like how the lace is from home, I just wish my family could be here today. Bobby and I are planning on going to Ireland once he is discharged from the army."

"That will be such a wonderful trip for you, Lilian, to go back home and see your family again. It's been a long time."

A knock on the door interrupted our conversation to inform us that the wedding was about to commence.

I handed Lilian her small bouquet and held out my arm to her.

"Shall we Lilian Comerford, soon to be Mrs. Browne?"

Lilian drew a deep breath and we walked through the door.

"It's really happening, isn't it? I am not dreaming?"

"It is really happening!"

From the moment the doors opened, Bobbys eyes never left Lilian. They happily said their vows and ran out of the Church onto the street to shout their celebrations to the world.

Will and I threw rice over them as they kissed and the moment was captured in a photograph. Will happily revealed a bottle of champagne hiding in his jacket. He popped the cork and splashed the sparkling drink all over us as he cheered.

"Will, where did you get that?" I wiped the champagne from my face.

Will tapped his nose, "Yes dear."

"In no way does that answer my question."

"Yes dear!"

Laughter filled my ears as more champagne splashed above us, sprinkling down onto our faces. Will's eyes caught mine and he pulled me closer to him. He handed me the champagne and I drank from it, feeling its fizziness run down my throat and bubbling around inside me. I took a mental photograph of this moment, with Will by myside, his hand in mine and Lilian laughing beside me with Bobby.

I told myself to be thankful for all the tears I cried, for I never would have arrived at this moment with so much love in my heart.

OCTOBER 1945

In October 1945, I sailed home with other nurses and recovering soldiers from Calais to Dover.

Those magnificent white cliffs were the most welcoming sight. They eased my heart. I was finally home. My home. Safe. A survivor of a long war. No words could ever convey these six years of my life. I could only but feel my emotions, not explain them. They could never be explained.

I was home and that was what mattered.

I stepped off the ship and greedily took in a deep breath of English air. Free air. Yet, a deep sense of detachment fluttered through my core. Everything seemed to have immediately ended for me.

Was this not what I wanted? Did I not pray day and night for this war to end? Did I not pray that I could have a moment to myself, to breathe, read, relax, sleep…live? Did I not desperately wish I could live my own life, a life of freedom and peace? Yet, why did I feel so alone?

This melancholy grew stronger with each wave that flew over me.

Nurses and soldiers hurriedly passed me by, desperate to get home. I stood on the busy pier, gripping a suitcase either side of me. My knuckles were almost white. No more would I be surrounded by these nurses and soldiers. No more would I see their faces, greeting me each day.

No more would I live with brave women, caring women, strong women – wonderful friends. No more would I care for brave men, strong men, broken men. When would I see them all again? Would I ever experience their company again?

It was as though I was losing a part of my family.

A sharp pain shot through my arm. My knuckles were completely white, with red indents in the shape of my suitcase handles across the palm of my hands. I released my tight grip and followed the crowd towards the train.

While on the train to London, I received strange glares from the citizens around me due to my nurse's uniform. People were reluctant to allow nurses or soldiers to sit next to them as they were of the belief that 'the war was over now, it's time to move on.'

The civilians on the train did not want to look at the wounded soldiers. The soldiers with missing limbs, scarred faces, burnt hands and arms, or uncontrollably shaking. The very soldiers who sacrificed themselves for this world.

The civilians did not want to be reminded of the horrors of the war that they suffered for the past six years. Their silence and avoidant stares were our 'thank you's' for giving up six years of our life for this war. Their reluctance to acknowledge our presence was the cherry on top of the overflowing cup of gratitude.

But these civilians failed to realise that it was the nurses and soldiers who were the most affected. We, the nurses, and soldiers, saw and did things no person should ever have seen or done. I pushed away the anger and turned my attention to the wide-open fields fluttering past my window.

Once in London, I made my way to the military hospital. My duties were no longer needed as the war ended. I was turned loose. My options included returning to training to specialise in an area of nursing, nurse soldiers in a convalescent hospital, or find a job somewhere else. St Angela's was still open to me, but did I want it?

The secretary asked for my military nurse badge. I removed it from the sleeve of my uniform and held it in my hand for a moment. Flashbacks of the past six years swamped my mind. Nameless faces of soldiers flashed by my eyes with their helpless cries filling my ears. Repulsive smells of iodine, antiseptic ointment, rotting skin, and blood crept into my nose.

I tightly shut my eyes and shook my head.

My breath became stuck in my throat and my mouth gasped for air, but my chest forgot how to expand. Let me breathe, I wanted to scream, but my voice could not be found. My throat burned with the trapped scream. I scratched at my chest and back to remove the ropes tied around me. The knots were too complicated to untie. I dared not move as each attempt to draw in breath tied the ropes tighter around me.

A loud bang forced my eyes open. The secretary stared at me as she slowly backed away. I felt like a dangerous animal. I quickly smiled to hide my embarrassment, placed the badge on her desk and briskly walked out of the building.

I ran down the concrete steps and down a quiet side street where I could slump my back against a wall and steady myself.

What is wrong with me? My breath came back to me in harsh inhales and unsteady exhales. Young nurses walked in clusters and entered the hospital to start their shift. Something that I had done so many times. Yet, I no longer felt connected with them.

Another wave of panic raced over my body. I could not be a nurse anymore. I could not go back into training. I could not specialise in an area of nursing. I could not do it. I could not go back into hospital life.

After spending so much time wanting to be a nurse, I never wanted to see a hospital again.

Nobody wanted to talk about the war. Nobody wanted to acknowledge these past six years. Once the war officially ended and celebrations were over, nobody wanted to admit these past six years occurred. People packed away the war into a tightly sealed box. Life returned to normal as though nothing changed. People still shopped, worked, socialised, ate, drank, slept, laughed, talked, walked…lived. It was as if an amnesia fell upon the world. A collective amnesia.

The world did not care if I was affected by the war or lived through horrific events. The world did not care if anyone was affected because we all were hurting.

My pain was something for me to hide away and deal with. My pain needed to be concealed, ignored, rejected, denied, and treated as if it were shameful. My pain was no longer mine.

I needed to find a new mask, a mask to show the world I was happy, I was fine, I was a functioning person. My pain would only make others uncomfortable.

I too needed to place my memories into a box. Maybe one day I would have the courage to open it again.

My breathing steadied and I walked to the train station to go home. I was torn between anticipation and dread as the distance between me and home became shorter. An excitement lay within me as I desperately wanted to see my family. But I dreaded the sad sight of my father's empty chair at the table, his lonely green armchair by the fire, his unlit pipe with the scent of tobacco still lingering in it, his unread newspaper, and his aimlessly wandering dog, Chester.

What was home without my father?

The train stopped at my local station. A lonely figure stood on the platform. This person held the top of a floor-length fur coat, tightly closed with their bony hand. Their head bowed, making it hard to see the face. But once I stepped off the train, this frail person glanced up. She was unrecognisable.

"Lucy", my mother's wheezed.

I ran towards her and wrapped my arms around her in an embrace. Her bones seemed to stick out from every inch of her. I was terrified that if I hugged her too tightly, she would fall to the ground into a million pieces.

My mother refused to finish the hug for some time and pulled me in even closer to her. I heard her quietly hold in a cry and felt her body shake under my arms. I soothingly stroked her back. She broke from the hug to dab her eyes. Even here, after all this time, Webley's still did not cry, they persevered.

Beatty happily greeted us as he held open the car door. My mother held my hand in hers as we drove home. Not once did she look at me. Her hand squeezed mine each time a wave of tears tried to surface. But she would push these tears back down. This touched me right to my core. I tried my best not to cry. I knew she would not appreciate this.

When we arrived home, my gaze turned to the door of the study and anticipated the door to open at any moment. I waited, like a dog waited for their master to appear, my tail almost wagging. To my dismay, the door never opened. I turned away, my tail between my legs and held myself.

A creak in the floorboards echoed from behind me. I swiftly turned, my eyes pinned on the study door. I wholeheartedly believed my father would walk out any moment with a little smile on his face. That his death was all but a bad dream. The creak echoed again but the door never opened.

My mother stared longingly at the study door.

"I have not entered that room since your dear fathers...since the death. I cannot seem to make my myself enter it. If I ever need something from the room, Margot or a maid retrieves it for me. I suppose I never had much need to enter the room, it always was his hide away. Mine was the drawing room."

I gravely smiled at her, but her focus was entirely on the closed door.

My mother's blank eyes found mine and she exhaled a deep sigh.

"Tea is prepared in the Music Room. Margot should be joining us."

I followed my mother down the dark wooded corridor to the Music Room. Margot sat happily on the light blue couch, with her back to us. Adelaide sat beside her with a toy in hand. She had grown up so much. Margot twisted in her seat to greet us. She held a half-eaten sandwich in her hand.

My mother caringly smiled at Margot and took the seat next to her on the couch. I took the seat across from them. What a sweet sight to see! The two Mrs. Webley's enjoying each other's company.

Margot adopted a soft English twang, slowly drowning out her natural Germanic sounds. Proudly patting her bump, a huge smile spread across her face, glowing with her second pregnancy. Her smile grew larger as, "Lucy Loo," echoed from behind us. I jumped from my seat as George appeared before me.

Mother's smile, still appearing melancholic, watched George and Margot a moment before turning to me.

"Oh sweetheart, let me see your ring? I am excited to hear everything about this wonderful Will Fraye."

I outstretched my hand to her and watched her face as she lit up with immense happiness. She gently held my hand in hers and gazed at the ring. I began to tell her about Will and realised that once I started talking about him, I could not seem to make myself stop. The sheer sound of his name falling from my lips was enough to make me smile.

"When are we to meet this Will Fraye and have the wedding?"

"Soon!"

"Good, because I have everything organised. All you have to do is put on the dress and say, 'I do.'"

"Of course, you have everything organised," I let out a laugh.

BREATHE

Will arrived with his family the following week. I counted down the days until I could see him again.

A special dinner was held to celebrate the engagement. Will fitted in seamlessly into my life and my family. He did not need to do anything or be anything else for my family to accept him. His lineage and family wealth were more than enough for my mother to welcome him in with open arms.

"Wealth recognises wealth," was what my mother told me when she first met Will. I hated this comment.

I sat in my chair in the grand dining room, looked at the smiling and cheerful faces around me, eating enough food to feed a village, and drinking champagne and wine as though they were on tap. How had I returned to this life so quickly?

With every superficial laugh, practised smile, and generic dining room conversations, I faded more and more away from this type of living. This life laid out before me.

The next forty years of my life flashed before my eyes.

I saw myself sitting at a large dining room table, in an ornate room, filled with expensive things to impress people who did not matter to me. Drinking expensive wines and spirits, changing my wardrobe with the seasons, commanding staff, visiting my children in the nursery, being more occupied with keeping up with 'friends' than spending time with my own kin, hollowly laughing at ill-humorous jokes and desperately keeping up the image of being the happiest woman in the room…the most beautiful woman in the room.

A woman can only be two things once she was married - happy and beautiful.

I did not think I could do this. I could not be this woman.

No matter how minute my movements or facial expressions were, Will intuitively picked up on them. I turned to him, and he clinked his wine glass with mine. He held my gaze and my mind slowly came back to the present.

When the meal finished, Will and I snuck away from our boasting families and walked around the gardens. The moonlight lit the path for us as we talked and laughed into the early morning hours.

Many nurses and soldiers, like Will and I, felt isolated when they went home. When they were at war, they were constantly surrounded by people who experienced what they had experienced or dealt with even worse things. Neither money nor status mattered as they all had a unique bond with each other – war.

We selfishly became a somewhat elite club as not everyone could say they were there for D-Day, the Blitz, or witnessed the German soldier's surrender with their own eyes. One can never get away from those experiences and bonds.

Regardless of people's situations, everyone was treated equally, whether you were rich or poor it did not matter. People died regardless of their place in society.

However, when we came home, class and money suddenly had value again. It repulsed me.

END OF AN ERA

On the morning of my wedding, Lilian and my mother helped me to get ready. My dress was my mother's, but I asked Aunt June if she could make some alterations to it.

Delicate lace clung to the bodice of the dress, accentuating the waist. The neckline swooped down in a Queen Anne style. Four pearl buttons cuffed the lace sleeves. Pearl buttons ran along the spine of the dress.

As a child, I stared at the picture of my mother in this dress. I always dreamed of wearing it, twirling around in it, holding a bouquet of flowers in my hand, with my hair tied up in a French knot and pearl earring dripping down my neck.

I never dreamed of my wedding day, but only dreamed of wearing the dress.

I stood in front of the mirror and beheld myself. The woman in the reflection looked nothing like my old self. She was no longer a girl but had blossomed into a grown woman. These were my final moments of being Lucy Annabelle Webley. For the rest of my life, I would become Lucy Fraye. Mrs William Fraye. Let that sink in. But I would always be Lucy.

The shape of my body. My curves. I admired the healthy weight I had gained since coming home. I looked healthy. Happy. Oh, so happy.

I sat down onto the dressing table and Lilian expertly pinned up my hair and did my makeup.

My mother placed my favourite green and blue gemstone butterfly hairclip of hers, on top of the small bun at the back of my head kissed the crown of my head.

"Someday, when you have a daughter of your own, it can be passed onto her on her wedding day."

I held my mother's hand in mine and relished this moment, taking a mental picture, smiling at each other through the mirror. My mother was never a woman who openly showed her love like this, and I wished I had more moments like this to make her feel proud of me.

The Abbey bells tore us away from our tearful moment and reminded us of where we were. We quickly freshened ourselves up. My mother flustered about, fixing my dress and veil making sure that everything was perfect. I took a deep breath in the mirror to calm my nerves, but it did not work.

I held out my hand to my mother and she gladly took it. I felt her strength and calmness pass through me, and I stood taller. Lilian held the door for us as we made our way down the great stairs.

My mind drifted to those that I had lost over the past few years. My imagination went wild wondering how my day could be made better if those that I had lost were here.

I pictured a smiling Arthur, proudly holding Arty on his lap with Molly's hand in his, sitting next to George and his family in the Abbey. I pictured Beatrice and Betty sitting with Joan, Rita, Whilma, and Dorothy, laughing, and chatting with each other. I pictured Matron Burke shyly sitting next to the girls.

I pictured Nell, helping me prepare for my wedding and linking arms with my mother and we made our way to the abbey. I pictured my father waiting at the doors of the abbey, with a pipe in his mouth, cracking jokes as usual to calm everyone's nerves.

I also pictured Adam, with Jonathon in his arms, smiling reassuringly at me as I walked towards my future.

Music echoed from the abbey, with the sweet melody of the choir pouring out through the stain glass windows. The wind rustled through the trees, shaking the Autumn leaves. I watched the red tinted leaves silently fall like natures confetti from the old trees. I stood and stared at the ancient wooden doors of the abbey in front of me.

The love of my life stood on the other side of those doors, patiently waiting for me.

Lilian handed me my bouquet and held onto the ends of my veil.

My mother fixed my dress once more. Her eyes afraid to look into mine.

"Your father, he would have been...he would have been immensely proud of you today, my darling."

I held her hand to stop fussing with my dress and placed a gentle kiss on it.

"Are you ready to walk down the aisle, Miss Webley?" Lilian beamed.

"I'm ready."

The doors opened to a serenading solo violin accompanied by a piano, filling my ears with mesmerising music. Every seat in the small abbey was occupied by familiar smiling faces. My mother's hand steadied me as we walked down the narrow aisle. My trembling thankfully stopped and was replaced with bursting excitement the second I locked eyes with Will.

He stood at the top of the room beside a cheerful Bobby, who was whispering words of encouragement into Will's ears. Will's eyes and attention were only on me, and mine rested solely on him. How did I get so lucky?

My mother carefully placed my hand in Will's. His hand felt strong. So certain and steady. There was no trace of nerves.

The Vicars voice echoed through the Abbey and the room was instantly revoked to silence. "We are gathered here today..."

The moment I became Mrs. Fraye, Will took me by the hand and led me out of the Abbey. Some of the soldiers that were under Will in his platoon stood and clapped the entire walk down the aisle. They howled and cheered, which caused some looks of disgust from my mother's ladies' group. However, they sent me into a fit of laughter which made Will smile even more proudly.

A celebratory photograph captured the wedding guests gathered around Will and I as we stood outside the abbey. A gust of wind blew Autumn leaves everywhere. They fluttered about the afternoon sky, with the sun bringing to life the red and orange in the leaf.

This must be what happiness and peace feels like. I wished I could bottle this very moment.

We returned to the house with music, laughter, and conversations flowing from every room. I never ventured too far from Will. We were practically joined at the hip. I spent the day in constant laughter and smiles as Will made it his duty to ensure the day was nothing but happy.

I loved him even more in those laughter filled moments.

The celebrations continued into the early hours of the morning, with everyone swimming in a sea of wine, champagne, and Webley's Whiskey. The music never stopped playing, the dancing never ceased, and the food and drink did not stop flowing.

After this day, everything would soon change for me, my family, and friends. Will and I decided to move to America and start our life together there.

Lilian and Bobby were moving to Brooklyn and were expecting their first child. Whilma was moving to Scotland with her new husband, Dorothy was four months pregnant and leaving for Ohio with her husband, Rick. Joan started her new job in the Maternity Ward, at a hospital in Essex. Rita eloped with a Canadian soldier before the war ended and they were moving to Montreal.

The girls and I stood in a circle saying our goodbyes at the early hours of the morning. We reminisced for some time about our St Angela days, causing us all to laugh at the wonderful memories we had made together. But naturally, the tears soon followed as we said our goodbyes.

These wonderful women were my family, my home, my life, my sisters. Their strength, bravery, courage, honesty, loyalty, and support moulded me into the woman I became. We hugged each other and said our final goodbyes, making our promises to keep in touch.

Lilian and I stood waving at them as they walked away. I put my arm around Lilian, and she leaned her head onto my shoulder as we watched the St Angela girls' silhouettes fade into the night.

It was the end of era but only the beginning of a new one.

AMERICA

Will and I stayed for a while in England. My father's first year anniversary was upon us. I wanted to be there for father since I was not there for his death.

On the days approaching the anniversary, my mother took to her bed. She rarely left her room and ate little. I wished I could take an ounce of her pain away. When father's anniversary arrived, and mother joined us for breakfast, she did not eat a single crumb but only stared at his portrait on the wall.

I looked at my father's chair, which now seated George, and I knew he would make a great head of the Webley estate.

Will and I stayed in England until the beginning of December. It was time for us to move to America and begin our lives together. My mother and George brought us to the train station. Mother held onto my hand until I stepped onto the train.

She held onto me as if it were our last goodbye.

I reassured her that I would come home again and that she must visit me. She did not say a word, but smiled and hugged Will and me.

The train whistled and Will caught my hand and gestured for me to get on the train. I stood in the doorway and waved goodbye to George and Mother. Tears slowly drifted down my cheeks. I was leaving them once again.

We boarded our ship in Southampton and made our way to America. After ten days of smooth sailing, we arrived in New York. I felt as though I stumbled into a whole new world. We stayed in the city for a few days until we went to Will's home place.

Snow sprinkled across the lawn and house, with tiny icicles dripping from the tall trees. The front door was hooded by three columns, with a balcony overhead. Bows of holly hung from the balcony. The front doors opened to a white hallway, with a swooping staircase.

I felt as though I entered a prestigious hotel but something about it felt like home. A small party was held for our arrival with Will's friends and family joining us.

To my surprise, I had letters already waiting for me.

Webley Hazelton Manor,
3rd December 1945

Dear Lucy,

I hope you have made it safely over to America and that you were not too seasick. It can take some getting used to being on a ship for a long time. But ships and seasickness are not what I am writing to you about....

It pains me to write this, but Mama passed away last night in her sleep. Doctor Fernsby said she died of a broken heart. When we returned to the house after you left, she spoke of how lost she was since father's death and even more so now that you left.

She spent the following days roaming around the estate with Adelaide. Margot and I believed she was going to put her focus now onto her grandchildren and find purpose there. What we did not realise was that she was in fact saying her goodbyes.

She passed away in her sleep holding a photo of father, Arthur, you, and me. It was taken before Arthur and I left for war.

Mama has not been the same since father's death and I know she deeply missed him every day. At least, they can be together again.

She is to be buried beside father, with Arthur and Nell. The funeral will take place by the end of this week. I am sorry to reveal this sorrowful news to you, Lucy. It pains me to know this will be one of your first memories of America. Margot and I give Will and you our best wishes. We miss you dearly.
Your loving brother,
George.

The other letter had my mother's writing on the envelope.
Webley Hazelton Manor,
1ˢᵗ December 1945

My darling Belle,

It amazes me how you will open this letter and read it in America. So many wonderful miles away from here. But I hope you do come back home sometime in the future and remember your childhood days in a happy light. I hope you are blessed with beautiful children like I have been and proudly show them where you came from. Please tell them about me.

It is time for me to go, my sweetheart. I am ready to leave this earth and be with those that I have sorrowfully lost. I have known for some time now that my time here was coming to an end. One day you will understand this.

My heart has been broken so many times in my life and it cannot take any more. When Nell and Arthur died, I experienced a horrific sorrow. Words can never give it justice. A child should not die before the parent. But when your father died, my heart shattered into a million pieces. I knew the pieces could never be put back together again.

Every day that passed by without him became tremendously difficult for me. The day that Charles died might as well have been the day that I died.

I am so incredibly proud of you, Lucy. Your courage, determination, optimism, and strength have continually inspired me. You have grown into an incredible woman. I want to thank you for making my life so beautiful. Every single day of my life that you have been in it, was always wonderful. I want to thank you for that.

The proudest day of my life was the day you came home from Europe. Like a caterpillar, you transformed into your very own person. You were filled to the brim with nothing but compassion, love, and optimism. You may not have seen your strength, but I always did.

Your father often to spoke about his 'little Belle' nursing. He told people how it was you and the nurses who were winning the war for us. The nurses were the real heroes. Without the nurses, the men could not carry on. Both he and I were so proud of you. I wish I told you that more.

Yesterday, you left for America and many exciting adventures await you. Please experience everything that you can possibly get your hands on. Try and do as much as possible. Make the most out of your life. I wish I had.

Experience and memories are the most precious things that you can ever own. Do not waste your time looking back on all the things that could have been or the things that sadden you. If it does not bring you happiness – remove it. I wish I practised this more.

Over the years, I have tried my best to pass on my wisdom to you and your brothers. One piece of advice that my mother gave me and has stuck with me since is, respect.

Always have respect for yourself and others.

Do not worry about trivial and meaningless things. Instead, treat respect as your currency – it will get you further than anything else. Take time out every day just for you. This is especially needed for when you have children. Forgive but more importantly, forget. You do not know everything – accept this and you are set up for life. Ask for help when you need it. Make time to cry, do not bottle it up and put it on a shelf for later. This is something I wish I had practised more. Do not tire your heart with too many rules. Most importantly, laughter is the healthiest thing for you.

I just wish I did it more often. There is so much that I wish I did more of. But what use are regrets?

There is so much that I want to tell you and advise you on, but there comes a time where you need to learn your own lessons. The thing about advice is that it comes from one's experiences, mistakes, and findings. In order for you to give it, you first need to live it. My best advice to you is to live your life to the best of your abilities, my sweetheart. You can only do your best.

I will always be with you, my darling Belle. I can watch you grow even more from my new viewpoint. When you start your own family and build your life, keep me with you. You can keep me alive in your memories and nurture me in your heart. There is no need to be scared or upset, for I will always be with you. Every step of the way. All you have to do is think of me.

I know it is hard for you to understand right now, but I am ready to go.

Love always, Mama

1998

"Granny?" Emmy entreats, arousing me from my ruminations. "What was it like living in America?"

Emmy has moved on to another photo-album. The pictures are saturated colours. I bought my first coloured camera in 1946 while in America. The bright colours bring the pictures more to life, like a hazy summers' day memory.

I smile at Emmy as I watch her eyes flutter across the pictures.

"Life in America was something that took a long time for me to get used to. From the way of living, the accents, how people talked to each other, the fashion, how people behaved, and to the food. Everything seemed foreign and strange. Post-War America was a fantastic time. America was tremendously proud of the victories that they achieved in the war. People embraced peacetime with open arms. Factories and businesses that produced war-time equipment now changed to making peace-time products. The economy was booming."

"Life was good in those days!" Lilian smiles at the colour pictures.

I point out the houses to Emmy in the pictures and watch her face light up as she discovers more meaning to these pictures. Isn't it strange how one picture can mean the world to someone yet nothing to another?

Emmy turns the page of the photo-album. Her eyes move across the pictures, soaking up each one individually.

"From the day that I arrived in America, your Grandad was so excited and proud to show me his country. That picture was when he brought me to his old University. Those pictures where when he took me to different parts of New York city to experience an even more intense energy than London.

"When we bought our first car, we went on a road trip. I took the driver's seat and your Grandad took the map, directing me here and there. I soaked up as much history as I possibly could on that trip. It was the first time that Will and I had been completely alone with each other, and it was wonderful. The sound of our trip was laughter."

"The pictures of your road trip look so fun," Emmy smiles. She turns the page and holds up a picture of me on sitting on the porch of my first home with Will.

"Were you happy in America?" Emmy intuitively looks at me. Her young face with elder eyes, wise beyond her years, instantly spots my hidden words.

"I enjoyed my time in America. It could never be home to me, but it became home for a short while. America was exciting and new. Life was great for us and America suited us for a time, but we both felt the need to leave and return to England."

Emmy caringly smiles at me, happy with my answer. She turns the page and reveals baby photos of Teddy.

For most of my pregnancy with Teddy, I was terrified. I began to ease into the idea of being pregnant once I passed four months. Will did not understand my fears but cared for me for the nine months.

When Teddy was born, I became extremely emotional and overwhelmed. I never heard Jonathan's cry and I always wondered what it would have sounded like. To hold Teddy in my arms and feel his heartbeat made me never want to let go of him.

"I missed England and wanted to raise my children in the countryside. We stayed with George and Margot until we could find somewhere to live." That was a wonderful time of my life.

Emmy turns the page revealing photographs of this house, my home, and her face brightens.

"Tell me the story of how you found this house?"

"You know the story! You've heard it a hundred times," I smile.

"Tell me again."

"George gave me his new car to drive," I reminisce. "I

became lost in the nature around me and I vaguely knew where I was, but that did not matter. Here was beautiful. Suddenly, the car began to jerk and I saw that I had run out of fuel. I stopped the car in a secluded laneway. I got out to look for help but there was not a house in sight. I walked along the road until it began to rain. It drizzled at first but with every drop it got heavier and heavier. This red-brick wall appeared before me. It was overgrown with bushes and trees, and I ran towards it.

"There was a gate hidden among the trees and ivy. An abandoned Victorian house revealed itself. I ran inside the house to find some shelter. The porch had a whole in the middle of its floor and many of the windows were broken. The front door was loosely open and I cautiously pushed it open. Through the door, I could hear water dripping all around me. I looked up at the roof and saw holes here and there. It saddened me to think that this house was once loved and lived in, full of life and people. Yet now, hidden by overgrown trees and shrubs, this home felt lost from the world, abandoned to fall apart here alone.

"Once the rain stopped, I carefully roamed around the house. This was an old Victorian house, solidly built with style and character. Surprisingly, the kitchen was mostly intact. A small hallway caught my eye and I followed it. I opened the doors at random, exploring this museum of abandoned things. Teacups filled with dusty years sat on tables with empty chairs. Books lay open on desks, waiting to be read. Curtains sadly hung from broken windows, desperately trying to protect the house from the elements. Coats hung on hooks, never to be worn again. Faded paintings told stories of by-gone times. The living room showcased the most magnificent light. Stain glass windowpanes on the French doors casted rainbows across the room. The stiff doors, warped with rain, led me outside to an Eden.

"Rose bushes clung to the walls of the house. These flowers had not begun to blossom, but I knew they would be magnificent. I followed the wild path to a small stream. A small wall stood between me and the gently burbling river.

I hiked up my skirt to my knees and climbed over the wall. My serendipity was suddenly disturbed when an old farmer called out to me, concerned I had lost my way.

"I quizzed him about the house and who owned it. He told me that it had not been lived in for years and that it was destined to fall down. I could not let that happen. So, your Grandad and I bought the house and began to renovate it. At the beginning, we lived entirely in the kitchen. We repaired the house room by room and electricity was brought into the house for the first time.

"It took almost five and half years to fully complete the house and I adored every second of it. Building my life with Will was one of the greatest adventures I have ever had."

I smile at Emmy who closes the final photo-album and places it with the pile of albums. My whole life, in pictures, can be measured in these photo albums.

"The phrase, 'a picture holds a thousand words', never really appealed to me until now," Emmy chuckles as she carries the pile of albums to the bookshelf. "Thank you for telling me your story Granny."

"We better get some sleep for it's already tomorrow," Lilian tiredly rubs her eyes.

Mae and Emmy help me out of my seat. My knees and back have become stiff and I try to stand tall. My eyes fall onto the familiar faces in each of the framed photos on the walls and shelves. I smile to myself at the gratifying fact that I had the chance to know and love each and every person in them.

Mae takes my arm and guides me out of the room and up the stairs. I take each step at a time as my aches and pains ripple throughout my wintering body.

I stop at my bedroom door and turn to say goodnight to Mae, Emmy, and Lilian. I hug each one tightly and feel their body in mine. I hold each of their faces in my hands before leaving the hug and try to take a snapshot of their features in my mind. My own private photo-album.

But I pull Mae back to me and hug her again. I need to see her face once more.

"I love you," I whisper.

"I love you too, Mam. Goodnight, sleep well."

I let her go and gently whisper 'goodnight' to them all. I stand in my doorway and watch them walk to their rooms for the night and close the door.

I can rest now.

STAY WITH ME

The long bay windows in my bedroom are open wide, allowing the midnight air to dance around the room. The full-moon casts a gentle spotlight onto my bed. My floral print curtains sway ever so gently in the cool night breeze, but I am nice and cosy in bed.

The house is completely, silently, still. I look around me, recalling the memories that occurred in this very room.

I can see a faded seven-year-old Mae peeping her sleepy head in through the door, late at night, carrying her teddy bear with sleep still in the corners of her eyes. She had yet another bad dream and her parents' warm bed was the place where bad dreams could not enter.

I can hear Teddy's little bare feet thumping on the wooden floor suddenly coming to a halt as he reached my side of the bed. A weight would abruptly land on top of me and a tiny voice would screech, 'Merry Christmas!'

I can see Will moving around the room, putting on his shirt and tie, getting ready for the day. He would walk around the room, humming to himself, gently waking me up.

I can still see Teddy and Mae carrying a tray full of breakfast, with flowers and a handmade 'Happy Mother's Day' card placed proudly in the middle. They tried their utmost best to not spill a drop of tea from the kitchen to my bedroom. When they grew older, the tray full of breakfast turned into a cup of tea and a card, yet they still had the same sense of pride and satisfaction handing it over to me.

So many simple and precious memories.

My attention turns to my bed, and I automatically put my hand out to reach for Will's. I am coldly reminded that he too is now a memory. I look at the empty space beside me and remember all the times that I woke up next to Will and watched his peaceful face as he slept.

A ringing sound echoes through my ears. It is soft at first but grows to be a deafening siren. My breath feels heavy and I feel my eyes begin to droop. A fog slowly creeps over my eyes. This fog has slowly been making its way into my eyes all day, but I have fought it off. Now, I let it wash over me.

Waves of familiar scents flow past me. I can smell aftershave, perfume and lavender soap, tobacco, carbolic soap, and daisies. I can faintly hear Arthur's hearty laugh and George singing 'Lucy Loo!' A hand gently strokes my hair. A smile forms on my mouth as I try to follow the sounds and smells.

My head and body grow heavier with each breath that I take, almost sinking further and further into my bed. I feel as though I have not slept in days. My tiredness tells me it is okay. I can rest now. Close my eyes and rest.

My door creaks open and Lilian slowly pops her head in and smiles at me.

"What are you still doing up?"

"Lil?"

"What's wrong?" Lilian runs towards me and catches my clammy hand.

"Stay with me," I whisper.

Lilian sits beside me on the edge of my bed and holds my hand. I watch as the tears slowly fall down her eyes.

"I should call Mae and Emmy."

I look around my room. Will's fresh smelling aftershave suddenly fills my nostrils. I take a deep breath in to fully immerse myself in the beautiful scent. A warm, hazy fog creeps over my eyes and I can rest now…

EPILOGUE

On the morning of Granny's funeral, Mam found letters in the drawer of Granny's bedside locker addressed to each member of the family and one for Lilian. They are goodbye letters. It seems Granny knew she was dying long before we ever could have known.

Mam hands me mine and I do not know whether I want to open it or keep it closed forever.

In the conservatory, Nell sits beside me, leaning her head into my shoulder. I hold the letter in my hands as I look out at the blooming garden. The morning sun shines through the glass gently wrapping a warm blanket around me. I watch Teddy and Mam in the garden, reading their letters through tear flooded eyes.

Granny's garden chair sits lifelessly in between them.

Lilian places a cup of tea onto the table for me and rubs my cheek before leaving the room with her letter. Since Granny's death, Lilian has been the rock for the family. She has been there for everyone, especially Mam and Teddy. Lilian remains strong for everyone, yet I always see the tears silently falling down her cheeks.

I look at my envelope and rub my thumb over my name in Granny's writing. I turn over the envelope and admire the red-waxed seal with a rose imprinted in the middle of it. I begin to wonder when Granny decided to write all these heart-felt letters. My hands shake as I remove the seal, and gently pull out the letter.

1st July 1998

Dearest Emmy,

If you are reading this, it means I have passed on. I ask you not to be upset, grieve, or cry over my death, but instead to celebrate the wonderful life that I have lived. You are one of the main reasons I have lived an incredible life. You will never know how proud I am to be called your grandmother.

I know it may be hard for you to understand this, but it was my time to go. My job was done. I was not needed anymore. My children have grown up into extraordinary adults and have gone on to have tremendous children of their own.

When my children were growing up, my role was to be their sole caretaker, to watch out for them, teach them, help them grow into the people they are today. When they had children of their own, my role changed to encourage them and pass on advice. But the time has come where I cannot give anymore advice or encouragement because you do not need it anymore.

Advice is a terrific thing, Emmy, and when it is given to you, be gracious and listen with open ears to the person that is gifting it to you. You do not have to necessarily take it but listen. You might need it in the future.

Emmy, you have grown into an incredible young woman. I believe whatever you put your mind to, you will achieve great things. You have the ability to do anything, be anything. Do just this!

I have lived a wonderful life and learned many lessons. These lessons only came from living. I want you to live your life to the fullest. If that means you wish to bury your head in books and learn about everything around you, then so be it. If you wish to travel the world and not stop until you have seen every plant, rock, and landmark in the entire world – then so be it!

Follow your heart, Emmy, and you will never go wrong. It will take some time to tune into your heart and what it is trying to tell you but know that it is worth it in the end.

Take some time to get-to-know you instead of searching for it in others. How can anyone else know you if you do not? Make yourself as interesting as humanely possible because you must spend your whole life with you!

Please do not be afraid of yourself or of being yourself – it will be the most courageous thing that you will have to do. As my mother told me, and I will now tell you, have respect for yourself and others. But most importantly, yourself. View respect as your currency.

Do not think you have lost me just because you cannot see me. I will always be around you, watching over you as you move through life. I will be there every step of the way, helping you in any way that I can. You may not hear me or feel me, but I am there.

I wrote you this letter as a final goodbye, something you can always return to when you need my words. My mother wrote me a letter similar to this, and it brought me such comfort. Some day you will be showing this letter and telling your stories to you children and one day to your grandchildren. Only then will you understand my love and pride for you.

Please take care of yourself, Emmy. Now that you have turned 19, you have your whole life ahead of you, and what a wonderful life you will have. All the doors have opened for you, and you have the choice to walk through whatever door you wish.

On your graduation day from university, have me there. On your wedding day, have me there. On your first child's birth, have me there. On your happy days and sad days, have me there.

Remember me in any way that you choose, be it a flower, a cup of tea, a song, a smell, or a photo. Keep me with you. That is how people live on when they have gone, it is through our loved ones bringing us with them.

I love you so much Emmy and wish you a life
full of adventures and happiness.
Love always,
Granny

THANK YOU

To you, the reader, thank you for purchasing
and reading *Remembering Me*.
Thank you for holding this book in your hands, moving
through its pages, making it to the end of the book, and reading
these lines. Your support has not gone unnoticed.
If you would like to leave a review on Amazon, Goodreads, or social
media that would be greatly appreciated. Your opinion matters.
Thank you to Colin Eyre for designing and
bringing to life the cover of the book.
Thank you to Catherine Kealy and Aimhirgín Byrne for their design
consultations, their edits and advice over the course of writing this book.
Thank you to my friends for their support through the
writing of this book. Thank you for all the kind words and
encouragements, the suggestions and advice, the spell-checkers,
the first-draft readers, and the many many cups of tea.
Thank you to my editor, Janet Still, without whom
this book would not be where it is.
From the bottom of my heart,
thank you.

~ Ruby Eyre ~

ABOUT THE AUTHOR

Ruby Eyre

Ruby Eyre is a new author from county Laois, Ireland. Remembering Me is her first book. Through completing her degree in Criminology and her Masters in Anthropology in University College of Cork, Ruby dedicated her spare time to writing and editing Remembering Me.

From a young age, writing has been an integral part of her life with music and history being the other loves. World War II has always held a special fascination and place in her heart.

After a short visit to Utah beach, France, in 2017, the idea of Remembering Me began and with time grew into this book.

Instagram - @_rememberingme_

Printed in Great Britain
by Amazon